# [ BURNING

# DESIRE ]

# [ BURNING DESIRE ]

## *Relentless Aaron*

ST. MARTIN'S GRIFFIN ✺ NEW YORK

This is a work of fiction. All of the characters, organizations, and events portrayed in this novel are either products of the author's imagination or are used fictitiously.

BURNING DESIRE. Copyright © 2009 by Relentless Aaron. All rights reserved. Printed in the United States of America. For information, address St. Martin's Press, 175 Fifth Avenue, New York, N.Y. 10010.

www.stmartins.com

Library of Congress Cataloging-in-Publication Data

Relentless Aaron.
    Burning desire / Relentless Aaron. — 1st ed.
        p. cm.
    ISBN 978-0-312-35938-6
    1. African Americans—Fiction.    I. Title.
    PS3618.E57277B87 2009
    813'.6—dc22

                                                    2009017011

First Edition: December 2009

10   9   8   7   6   5   4   3   2   1

*Dedicated to my friends in New York,*
*Atlanta, and my readership*
*throughout the world*

# ACKNOWLEDGMENTS

SPECIAL THANKS TO Tiny, Tony Rose, Max Rodriguez, Bernard Bronner, my editor, Monique Patterson, Julie, and Team Relentless.

# [ BURNING
DESIRE ]

# [ ONE ]

## DANTÉ

IT WAS SOMETHING to be proud of, how I'd made a name for myself, even if it wasn't merely hard work and focus that got me here. And, in the back of my mind, that's just what I think about—how lucky I am to be who and what I am. I can't help thinking that my grandfather had a lot to do with what I know and where I'm at today, considering how (from age eight until I was a teenager) he had custody of me. So while Dad was away for six years, Gramps taught me the family's handyman trade and made sure I knew how to act by using that leather belt on my ass early and often. As much as I dreaded the old-school ways of my grandfather, almost twenty years later, I realize it was good medicine. And, I might be imagining things, but ever since the older men in my life passed on, it feels like even more work has been coming my way. It's as if "the hood" was showing some kind of combined condolences toward my situation. Miss Sally wants me to fish out a ring from her drain for the umpteenth time, a new resident needs me to come in and seal any holes that *might* be the welcome entrance for the mice in her apartment, and Marcia Thomas needs me to change another lightbulb. Now, if you think those calls are silly, there's *way* more that are worse. Leaking faucets, air conditioners on the blink, seal this or fix that. And there's my favorite nuisance request that comes up from time to time: *is there a way to stop that smell from next door?* And "next door" usually amounted to nothing but the baby's soiled diaper or the dog poop that hadn't been cleaned up for a day. It all adds up to air pollution, no matter how you look at it. Sometimes the air in these buildings is just a step away from the Projects: thick enough to slice with a butter knife. But the whole concept of Park Chester is supposed to be on some agenda of *next-level* living. *Whatever that means.*

I've met plenty of families who moved out of the Projects and into these buildings thinking they were *movin' on up*, like George and Weezy. But after a few years of this, they come to realize it's the same old trap, just a different part of the neighborhood. Smart people doin' smart things, and dumb people keeping their titles. Still, just because I might be able to snuff out these simple maintenance issues they call me for, doesn't measure up to some of my clients who are older men and women. Some are too busy, and a few are just plain lazy. And me—I end up being the good-deed doer, or the *glue* that keeps our neighborhood together. I'll go in for a plumbing job and I'll end up fixing a wall outlet that some kid stuck a toothpick in. Think about the blocks and blocks of apartment buildings that keep me earnin' a livin, and so many tales, dramas, and tragedies to go with it. Domestic violence, child welfare issues, and even petty crimes that I turn my back on, or else I'd have to take things personal; or else I'd be labeled a *tattletale*. And who needs that?

Regardless, I still gotta be on my grind; I still gotta get paper. They call me, I get paid; no credit, no barter. So, how can I argue with any of this if there's legitimate money on the table? And, by the way, *I couldn't help noticing the ants crawling throughout your place—need me to handle that for you?*

MY LIVING arrangement has been pretty much the same ever since I left college to take care of my father during his last living days. We were the only New York members of the Garrett family, and we sort of depended on one another for those remaining eighteen months of his life, so a two-bedroom apartment in Park Chester worked out just fine. "Team Garrett," the neighbors called us in his healthier days, how we always knocked out whatever handyman issues came about; no matter what, there wasn't a job we couldn't handle. But then the prostate cancer set in for my dad, like his dad before him. Then the funerals came (more or less) back-to-back.

SO I'M solo now, and I'm getting the feeling I need to insulate myself some. Call me a sucker if you want, but your self-esteem points drop into the single digits when you lose someone close to you. I guess you'd have to live it to know it. But everything could've taken a different turn—I could've just as well worn the "I don't give a damn" attitude. Or I coulda been swallowed by drugs, or worse, suicide. So, considering the choices of a stand-up dude from the Bronx who wasn't forced by circumstance to rep a gang or group, I done pretty good for myself.

SINCE I do so much work for these different Park Chester residents (mostly women), I've been trusted with keys to their various apartments so that while they're at work I can go in and fix the problem. This was the case with Ms. Thomas in building 14, apartment 7B. There are times when she never realizes I came through. I'll do my customary knock, but when there's no answer I figure all is safe and I go right in. Ms. Thomas isn't the only one with a dog, either. She has a poodle that's mad noisy when I go into her place. But, for whatever reason, there was no barking this time. I figured lil' Sparky was out with Ms. Thomas, at the vet or with a friend. And, quiet as I tried to keep it, that was a good thing for my allergies. Allergic to dogs, don't like 'em, and that's all there is to it. Cats are even worse, since their fur gets all over the place and I can't help but breathe that shit in. Before you know it, I start sneezing and my eyes turn watery. I'm sure the lonely pet lovers of the world see it all different, but I got enough of life's weight on my shoulders to carry more. God bless 'em.

"SPARKY! *HEEEERE*, Sparky!" The moment I stepped through the door I called out for the dog, just to be sure the mutt wasn't about to ambush me and (maybe) bite my leg off. Paranoid, I know—but you'd have to walk in my shoes to understand how my nervous system starts acting up. It

starts in the brain, like my senses start tingling or something, and from there my body starts acting up. I spiral into
itching and goose bumps. The twitching and the sneezing
just take over, and it spirals from there. Like I said, call me
a punk, but that's just how it is. And I gotta *deal with it*.

So, when I didn't hear anything, I stepped right on in, as
if it was my own place. I always liked Marsha Thomas's
crib, but not until now did I snoop around some. It started
with my flipping through the two-month-old *Ebony* magazine on the coffee table by her vinyl-covered sectional
couch. Why do they *do* that to couches? I mean, if you
can't sink into the total comfort of the couch, *what's the
point?* And if you're preserving the couch for a rainy day
(like, maybe your sixtieth birthday?) and *then* you decide
to remove the plastic, just to experience the "full value" of
the furniture for the remaining days of your life, then it
seems to me you went through a lifetime of pain for two
minutes of pleasure! Ms. Thomas, the masochist?

I DIDN'T get to flipping halfway through the magazine
before hearing what I thought was a squeal from farther
back in the apartment. I ignored it the first time, but there
was a second squeal that seemed to graduate into a cry.
Stepping farther on into the apartment, with no daylight to
follow me from the living room, I noticed flickers of light
reflecting against the master-bedroom door. Common
sense told me it might be a TV that had been left on. I tried
to switch on the hall light, but it didn't work. So I found
myself saying, *Duh, Danté. Why'd you think she called you
here in the first place?* Still, the back of the house and the

rest of the hallway drew me ever closer until I reached the
entrance; until my mouth fell open and my eyes grew wide.
No longer blinded by the dark, I could see Ms. Thomas lying on the bed naked, and flickering on the TV at the foot
of her bed was an old recording of *Soul Train*. How did I
know it was old? Not only because they discontinued the
show, but because Marvin Gaye was singing live to the
crowd. And *that* nigga dead. So, unless the squeals were of
audience members on the TV, it was easy to guess where
the noise came from. And now it was obvious—*obviously
luring me in*, that is. The imagery made me think of some
old 70s blacksploitation flick. Or even the glow-in-the-dark
indoor golf franchises with the black lights all over the
place so that just about every speck of dust would show up
in neon. The only difference here was that I was at the center of it all, about to glow in the dark my *damn* self.

Meanwhile, there was this glistening hue of purple that
changed what I knew to be Ms. Thomas's mocha-brown
skin. The reality was that the lighting on the *Soul Train*
stage had a purple hue, as if the TV needed some correction. The other reality here was that Ms. Thomas was fin-
gering her snatch, more than engrossed in the act as her
body seemed tense, stretching, frustrated.

As of now, I thought her eyes were closed, or that she
was focused on Marvin *gettin' it on* with his own magne-
tism. I thought that my presence had gone unnoticed and
that the rich odor of her sex went undisturbed. How wrong
was I when I tried to backstep and tippy-toe away. Maybe it
was my tool belt knocking against the wall or something,
but those beautiful, sensual forty-six-year-old eyes of hers
opened even wider and appeared to dare me to take another

step back. And the dreamy state I was in turned dizzy when she sang:

> "*Come on, come on, come on, come on,*
> *come on, baby.*"

—And I knew good and well she was talking to me. But if there was no other indication that this was the case, there was always the twitching in my boxer-briefs, a reality I could *not* get around even if I tried.

"Sorry, Ms. Thomas. I knocked, I *swear*." Stuttering and disheveled, I respectfully turned my eyes toward the dark wall nearest to me, ready to break the record for the hundred-yard dash to the apartment entrance.

"*Excuuuuse* me!" she cackled as I attempted to remove myself from her presence. "Danté, darling," she cried out in an off-key, singsong kind of way. "Don't you be a little coward now. You're not a *coward*, are you?"

I got a little bold and backpedaled to her bedroom threshold. Okay, I'll admit that I had peeped at her grapefruit jugs and that bottle-shaped figure with the outrageous ass, but I never gave a second thought to being in her bedroom while she was playing with herself! I never thought I'd be introduced to these brand-new sensations in my loins, not to mention the airborne scent of Ms. Thomas's fruity body juices. And now that I thought about it, if she was offering me the view *and* paying me, then why not get my gaze on? Really, I never had a problem with the ladies. I got no kids so far, and I'm pretty good-looking (if I do say so myself), with my thin, flexible, 168-pound body and my matted crewcut always groomed like my goatee. Look at a *GQ* magazine and look at me, and you can agree I belong there.

Just as confidently I replied, "Ahh, Ms. Thomas, I am the *last* person you can call shy. I just, well, I'm respectful of my elders." I didn't think she saw the smirk on my face, but nevertheless, she propped herself up some and bounced back quick.

"Elders, huh?" The urge for retaliation was fresh in her eyes, like a challenger in a sword fight, only without the blood and gore.

She went on to say, "I wasn't too old *last* week when you were here."

The question mark on my face was as sincere as her voice was determined.

She went on to say, "Oh, don't act like you don't know what I'm talking about. I saw you checking me out, Danté; checkin' my ass out as I left the room. Don't deny it."

While I didn't give in, I was ready with a lie.

"I don't *think* so, Ms. Thomas."

"Well, my eyes don't lie, you strappin' young Mandingo you. And I'll put a month's rent up as a bet that you are *not* a coward. I think you're smart enough to know what I want. I think you're strong enough to give it to me. And I know you're equipped to do the job right. So stop bein' so nervous. Step into my bedroom and relax a little. Kick your shoes off and let a real woman give a hardworkin' handyman a massage. No strings attached. Promise."

*Smart enough? Strong enough?? Am I equipped to do the job right???* Was she kidding? She must've thought I was stupid to go for the psychology tricks, tryin' to make me feel deficient, so that maybe I'd feel I had something to prove to her (and myself). Besides that, her words were poppin' in and out because my capitalist-conscious mind was still calculating her wager of a month's rent, and the challenge that came with it.

*Does she mean that?*

I LEFT Ms. Thomas's apartment well after nine that night, feeling a little out of place from the drinks that followed dinner. And if it wasn't dizziness I was feeling, then I was probably what you call *mellowed out* or *spent* after our first-ever sexual encounter. All the while I kept thinking that I know better—the idea and the act of sex is supposed to be gratifying, satisfying, and electrifying, with partners who can't *wait* to return for more. I mean, you'd think at *least* we should be in love. And yet, it wasn't that way for me. Instead, it was *her* orgasm that was an explosion, compared to mine; the mere oil spill. Hers was the desire that (in hindsight) seemed to be that dire need, while, on the other hand, I couldn't wait to get it over with. And here's the worst thought I was left with—I'm not sure if it was the egg scent that somehow rubbed off her body and onto my own, or what I took to be some flowery cheap perfume she wore. But either way, it was a push-and-pull endeavor that was much too difficult to enjoy.

Now, besides all that, there was a downside that left me with a kind of mental dehydration where I carried some ugly weight on my mind; as if something was dragging me down from the pleasure that I would usually enjoy after sex. It was easy to know that I didn't love this woman, that this was but a thrill and that there would be no future between us. However, my best guess in regard to the emotional spin I was going through amounted to nothing more than *giving*. I had given something away when I stepped past that threshold to her bedroom. I had exposed my greatest assets when I undressed before this woman—so clever with her sensuality and promise of ecstasy squared. I had invested my time and energy when I lay with, touched, fondled, and penetrated this woman. But as different and as intoxicating as she made it seem at the outset, the truth was more evident than ever once I came. After I came I could think clearly, and the thoughts were not clouded by desire or my lack of sexual satisfaction. In the end, the fact was that her lovin' was just *ordinary*, with *extra*ordinary or a different wrapping—that's all. And, she was right in saying that there was no attachment, not emotionally and not physically. I didn't feel a thing, even with the great dinner she later cooked, or the awesome back massage she gave me *before* the sex.

But there was one memory I think I did intend to keep, that engrossing, juicy-wet blow job she executed. I think about it now and I can say, *Okay, so maybe there was a plus to this encounter.* Regardless of how selfish it was.

It was an impulsive moment that caught me off guard and pulled me back in like a fish—another thrill that I surrendered to. After all seemed to be said and done, I still had on my boxers, sitting at the dinette table with my bare chest and with one last scoop of apple pie and vanilla ice cream.

Ms. Thomas said, "After all this, you *still* haven't changed the light bulb." And the way she said that was so authoritative, as if I'd done something wrong and there was some means of discipline I'd face; someone she could report me to, or that my reputation might somehow be jeopardized. I honestly thought she was kidding, but there was that stern disciplinarian's look in her eye that (I have to admit) intimidated me some. I haven't seen that face since my third-grade teacher, Mrs. Fraoli, disciplined me. Nevertheless, I kept my urge to fire back a secret, and I busied myself with that last scoop of dessert before immediately getting up on my ladder to change the light bulb in her hallway. True story here—she snuck up on me, slipped my used beef from my boxers, and began to suck on me like this was a normal activity. And how could I argue with what had to be the most spontaneous, exciting, and sensationally impulsive sexual encounter that I'd ever experienced? Not to mention the moments when I nearly buckled; nearly thrown off balance as I continued working on the fixture overhead.

I eventually came down from the high. I was not "converted" into a lover. I was not convinced that our indulgences were worthwhile enough for me to return for more. And, if anything, Ms. Thomas helped me get some backed-up weight off my shoulders (or out of my loins). So, I might call what happened in her apartment a win-win event. But, no bullshit—I could've gotten the same satisfaction jerking off in the shower.

# [ T W O ]

THE DAYS THAT followed seemed to drag like a bad dream. The memorable scent of her wasn't helping things. It was like a knot in my stomach, or in my brain. And I'm thinking it was the raunchy sex; not because the sex itself was raunchy, but because that day I had put in some long hours and didn't get a chance to shower. Not that she cared, either, because despite all (and that my feet were just *funky*), this woman had no shame, sucking my toes like Tootsie Roll Pops. Had me squirmin' around on the bed like I was in withdrawal.

Above and beyond all that, there were the lingering memories, and finally, she was still calling me and leaving messages as if this was gonna happen again *real* soon. I found myself, on more than one occasion, talking not *on* the phone but *to* the phone, saying, "Bitch, is you crazy?" And while my mind is playing tricks on me, it's still work as usual—I'm still fixing plumbing, electrical shorts, a soggy-plaster-wall issue, and even replacing someone's air-conditioning unit. One client's clothing shelf is coming apart, an elderly woman needs the doorknob tightened on her bedroom door, and at least one complaint of chipping paint needs my attention. Sure, for some people who paid $30K to $50K a half-dozen years ago, moving to Park Chester might've been the achievement of the American dream. But, firsthand, I was one of the handful of people (handymen and superintendents) who got the front-seat view to this crumbling empire. There's the mildew, the electrical problems, the raw-sewage issues that attract the abundance of roaches and vermin, and so many other realities that middle- and low-income renters have always been accustomed to. But I'm also accustomed to dealing with these realities. So, it's nothing new to me. If anything, my mind is occupied with immediate goals and dreams of my future. The occasion with Ms. Thomas only gave me more to mutter about, with my mind so busy replaying the hows and the whys. I'm even cursing myself for falling into her trap, and I'm promising myself *never again.*

OUT OF nowhere, I stopped in to see Pastor Bishop at St. Raymond's Church on East Tremont. After Pop passed away I frequently went to see Pastor Bishop. He listened to me, consoled me, and eventually suggested that I keep myself busy. He already knew my work, on account of my coming in to fix pews, a leak in the kitchen, and some bookshelves at the church; not to mention that he's one of my best-paying accounts.

"But that's your work, young Danté." He always called me *young Danté,* which felt like words from a wise man, as opposed to the utterance of a local preacher. "I'd like to see you get into some extracurricular activities. Have you seen a good movie lately? Maybe a party?"

"I haven't had much time for that, Pastor. Just always working."

"But you've gotta enjoy life, young Danté. All work and no play makes—"

"Yes, I heard that before. All work and no play makes Jack a dull boy. And my life is *hardly* that. Never a dull moment," I said, in my own personal "joke moment," but at the same time not even *thinking* about what was so heavy on my mind.

"Well, how about a night of bowling? Got plans for Friday? Maybe you have a sweetheart you could invite to our bowling night?"

"Friday . . ." I thought about this, more than sweeping aside the thought of women. "No plans. And no sweetheart."

"Then it's done."

I ALMOST forgot the offer come Friday. A boiler broke down in building 13 and Ms. Cornwall's stove was on the brink. Fixing the boiler took half a day. It took another two hours for me to get a green light from the super to replace Ms. Cornwall's stove, and by the time I returned from Home Depot it was four thirty. Getting the stove up to her apartment took another hour. I had it all installed and working by six thirty. Exhausted, I left Ms. Cornwall's apartment with a deep breath and a need for a shower and a meal. It was in the elevator where a woman spoke to me as I tried to manipulate the empty box that had contained the oven.

"Hey there. I remember you," she said. "You fixed our tub a month ago. Eighth floor? I'm Stacy. Yvonne Singletary is my auntie."

I managed an uncomfortable smile, knowing how I must've smelled and being in such closed quarters with a woman who was obviously dressed to go out somewhere. In the meantime, I also found my face squeezing into its own want for a connection. I'd have been lost if she'd left it at "fixed our tub," or "eighth floor." But Mrs. Singletary was a woman you don't forget. She was always so fashionable (when I did see her), and polite at every encounter. What's more, she tipped *well*. I remembered caulking her tub and that it was so sparkling clean, so much different from some other bathrooms, tubs or showers that I've had to repair. Some were horrendous and hadn't been cleaned *at all*. I mean, what did they think, that these were self-cleaning and that the dirt from their bodies just disappeared? That's the one thing I had to get used to when doing jobs for people: I'm invited into the privacy of their homes, and sure (set aside the sex-starved Ms. Thomas), it all seems so blissful while I'm there working. But, behind the closed doors of these dwellings was anyone's guess. Habitats of various ways of life, religions, and practices. Some people maintained a healthy lifestyle but were lacking in other ways. Others lived cluttered lives but seemed to know where everything was at the drop of a dime. And still others were anal about their cleaning and hygiene, forcing me to come out of my work boots whether it was white carpet or tarnished wood floors. Even if the floors weren't all that hot I'd have to oblige my customers. Whatever the case, I was left to make sense of it all, but forced to ignore people's paranoia and negligence. There was just no winning with people.

I DIDN'T pick up any *anal* sensibilities from Mrs. Single-tary. And so far, she didn't appear to be another Ms. Thomas. She was just one of those people who seemed to have it all together. And here was the product of that environment?

*Not bad.*

"You're her niece, you say? I'm sorry, I don't think I remember you."

"You didn't really see me. But I saw you." The way she said that was so *cute*. Like she had the upper hand on me, or knew something I didn't. I smirked some, but I also sized her up within that next second—that moment of assessment that I like to impose. But, just as quickly, I went on with the small talk. "I'm from down south—just outside of downtown 'Lanta. But I'm stayin' with Auntie for a while."

I took all that in as unimportant information, but I then said, "Be careful out there. The rain is supposed to really come down later tonight."

"I should be back by then; just going out for a little bowling. Thanks to some *coercion* from my auntie."

*Bowling.*

And that's when it hit me. "That's right. Today's Friday," I said, more or less to myself.

"Oh, you bowl?" she asked.

"No, but Pastor Bishop invited me to Harlem Lanes to-night for some kinda bowling event. Something to do with his church."

"The pastor from East Tremont? Harlem Lanes? *That's*

where I'm going." Then Mrs. Singletary's niece did some quick calculating. "You know what, *that's* why Auntie was being so damn evasive about the details. This is some *church* event, ain't it. That's why—"

"Well, not necessarily," I explained. "Harlem Lanes has a lot of lanes. I mean, a *lot* of 'em. There's always a party going on there. It could just be coincidence that the church is there on the night you're going."

She twisted her lips in deep doubt. *"Coincidence,* huh? I just *bet* it is."

THAT RUN-IN I had with Mrs. Singletary's niece was more than ironic. I had just arrived in Harlem, rushing down after my shower and a quick bite to eat. And who do I see in the lobby of the building where Harlem Lanes is located, apparently about to leave.

## STACY

He came sprintin' through the lobby doors until the sudden halt. Scared the livin' daylights outta me, until I realized it was Danté.

"Hey, what's up?" he announced while brushing the rain off his jacket. "Stacy, right?"

*Okay, I guess that's a plus. Remembering my name.*

"Oh—*hey,*" I said. And I could feel my face brighten up to greet him, but at the same time I didn't feel like explaining to him that I wasn't a happy camper.

Still brushing those raindrops everywhere, Danté eventually addressed me.

"Everything alright?"

"It will be, as soon as my cab gets here," I said, rolling my eyes.

"Finished that quick? I mean, I just got here."

*Okay. And you don't have to be a rocket scientist to figure out that I ain't been at Harlem Lanes for more than an hour. Hour and a half, tops.*

"I was finished before I started," I told him, try'na be nice even if my thoughts were scathing. "Turns out it *is* a church event. With a *whooole* bunch of skirts and shirts and ties and—"

"Oh, come on, it can't be *that* bad," he suggested. Then Danté with the jokes: "We could always hop around the corner to One-two-five and pick up a tie and skirt. We'll fit right in."

It was easy for me to make a face to say, *Not funny.* But somewhere down deep inside I felt his comedy.

"So, then, you didn't even get to bowl," he went on to say. *Danté, the rocket scientist.*

"Nope. I was feelin' real out of place up there. Like the black sheep or somethin'."

I could practically see him take a deep breath, as if he was feeding into a whole new plate of responsibilities. I was also smart enough to know that it's not like you could get to know a person halfway. And it only became more complicated when it was a man/woman relationship.

"Come on, Stacy. Don't let me go up there alone. Then I'm gonna be left to feel the way you're feeling. Plus, you'll already be in a cab, probably laughing at me all the way back to Park Chester." I snickered in between his words. "Let's be two black sheep and make something out of nothing. Whatcha say?" Now his hand was on my arm, encouraging my reply. Cute. And it had to be, 'cuz he ain't know me from Adam and already got his hands on me?

"Ahh, I don't know. I kinda had my mind set after leaving there. You go 'head. You can handle it. You're a big boy."

"Okay, well, I won't force you into something you don't wanna do. How about we do something you *do* wanna do? I mean, no sense in me going up there to be the *only* black sheep. And besides, what would your auntie say if you left her number-one handyman out here all alone, all this hard rain and—"

With a chuckle, I said, "You know, you really know how to put it on a woman, don't you."

"Is it that obvious?" he asked, and now he was posing with what I guessed was his very best mack-daddy act.

Finally, a laugh erupted from deep down in my belly, and then we were both laughing, even as another couple was rushing in from the rain. It felt so good to laugh after all the hell I'd been through. Long story.

"So whatcha say we get wet. My truck is right across the way; or, ahh—I can pull it around if you're afraid of a few raindrops."

I'm sure the face I made could've stopped an entire football team. But I like to back my talk with action. I pulled my jacket tight, prepared and game for just about anything a *man* could do.

"Which way, Marco Polo." But as I said this, I was already moving out, practically leaving him behind in my dust. I turned to see the surprised *crazy* look on Danté's face. Like I could read his mind.

*Damn. He ain't gotta prove nothin' to me. I was only kidding!*

He caught up to me real fast, and we were eventually side by side, practically sprinting. So there was no sense in me backin' down now. We suddenly got into this lil' foot race! *Really!? This dude don't really know me!?* Now, I'm not the fastest runner in the world in heels, but put Stacy in some Air Jordans and see if I don't recall my high school track meets, *okay?* And *so what* if I never competed or that I was just try'na get closer to Russell Tomlin. Point is, I was hangin' in there where and when I had to, and even now I was feeling nimble, hopping over puddles just like he was, over the island that separated north- and southbound traffic, till we easily crossed over to the other side of the street. Sure, he was passing me, but at least I was feelin' good about this first impression: *Don't take Stacy for no sucka. Nothing is gonna slow my stride.* It was so good to find that side of me again: the confidence to take certain risks in life.

Eventually we were inside Danté's truck and he was (out of nowhere) making excuses about its appearance, reaching to pick up tools and pipe fittings from the floor on the passenger's side.

"That's okay," I told him. "I'm good."

"Not exactly set up for a date here. Sorry."

"Uhh, *date?* No. I don't *think* so."

"I mean, I really wasn't expecting to entertain any—"

"Um, *Danté*? I'm not talkin' about your truck. I'm talkin' about the *date* part. This isn't a *date*. You're not *entertaining* me. In fact, we never ran into each other tonight. *O-kay*?"

"Uh, sure." His response came out something like a weak sigh.

And no he is *not* lookin' at me like I'm *coo-coo*?

# DANTÉ

One side of my brain was saying *coo-coo, coo-coo*. And there was probably a red flag that I should've paid attention to. But there's this *other* side of my brain! And sometimes it takes over without warning, like that day in Ms. Thomas's apartment. This was one of those times.

*Damn, this woman is fine*, I thought to myself. The way she just froze; stopped everything, including all the coming-in-from-the-rain blues, just to address me and (maybe) my little slip of the lip. Her eyes were so direct and daring, but also so large and beautiful. Her nose was sharp enough to cut me, but at the same time, her nostrils flared some and invited an eyeful of my attention. It was at this very instant that I had a much better look at her copper-tone skin and the shapely body that was now a passenger in my fairly new Chevy Blazer. It was only now that I realized I was at-tracted to this woman. And maybe *that's* even a lie (or an understatement). To be certain, I wanted to experience the hidden side of Stacy and see just how connected we were. I wanted to get my hands on Stacy and get close enough to smell more of her. And yes, I wanted to be *inside* of Stacy. So *what* if the timing might've been too soon; taking into account my recent swim with Ms. Thomas. I mean, who the hell was keeping track anyway?

And the other thing to consider was that you couldn't let opportunity pass you by. One moment Stacy might be available, and the next thing you know she'd be married off to someone (in my opinion) less worthy. And although I feel myself to be that hardworking, *worthy* candidate, I do have a selfish side. Stacy might just be all the redemption that I needed to let loose my burdens—the residual mental baggage I shouldered from apartment 7B. And now that I think of it, I'm wondering if that's what drove me to attraction, the comparison between her and—? *Naaah!*

Meanwhile, the tongue lashing that Stacy dropped on me still hadn't worn off, even if I was looking at her much differently than a few moments earlier. Except now, I found myself reviewing my every word and action—like walking on eggshells. And I was left to assume that the mere mention of *date* had to be the buzz word that flipped her switch. I remained speechless, wondering where all this came from, because surely there was something else other than my being too forward.

I SHOOK my head to show my understanding. But the faint *coo-coo, coo-coo* was still there in our midst as I started up the truck.

"I guess you wanna go straight home?" I mentioned this, but I was hoping that she'd disagree. *Why do I play these games? Why don't I just tell her what's on my mind?*

Stacy was already checking her lipstick and fixing her hair in the mirror. I couldn't help noticing how focused she was and how quickly she pulled herself together. That's when she turned to me.

"You wanna know what I notice most about men? The *majority* of men?" She turned her attention back to the mirror as she completed her statement. "You all are straight-up suckas when it comes to the females. *Especially* if y'all haven't tasted the ice cream yet." Still in the mirror and shaking her head as though she were disappointed, Stacy didn't appear to need a response. And, I was honestly conf'*rused*. So what was she saying? That I wasn't aggressive enough? Or that I let down too easy?

"Danté, take me somewhere for a drink."

Turning the truck out of its parking space, I said, *"Surely will, Miss Daisy."* Going for a laugh (and a *wee* bit of risky sarcasm) I uttered the words with a southern servant's accent.

WHEN YOU'RE in business for yourself you find a lot of perks to come along with the job. I suppose that's what it is for any business model. For me, the resources spread far and wide because, although I deal with a lot of our middle-to-low-income families, many of the people I do jobs for hold down important positions. Sometimes people shift jobs, but the resources never stop coming, so long as I am dependable and I do the best job possible. People are generally happy with my work and (besides paying me) they always seem to do something more. Mrs. Taylor always gives me some of her homemade apple dumplings. But she also manages a Foot Locker downtown, which means *mad* discounts on any footwear I buy. Jim Allen has a fish-and-meat market around the corner. So, even though I'm living the single life, my chicken and fish meals are always healthy. Donald Gilmore and his wifey, Liz, own the gas station around the corner. And while they don't do diddly-squat for me on the high price of gas, they *do* break me off *major* when my truck needs help, all because I'm dependable when they need me to fix something. And for my entertainment, I got at least two movie-theater employees that get me in, but I call Mary Lewis the "big dog of entertainment." Mary's another client of mine, who also does the accounting for Cablevision's executive offices. And since that company owns just about every major venue in town, like Madison Square Garden, Radio City, and The Beacon Theater, I always get offered complimentary tickets to box seats at Knick games or orchestra seats at the Christmas shows, plays, or just about any concert that comes to town. Better *believe* I be waitin' for Mary to need Mister Fix-It!

So Mister Fix-It is our family business, and it requires very little maintenance. I do no advertising since word of mouth really gets around. And Mr. Wise handles all the rest, like taxes, accounting, and all that. But, just as it was with every other resource, Mister Fix-It also introduces me to an abundance of human resources, such as my first date with Stacy. I met her auntie because of the work I do. I ran into Stacy in the elevator because of the work I do. And there's no way I would have acknowledged or recognized her at the bowling alley if it wasn't for my line of work. So it was only fitting that my relationship with JP's Restaurant (on City Island) would complete the night. It would be convenient both for the *drinks* that Stacy suggested, as well as food, if necessary.

Once we got comfortable at one of the isolated booths, I asked "So, are you saying you were kidding about the idea of the *date*?"

"Actually, no. I wasn't kidding. If my auntie knew I was out seeing men instead of bowling, or that I was on a date at the movies, instead of getting my hair done, I'd have some weight on my shoulders. Auntie is anal like that, and I don't really need that in my life right now. Can you believe she still thinks I'm a virgin, and that she's preserving me? She calls me and checks on me like a probation officer or something. And even before I *do* go out, she's gotta take down notes about my schedule, what I'll be doing when, and with who." Stacy gasped at the end of her words, and she began to reach around in her purse.

"Man. I don't get it. Why don't you just lay down the law? Remind her you're an adult?"

"It's not that easy. She's providing a roof over my head right now. No rent. Very little overhead. So I gotta abide by her rules, if you know what I'm sayin'. But trust and believe, I been wanting to do that for a minute now."

"Okay, I'm confused. So why couldn't you just tell me about the situation between you and Auntie? What was all the drama for in the truck? On one hand, you don't want the mention of a date. And in the same breath, you were calling me a sucka."

Stacy chuckled, now with her little palm mirror in hand, checking her makeup there in front of me.

"Oh, that's funny to you?" I asked without want for a reply. And so, now it was time for some of *my* drama. The waitress had just approached. "Can I have the check, please?"

Stacy was quiet for the instant. It seemed as if she had

an explanation for her ways and that she was about to be humble. But I didn't wait. I simply handed the waitress my money, including the tip. And while the exchange was going on, while Stacy's explanation was waiting to be told, I had another engagement.

"If you don't mind, excuse me, I need to use the *little boys'* room," I said, complete with my angle of sarcasm. I could see on Stacy's face that my work was taking its toll. *Good*.

BACK IN the truck, still in JP's dark parking lot, the rain had tapered off some. There was a light drizzle, enough to shower the windshield so that the neon JP's sign and everything outside was smeared. And now, Stacy was trying to clean up the mess she had started two hours earlier in Harlem.

"I was just sayin' that because of the *look* on your face. I mean, I don't *really* look at you as soft, or a sucka. Maybe I shouldn't have used those words. But, were you *serious*? I never expected you to fold that easy. Plus, like, you din' even *argue* the issue. You just shut up 'n' drove. I mean, is it that easy for a woman to get out of your hair? What if I *was* attracted to you, and I was just *testing* you to see your response?" Stacy let out a sharp buzzer sound from her lips. "Game over."

## STACY

I hated to come on so strong with this cutie-pie, but I've had too many experiences with men (or *so-called* men) where I've been the lush; where I've been the pushover. But after the last one? I said, *No more.* If it was up to me, a nigga had to know that I was ready to go hard at the drop of a dime. This way they wouldn't get confused and try to act up or act out, or worse—try'na put they hands on me. 'Cuz then I'm all about the hot ghetto mess. Try'na tell 'ya.

And here he comes with his spit game. Let's hear it:

"Well, Miss Stacy, first of all, I really am not in any kind of shape to be a part of anyone's *test.* And not—" I tried to interject, but he cut me off to keep with his point. I can't lie; as much as I didn't appreciate it, I've always said I sometimes need a boss to shut me up. 'Cuz I can be a handful. "And not only that; for a long time now I haven't been in the market for a woman where I can show my top game. So, for me, it's whatever *you* say. You wanna know the truth? I'm a pushover these days." Danté shrugged at the end of his explanation and changed the radio to WBLS. The quiet storm was playing "Is it a Crime," coincidentally one of my favorite songs from Sade. Without looking him straight in the eye, I couldn't help how disarmed I felt, and how my bold position had melted. Shit, he damn near made me forget whateva agenda I had—so far he didn't seem to be putting on an act. Either that, or he was really good with this relationship stuff. And then he had more to say. I inhaled, tryin' not to be so obvious. All I could hope for was that he didn't see through me and that I was taking the chance to play with his head. If he did, then he was definitely turning the tables now.

HE SAID, "And not that you were supposed to know this—*I know your auntie does*—but I had a couple close family members pass away recently. So my spirits are down some and I'm not as alert as I might be at another time in my life."

I didn't dare wait another second before I blurted, "Ohhh, Danté. I'm *so* sorry. I never—"

The conversation and the tension eased so much after that bomb, and I felt like all my defenses were down and that we were building our new relationship from scratch. I was so brokenhearted to hear about his loss—some real talk that was—and now *I* was on the verge of tears. I mean, I felt like things suddenly got so heavy, with Danté's life drawn out like some ancient painting on me—the canvas—and he was the master artist Vincent van Gogh. Thing is, this was something *I* might've done, especially when I feel the demon inside of me. But then, thinkin' about it all, I probably deserved every bit of guilt I was feeling, considerin' how I just tried to play him. Callin' him a *sucka* and whatnot. So, I figure maybe it was only right.

After a time the two drinks we had shared inside the restaurant began to wear, however I could feel myself turning to putty in Danté's hands. Even while we were still parked in his truck I could sense sorrow from his aura; no tears, just the whole head-down and filled with remorse. It had a powerful effect on me, whereas I just wanted to lean over and hug this man, someone I hardly knew. One thing I did know was that I had to stop pretending. I'm *way* less than the scandalous bitch I sometimes project, and for the most part I like to keep it real at all times. So, maybe this was something like Universal Law—what comes around, goes around.

———

I EVENTUALLY reached over and rubbed Danté's hand, tryin' to soothe him. Then I reached for his shoulders. It was the first time we got to *really* connect, so I felt that trembling when I get all nervous with a guy. I hesitated and took big swallows of air at that point.

"You okay, Danté? You need anything? Anything I can do?"

He cleared his throat and didn't look at me straight on. His hand went to his face so that I couldn't see his eyes. I could only imagine the pain he'd endured in the past months, and I got to askin' myself why I had to test him like I did. *Damn.* My hands automatically rubbed more of him until I was feeling up his neck. My other hand smoothed along the opposite side of his face. Eventually, I pulled him into my embrace. It was a little difficult in the front of the truck with the emergency break and all, but damned if I wasn't gonna maneuver here to try'n make things better.

"It's gonna be alright, boo. I didn't mean to come at you so hard," I said. "And I should know better, because I been there."

Danté hugged me tighter and I felt his empathy toward *my* past issues, but I wasn't interested in talking about *my* past, since that would confuse things. After all, wasn't this moment all about *Danté*? Pacifying *his* sorrows?

At *least* ten minutes of cuddling passed before I broke down. No act here. Danté really had an impact on me.

I couldn't help what came out of my mouth next:

"Do you want some company tonight?"

# DANTÉ

In my mind I choked back the questions, wondering how she would work *this* out with her anal auntie. Not that this was a promise of the inevitable—my mind racing with images of Stacy bent over the vanity and sink while I'm looking in the mirror, admiring my own work as I did the punishing from behind. But, I'll be damned if we weren't off to a real good start.

I couldn't answer her right away, since that was *exactly* what I was thinking. Instead, I turned to look out the driver's-side window. Next thing I know, as though she was trying to assist with my decision-making, Stacy had her hands in my lap. My eyes wide, my face still turned, I couldn't *believe* what was happening. I didn't know whether to stop her because I wanted to show respect, despite the bowling-alley nonsense, or if I should grab a chunk of her hair to encourage some of the raunchiest moments of my life. And then I guess I'd say, *To hell with it—it was good while it lasted*. And of course, if I did that, why would I want to have any extended relationship with her? I mean, did she do this with all the guys? Or was it that my performance was so moving and me so convincing and handsome and so eligible that she needed to make me feel better by *any means necessary?* By this time, it didn't matter because Stacy, the pretty-ass, aggressive, shapely woman who I got to spend time in the elevator with, the disgruntled girl who had sidetracked my night of bowling—*my client's niece! for God sakes*—was taking me half erect in her mouth like this was a job interview. And now that she wasn't looking, it was alright for *me* to look, and *damn I hated to have these thoughts*, but it was so *redeeming* to see her head bobbing up and down in my lap, with her wet and attentive gums accepting some and then *all* of my rock-hard dick in her mouth.

Some-all-some-all-lick-lap-lick-lap . . .

I didn't, couldn't, *wouldn't* have a word to say. I just shut up and let nature take its course. And wow, did this ever feel natural. At one point Stacy turned her head some to see my face. But by this time I was leaning back and ever engaged in the moment. I didn't know where this would lead, and I had no idea if this was the beginning of a great relationship or signs of a failed one. However, who in their right mind would be concerned about all that at a time like this?

"AHH, STACY?" I muttered her name while at the same time holding back an ejaculation with all my might. No *doubt* that would have been a mistake. This was impulsive. She was a willing participant. And, unless some act of God got in the way, there was no way I would pass up more of this. "Can we—can we hold off from this? I wanna take you up on your offer about tonight." I said this with the moans and grunts of a confused epileptic. Sure, I wanted more, but within more-comfortable surroundings, *please*?

Stacy let up from my lap, not without the sounds of her smacking those overworked lips. I suppose it was good for her since her eyes were reduced to slits and her deep breath seemed to want for more of me. And while Stacy grabbed up the bottle of water she'd started earlier, I got to thinking, *Damn, that was some good head.* I praised this girl to the high heavens as I wiggled the car out of park and eased out of JP's. *Thanks, JP, for the use of your parking lot.* It was so convenient for that impulsive moment. But in the back of my mind I couldn't help knowing I was raised better than this and that this was *way* out of character for me and any interaction I ever—I take that back. As I thought this, I also thought about Ms. Thomas. Maybe this was a virus going around and I was the carrier?

"What will you tell your aunt?" I asked on the parkway back to Park Chester.

"I got a girlfriend who will vouch for me. She'll bitch about how her car broke down and how she needed my help to push it back home. We'll do it on a conference call so Auntie will think we're in the same house at the same time. *Shit,* I'll say everything and anything for some more of *that,*" she said, waving her pointer finger at my loins.

Funny how Stacy said that, as if my dick was the next best thing after ice cream. And this girl's scruples were the worst; but *wow,* I loved every minute of it.

THE RAIN had all but subsided, and around 11:00 p.m. back in Park Chester, the neighbors were starting early for this weekend's Puerto Rican Day parade. The salsa and reggae-tone music was loud, coming from many different sources; most from speakers wedged in apartment windows. Already there were Puerto Rican flags either taped across the hoods of cars or mounted and proudly streaming through the streets of the Bronx. Somewhere, the scent of weed was wafting in the air. And to think this was only Friday. This was about to be a hot weekend, in more than one way.

Thinking that the weekend and the parties were the reason it was so easy for me to find a parking space, I was able to keep the truck close to my building. I did the whole gentleman's gesture of running around to open the door for my *date*, and I escorted her, arm in arm, down the pathway and to the entrance. The heat was more bearable tonight thanks to all the rain, but I couldn't help knowing what we faced in my apartment. All the while, the anticipation was boiling in my stomach to know this absolute dime was by my side, and how she practically *promised* me the pussy would be mine all night long. *I got a girlfriend who will vouch for me . . . Shit, I'll say everything and anything for some more of* **that**.

Wow. It couldn't get any better than this: like an incredibly alluring vacation brochure that was about to deliver on all its promises.

"Listen, I hate to make excuses, but my car is the clean side of me. My apartment, however, is a whole *'nother* story. Remember, it's been a man's world for some time now."

Stacy shrugged. She said, *"Whateva."* But as she did, I could see her eyes reviewing the bulge in my pants. We were stepping into the elevator and before the door even closed, Stacy pulled my arm so that I swung around. Her mouth glued itself to mine and her tongue pried and searched and tossed with my own. *Wow*, was this ever the impulsive vixen to make my day—my week and my year. And before I could *think* of something to say, we were against the elevator doors, the walls, and just about to waste no more time before I realized where we were and before I heard the doors slide open again. Stacy and I were about to hit the floor and go at each other when old man Curtis came into view. *Oh shit*.

"Alright now, you younguns. 'Nuff a that foolishness in the—is that *you*, Danté Garrett? My *word*, what would your *father* say?"

I was already pulling myself together and I encouraged Stacy to do the same with the nudge of my elbow. It was nothing more than Stacy's shirt and my zipper. We hadn't gotten so far as to offer the ultimate exposure to the old-timer, but I'm sure his imagination was through the roof, knowing that *something* raunchy was goin' on.

"Excuse me, Mr. Curtis. We were—we—"

"No need for explainin', young man. Just *please*. There's a time and a place for everything. Show some *respect*." Mr. Curtis reached toward the buttons to select his floor, but not without getting a *good* look at Stacy over his eyeglasses. Meanwhile, I'm telling myself, *Damn—the elevator hasn't moved. I didn't even get to push the button*. And, *Thank God he doesn't like her aunt*.

One day about three years earlier I had to sit through about a half hour of Mr. Curtis ranting about how Mrs. Singletary had turned him down for a date. And my mind calculated that, and the idea of Stacy only recently moving in with her aunt. All told, he might not even *know* who he was looking at. Beyond that, he was probably getting his *dirty old man* on with that one slick gaze passed off. No harm done.

"Alrighty now. Y'all be good, and try—try and keep the noise down, if possible." Mr. Curtis cracked me up with that one. *If possible*. The music in our midst was already madness, with the whole *b-bump-bump, b-bump-bump* from a whole lotta somebodies feeding into the early Puerto Rican Day euphoria. But it didn't matter to me since I was on a mission right now.

AS SOON as we got into my apartment, the heat consumed us as if we'd walked into a sauna.

"It takes me a minute to cool the apartment down. No sense in leaving the air conditioner on all day." But, while I said that, I also cursed myself for being the conscious consumer, not the *experienced player* women might expect to see these days. It sure would've paid off to not play consumer-conscious and to leave it on *today* of all days!

"Please. We in the 'hood, Mr. G. This ain't nothin' to me," said Stacy. "In fact, we don't even *need* air conditionin', 'cause it's about to get hot up in here *anyways*. And we— really don't—have time—for all—of that."

*Wow*. She had already kicked off her shoes, worked her way past the miscellaneous tools I had near the doorway, and basically attacked me. She was already in my arms, my embrace, and my mouth. *Wow*. Stacy was the most impulsive, spontaneous woman I'd met to date, and I didn't mind a bit. She pulled my shirt over my head and nibbled at my chest. And while we were attached at the lips, I lifted her through the hallway and farther into the apartment. I had to maneuver past the workbench I had set up earlier to cut a few plumbing fixtures, but we made it to my couch. I would've chosen my bed, but (1) the bed wasn't made and (2) I wanted to have *something* left that was private, consid-

ering this woman was inviting herself to just about everything *else* belonging to me.

The moaning, the friction, and the intense heat came
second to our sweaty faces. I couldn't wait to slip her
blouse up and over her head, and no sooner did I eventually get my hands full of her slick, C-size breasts. Her
breasts were instantly becoming my new addiction, and
they reminded me of the Halle Barry, Janet Jackson, and
Beyoncé types we always see in the media. Those images
are just shot at us through every means, whether it's TV,
magazines, movies, or the Internet, as if they were all loaded
in shotguns and aimed at the next pair of eyes. And not
that those women defined utter beauty (for me), just that
touching Stacy's body gave me that kind of impression.
Tight. Pointed. Shapely. Way different from the sagging
madness that Ms. Thomas had in my face just a week or so
earlier. And now Stacy's breasts were in my face like hot
honey biscuits I wouldn't mind stuffing into my mouth;
and then they *were* in my mouth. Salty from sweat and bit-
ter from some residual perfume, I didn't care either way.
I was enjoying these substantial amounts of flesh feeding
my moment of ecstasy.

*"Murder she wrote*
*Murder she wro-o-oooote"*

The soundtrack that fueled our tossing and turning was
more than mere music; there were also sirens and blips
from nearby police activity in the streets. Those trucks
driving by with their boomin' systems set off some car

alarms in their wake, and so there was some of that. From the apartment upstairs there were heavy footfalls that made my ceiling rumble, and perhaps that was a motorcycle (or two) with the revving engines outdoors. And *none of it* mattered. It was all coincidental. The only thing that *did* matter right now was the embrace that Stacy and I were locked in when she moaned, "I like it raw." I was trying so hard to prevent any premature ejaculation before the impact of our fun hit the tipping point.

*Yeah, I know there's supposed to be courting, Granddad. I know old-fashioned wins every time. I remember whatcha told me; but this girl is so different. She just makes me forget everything I ever knew. She changed my whole way of dealing with the opposite sex, and she did it in record time.*

I even had to stop at one point and pull out to adjust my thinking, but the truth was I was about to explode! Stacy, in the meantime, rolled onto the floor, her hands pulling at her hair in frustration. At that very moment she looked so *damn* good that I went back for her. And right there on the floor I delivered hungry, intense thrusts as Stacy moaned and cried out her want for more. She shouted, *"Take it! Take it!"* But she didn't have to encourage me. I was *already taking it*, and *working it*, and *punishing it*, with a focus that (if nothing else) this encounter would *never* be forgotten in our lifetime. Yes, it was so suddenly my mission to fuck her mind and body in ways they had never been fucked in the past. Her loud wails, the grabbing at my floor rug, the couch, and a nearby chair convinced me that I was indeed accomplishing that mission. But not until Stacy began to cry in those long,

*hard* sobs was I clear that Danté Garrett was an important evolution in her life; a life in which I didn't mind
playing a role. But, even at that late revelation, I stayed
the momentum and drove myself thoroughly past even
my own expectations. If she was faking up until this
point, I'd *surely* know it! She reached back and grabbed
my ass, basically wanting me to maintain the pressure,
the friction, and everything I was doing to her. And I did
that again and again, thrust after long, wet thrust. I finally
went over the top, grabbing her waist and arching her
back, so that I could get to the deepest parts of her.

# STACY

This was so new for me. Not the aggression that I came at
him with. Not the feeling of moving too fast, or the idea
that we were practically strangers. None of that was as
much of an issue as this man filling me and reaching my
very core with his thorough, masculine drive. I've been
with men before, so it wasn't the strength or the size or even
the punishment that was so usual. I didn't get that from
Danté. Danté was hittin' me with something so different,
so unexplainable. And all I could do was reach for something to hold on to so that I could arch my back some more,
so he could have more of me. And I don't know why I was
thinking this, but, with all this going on, I found myself
*testifying*! I could almost hear myself sayin', *Lawd have
mercy, please don't take this man out of my life!* I mean, the
way he was workin' it, he could do no wrong. I swear, he

could put a gun to my head and *rob* me if he wanted to, so long as I could get some more of this good dick! *No problem!* After so many thrusts in and out of me, the punishment mixed with ecstasy, my tears of joy were confused with my cries and moans, Danté was *still* continuously muscling his way into me until I eventually came harder than ever before. I mean, it was like I was peeing myself, only there was a rush of thousand-watt voltage that came with it.

ALL I remember was how we both collapsed on the floor, glued together, sweaty and spent, and lovin' it. The music was still pounding from this way and that, even as midnight passed. But instead of its being annoying, it only served as the soundtrack to the numbing spell Danté had on me. Danté—even the way his name rolled off my tongue tasted like newfound love. And probably, for as long as I lived, I wouldn't ever forget the robbery and the ecstasy that took place here in his apartment. I wouldn't ever forget the surrender or the absolute elation I felt laying there in that same helpless daze in Danté's arms.

## DANTÉ

I hopped up to cut on the air conditioner, then went into the bathroom to grab a washcloth for the two of us. After I helped wipe her once and twice and three times, I came back to carry her into my bedroom. No way did I care about how my bed looked now, since the two of us had basically consummated the relationship and what we meant to each other (however spur-of-the-moment), all in the past couple hours. It was both blissful and promising. She was willing and smart, aggressive and passive. She also looked great: great body and intoxicating attitude. If there was anything to hide, I didn't see it. But then, I guess I wouldn't, as blinded as I was by the lust and passion. If there was a red flag to find, I didn't see it, or didn't care.

Looking back on it now, I definitely should have cared.

# [ T H R E E ]

IF YOU LOOKED into the rituals of those day-to-day activities you'd see that Danté Garrett likes to schedule most of his appointments for the afternoons and early evenings. I like to surf the Internet in the late evenings, where I read all the up-to-date articles they print in magazines without having to go get them, only to clutter my apartment any more than it already is. If not that, I catch my favorite house-and-garden shows on cable—even if they're telling me stuff I already know. During the early morning, if there's no work scheduled, I'm catching up on sleep. Otherwise, you'd never find me hungover from club or bar hopping, and I don't do many nights out to the movies. The bootlegs are fine by me, since nowadays they are just as good as going to the theater. And the theaters? That's another thing. With all the people who frequent the movies (especially at the one closest to where I live), you'd think there was something more to do than to go and show off your girl, or to show out. Fights, stabbings, shootings: all of it over a woman. So I don't mind being a hard worker and a homebody. If I can avoid trouble I will, unless it confronts me one-on-one. Then it's up to God who lives or dies.

But with my routine and my schedule, there's no way I am up and about, cleaning my house, dishes, and clothes at seven thirty in the morning. I am *not* dusting bookshelves, cleaning surfaces, or organizing stuff that's been out of place for months and years. And I am *definitely* not cleaning my tub and shower as early as eight in the morning. But that Saturday—"the morning after"—was *so* different. The encounter with Stacy had me feeling like a marathon man! I did *all* that, and then had energy to run to the store for a few extra things while Stacy slept like an angel. And to think I intended to revolutionize *her* life! It was *me* who was the *changed* man! After all the cleaning, I made eggs and bacon for the two of us. I even went the extra mile to make tea, to squeeze some fresh orange juice, and to slice up a tomato, pepper, and onion so that she could join me to sprinkle some fresh veggies atop the eggs with some sharp cheddar cheese.

"You eat this way all the time?" she asked once she was able to open her eyes. She didn't seem to mind being naked there in front of me and I couldn't get enough of the sight, *or* the scent of sex that still hung in the air.

"No *question*. I mean I don't usually do it for *two*, but I definitely do it. I like to eat healthy. If the body's treated right, the mind will treat everything else right. You should taste my fried rice. It's off the hook."

"I see," she said, letting me see her eyes traverse from my face down to the hidden jewels in my shorts. "Well, everything else is already *off the hook*."

I laughed and said, ."You so funny." Then we ate like hungry mammoths.

"So, do you get down like that *all* the time? I mean," she swallowed what she had in her mouth, "you were an absolute *animal* last night."

Not answering her question yet, I asked, "Was I too much?"

"Too much? *Maaaan*, if I can get dick like that *every* day, I'll follow you to the moon and back, *ten times*." Stacy exhaled real noticeably.

I chuckled with my mouth full of food and managed to ask, "Are you always this forward?"

"Shit, *yes*. If there's something on my mind, I hold my tongue for *no one*. And if there's something I like, or that I want *more of*? Better believe I'm a *happy woman* if I get it. Now I might have to do what I gotta do to keep a safe roof over my head, but at the end of the day, *I'ma get mine*." Stacy practically sang her praises and desires while I continued to study her. I couldn't see any cracks, even if she was over the top with her life's demands. The thing that I admired about her most was her ability to be the perfect lady, like when we were in the elevator that first day we met, but how she was the aggressor when we were escaping the bowling alley and rushing through the rain. And she could also stay grounded and keep it 'hood when necessary; how she shrugged off my hot apartment and didn't quibble about the imperfections in life—the mess in my truck; the mess in my apartment. She was a chameleon, I guessed. And that was fine since everyone was unique in their own way.

Something struck me, and since she seemed to be allow-ing access, I didn't mind asking.

"Stacy?"

"Mmm-hmm?"

"I was just wondering: you appear to be *all that*. But, why don't you have a man? Why hasn't anyone scooped you up?" *What's wrong with you that I'm not seeing?* I wondered to myself. And then I *had* to ask, "And then I *really* need to know what was up with the whole *'I like it raw'* comment."

"I guess they too afraid of a woman who *knows* what she wants."

"But what about your past boyfriends? I know you had to have few of 'em?" *Pretty mothafucka that you are.*

"Okay, you hittin' me with a whole lotta questions, Mista' *Ned Stopple*. How about I ask *you* a few questions? How about I rate *you* on a scale from one to ten? I mean, why *I* gotta be under the microscope all a sudden? I mean, how chauvinist of you."

I thought to apologize after her comments. But then I remembered how she had called me a *sucka* the night be-fore. So instead of following my reflexes, I said, " 'Cuz a nigga like me got a lot to lose. No babies, my own business, money in the bank, and the whole *gentleman in the 'hood* thing goin' on, *plus* the dick is good. *What!*"

Stacy giggled. "Now *that* was good. You really had me goin' for a minute there; like, for *real*. I been around some thugs and," she snickered again, "that was *good*. I was 'spe-cially turned on by the whole way you moved your shoul-ders and head—like some *real* thug-shit." More laughs.

*Oh no, she didn't play me.*

"Alright, so I never claimed to be a thug, Stacy. But, if

you're gonna beat around the bush about who you deal with, you can at least tell me why it was so important for us to fuck in the raw. I mean, you try'na get pregnant or something?"

A chuckle, then she said, "I'm very trusting of the right person. I think you're the right person—'less I'm wrong? And I don't do it like that with everyone; matter fact, the last time I been with a man was months ago. I felt like a virgin last night. Especially when you came in me. I can't *wait* to have your baby."

"WHAT!? I thought you said—"

Stacy cackled like a heckler at Caroline's.

"Calm down, playboy. I was only kiddin'. Like I said last night, I use the IUD. No worries. And no babies."

*"Girrrl!"* I immediately tackled and tickled her until she eventually gave in and said *uncle*.

When we were normal again, she said, "But seriously, I been givin' you the benefit of the doubt on that. Not just that you look and eat healthy; you just add up to all the man I need, that's all. And besides, you get an A for your *outstanding* effort in bed."

"Girl? *Outstanding* is spelt with a O."

"So I missed a few English classes. Plan on disciplinin' me, *Mista* Danté Garrett? Can a lil' ol' girl like me offer you an apology? I mean, you just came and scooped lil' ol' me up off the big bad streets of *Haah*-lem, and I'm *ever* so grateful. . . ." Stacy moved the tray aside and maneuvered her body so that she was closer to me. "So, you mind, *Mista* Garrett, if I just show you *how* grateful I is?" Amid my heavy breathing, Stacy wasn't waiting for a response, and she proceeded to level her head so that it was down in my lap; and once again her spontaneity was *killing me*! I hated the way she was *playing me*—like a *fiddle*! And I couldn't help but wonder who this woman *really* was. But at the same time, she was turning me the fuck *on* with how she was acting. The whole southern-belle bit, complete with that down-south accent. What would my elders say to me now? *There you go, boy; suckered again.*

AND NOW, more dictation. More salacious sounds; and again, Stacy was engrossed with the length of me in and out of her mouth, making that SuperHead bootleg I saw look like an amateur home video.

To put it mildly, Stacy had me feeling like Super*man*. And by all the signals she basically gave me permission to do what I wanted with her. So, I went down that road and directed her to stand up. I helped her off the bed so that she easily worked her way to a kneeling position on the floor before me. Meanwhile, she continued with her incredible work. I mean *incredible* work. And somewhere during my uncontrollable emotions, I looked up to the heavens that promised to be above and beyond the ceiling of my bedroom, wondering if Pop could see and, maybe, even *feel* how damn incredible this was. And as I was about to reciprocate, trying to reposition myself so that I could bless her with some of the same, Stacy stopped me in midmotion. Even while she was still extrabusy down there, she took my hands and molded them around her neck, encouraging me to—what the *hell*? She wanted me to *choke* her?

*Lord have mercy!* I quietly exalted, wondering what I was getting into and what else this woman was capable of.

Needless to say, Stacy never fully answered my question about other men, and why she—pretty, smart, and aggressive—was so available, without a man by her side. After all, wasn't that the *natural way* of things? And yet, regardless of my unanswered questions, I surely didn't argue with anything; just went along with the program. And I didn't really remember to revisit the issue, either. I can't imagine what threw me off and made me forget.

During the next month and a half I found myself getting phone calls from both Ms. Thomas and the ever-sweet Polly Purebread-slash-Video Vixen, Stacy. I didn't have the heart to tell Ms. Thomas to get a life or to stop calling me. For one: she's a good client. And maybe I had procrastinated in expressing the importance of separating the business from the pleasure. But then, I didn't want to hurt her feelings with the whole hit-it-'n'-quit-it attitude. It's almost always the woman who's gonna want that attachment after they've given up the goodies. But for us, if there's no love in the first place, there will likely be no love down the road. And the thing with Ms. Thomas was definitely a lust thing. My thing is that, as a man, I may not know what I'm looking for, but that doesn't mean I'm gonna stop looking! And then, almost always, the fault is ours. We'll do whatever we have to and say whatever we have to just to get inside, and we won't think about and won't care about the consequences. So maybe I'd be a hypocrite to bring that up now, *after* the evening we had together? *After* I came on her chest? It was a bit much to figure out, and to have to tell her, *Well, gee, Ms. Thomas, I loved crossing the line to mix business with pleasure, but we need to put an end to this. And besides, I'm fucking another client's niece. Who happens to be* more my age and more of the type I'd like to, say, spend the rest of my life with? You think you can handle that and **stop calling me?** You psycho bitch?

No, I couldn't bring it to her that way; wouldn't want it to get around that I was Mister Fix-It in more than one way. And yet, getting back to her would be necessary at some point since she was (I'm sure) getting desperate, calling me for things I *know* were not necessary jobs. However, my focus was on just two issues right now: my work, which was still piled sky high, and my new girl, Stacy, who I barely had time for.

Even this soon, I have to say that Stacy was the best thing that ever happened to me. Just the juice she brought into my life had me hopping onto job sites like I was *on something*. And some clients who noticed even *asked* me, *Are you smoking something, Danté?* And I'd have to respond, *Naw. I'm just thrilled to be alive right now!* And then they'd say, *Well, it's good to see you come back to life. I was worried about you for a quick minute.* But little did folks know, I was cured over and above normal! I was as happy as a pig in shit. But the truth was that Stacy was rockin' my world, both mentally *and* physically. Stacy was spending money on me, even though, thanks to Pop's life insurance, I had a little more than seventy thousand dollars in my bank account. Still, Stacy was showin' me love from every which direction, even though I worked those long hours and had very little time to spend with her.

"I know what you're doin', baby. I'm in this for the long run," she'd tell me. Or she'd encourage me, like when I was getting strife from a super over at building 10. Because he wanted most or all of the business to come to him, he

*****************
Items Checked Out
*****************

JOHNSON, SHATYRA
26592001229075

Title:          Burning desire /
Item ID:        36592050010651
Call Number:    F RIELE
Out:            07/27/2017 11:19 AM
Due:            08/24/2017 11:59 PM
Renewals        2
Remaining:

Current fine    $0.00
balance:

would make things difficult for me and, maybe, not allow me easy access, or he'd be less than helpful if I needed to get to the basement on an electrical matter. Funny how the supers never really have time to get to all their issues in a timely manner, but the moment the work gets outsourced to a handyman, they wanna make things extra difficult and raise holy hell about it. My thing is, organize your time and get to your tenants' problems in an expeditious manner so that they don't need to call me in the first place. Another thing you can do is get the job done right *the first time* and they won't need to call someone who's more professional, more experienced, and who has a better attitude with people of *all* nationalities; not just my *own*. *Hello?* I found myself ranting like this from time to time, and Stacy just happened to be there—the pillow to cushion my complaints.

"Baby, just continue to be *you*. They gon' have to get over it," Stacy would tell me. And she'd massage my neck and shoulders and put me to sleep after a long day. Next thing I know, she's out the door, rushing off to beat Auntie's curfew. Not until the morning would I wake up to realize she'd done even more cleaning in my apartment, making things more organized and convenient to find. She eventually situated all my bills and other paperwork. At one point, my place looked like a custodian's shop; but now, after Stacy came into the picture and put her "woman's touch" down, it was a comfortable home again. I felt like I could breathe and that my life was back in order. The only thing I could never figure out is why there was always change on the floor. I mean, pennies, nickels, dimes, and quarters, lying on the floor like it rains loose change every day. And although I never really gave it too much thought at the time, it was but another of those red flags that I should've paid attention to.

Besides that, I had to admit my place had changed for the better. With a laugh, I could recall times in the past when I had to ask myself if I'd ever see my apartment again. But nowadays, I'm asking God, Cupid, (or the universe as a whole) how I was blessed with such a wonderful woman. It wasn't as if we went out every night, but we managed to squeeze a few dates in here and there. We did the movies, dinner at Mobay on 125th, and even though I was beat from a long day of work, we actually made time to revisit Harlem Lanes one Friday night. On a number of occasions we just stayed in while I made fried rice, salmon, or barbecued chicken. My menu wasn't a tremendous one, but the few dishes I could make (in my opinion) had five-star written all over them. It was two months into our relationship and I never gave it a second thought that the church might be having another of their outings such as the one that Stacy and I met at. So, of course, as coincidence would call it, Pastor Bishop ran into us at the desk where you get your shoes.

"Well, if it isn't *my man* young Danté."

"Hey, Preach. How's it goin'?"

"I should ask *you* that," he replied.

I looked at Stacy, considered what hell there'd be to pay if word got out too soon, and pulled Pastor Bishop aside.

"Ahh, *Preach?*"

He didn't answer, just raised his chin, in a sense bracing himself for whatever I was about to say.

"If anyone can keep something confidential, I know *you* can."

He nodded his head, still without saying a word.

"Yes, Mrs. Singletary's niece and I are seeing each other. She's making me incredibly happy, and *no* her aunt doesn't know, doesn't need to know, and *shouldn't* know until we're ready to tell her."

I could tell by his knowing eyes that Pastor Bishop could read between the lines.

"I get the point, young Danté. I only have one question— well, maybe two. How old is she?"

I made a face to express my surprise that Preach would insinuate the obvious. Then I said, "Preach, really. If there's one thing I'm not it's a predator. Stacy is twenty-one. Seen her ID."

"Okay. Well, you know I had to ask. She does look young."

"And your other question?" I said, on the very border of being short with him.

"Uhh, I was thinking I might see you at service this Sunday, yes?"

He had me cornered. No way out of it.

"Yes, Preach. I'll be there." If he hadn't seen us in the bowling alley, caught with our pants down, I might've passed on a church appearance as I had on so many occasions in the past. But I had no choice now.

"Everything okay? He's not one of those neighborhood gossips, is he?" Stacy asked.

"Naw. But now that I think about it, I don't wanna hafta put out more fires tonight."

Stacy didn't quite understand what I was talking about, and then she did, once she heard my request with the attendant.

"You have a lane on the first floor? I hate being around

all those church ladies, always up in somebody's business, if you know what I mean."

The attendant smiled and made the necessary arrangements so that I and my boo could bowl without having to look over our shoulders to wonder what church lady would see us and how long it might take for word to get back to Auntie. Meanwhile, the night was incredible and erotic all at once. I taught Stacy to bowl, handling the bowling ball with her, walking her through the posture, the form, and the stroke.

"Come to think of it, bowling is pretty much like sex: if your posture's not right, it doesn't matter how good you hold the ball."

"Is *that* so? Well, I think I hold your balls pretty good, don't you?"

"The *bowling* ball, Stacy."

"Oh, right. Of course."

"Mmm-hmm." I went on, trying to be serious: "And if you don't hold the ball right, it doesn't matter how good your stroke is—one thing is just important as the next."

"Well, if you ask me, you got the strokin' part down *just* right."

"You so *silly*, Stacy. Uhh, I think you're up next?"

Stacy threw a couple of gutter balls, but I wondered if that wasn't on purpose, just to get more of my *hands-on* attention. Then, for the next hour, I went on showing her how, until her bowling was close to harmonious with mine, like some neatly choreographed dance. And in all of that *hands-on teaching*, I don't think there's a body part of hers that went untouched on bowling night. And it wasn't like I embarrassed her or anything because the way the bowling alley is dark, lit only by neon and specialty lighting, more or less sets the stage for the fun we had.

Later, we made love with desperation and purpose. But something happened in bed that night, and it freaked me out. As a general rule, Stacy was to be home by 11:00 p.m., unless there was a special event going on, at which point Stacy's auntie would have to be fully familiar with the hows and whys. To me it was all silly, but if anyone saw how much of a panic Stacy would be in, they'd do like I do.

*Anything you say, boo.*

However, the window of time that Stacy had to work with often had her hopping up and out of bed so that she'd meet that damn curfew.

On that Friday night, not only did she sleep past her aunt's extended deadline, but instead of merely hopping up out of bed, she woke up screaming at the top of her lungs. Loud, wailing cries that shook me hard like an earth tremor. Seconds later, this woman was marching through the apartment in a desperate search for something. I wondered if I had missed something here and maybe someone broke into my place and Stacy had some insight on the matter. Then, before I could catch up with her, she was already headed back to the bedroom. Only, now she had a wooden baseball bat with her. *Where the hell did that come from?*

Aside from that, I felt the urgency here and wanted to hold and console Stacy. But there was just no negotiating with a naked woman who was curled up in a fetal position *hugging a baseball bat*! I can honestly say that I have never been through anything more frightening than to (at one moment) experience total peace, and then (a moment later) to be thrown into total shock, with deafening ears, dizziness, with my body suddenly going through "the shakes." But, the bit with the baseball bat took things to some whole other dimension.

The next day, Stacy didn't even have a reason for the sudden outburst; her thing was: *it just happened*. And my thing was: *that shit was crazy*.

I DIDN'T speak to any professionals or even close friends about Stacy's outburst, thinking that it was just a strange occurrence. And during the next couple of weeks the relationship between us was as normal as could be. I even went to great efforts to find extra time for a movie and dinner in the city, and we even spent an afternoon reading at a Barnes & Noble store way out in White Plains. It was my every intention to have her forget about things and the possible embarrassment that might come along with it. I didn't speak on it until I felt it was okay. The furthest I took it was to one day say, "If you need to talk to me about anything, you know my ears and arms are open." And I left it at that.

But the manic attacks didn't end there.

Ms. Garcia is one of my clients who works at a record label and, as usual, she invited me to a party. This time, the event featured Keyshia Cole and Donnell Jones. The last go-round, before Stacy came into the picture, Ms. Garcia and I went together to a four-hour all-expenses-paid cruise and concert featuring Toni Braxton. And *believe me*, the tension of those first-date jitters were in the air. First of all, Ms. Garcia was attractive, she was accustomed to getting her way, and although she's older and I'm still considered a young whippersnapper, the two of us were single. So I had every reason to believe that she was after me. But I had to *stay on the straight and narrow,* as Pop would say. And you best believe that Pop was up waiting for me that night, too. Although I'm not sure if he wanted to hear the *nitty-gritty* or if he was just checkin' to make sure I kept with the rules of the game. In the end, it was tough, 'cause Ms. Garcia's a sexy mama jama. But I kept my discipline. And I don't know what the difference was between Ms. Garcia and Ms. Thomas, except for the passage of time and all the strife in my life. Add to that Ms. Thomas's kind of laying it all out on a platter for me—I mean, how else am I supposed to act with a naked woman just lying there begging for it, challenging me, and (more or less) offering to ease my pain? I'd say I did exactly what was expected of me. But other than the *Soul Train experience* I had with Ms. Thomas more or less helping me through my depression, I had not broken "the code." And I think Ms. Garcia respected me for that and so grew our professional relationship.

When I asked her about these latest tickets and if she minded my taking someone else to the Keyshia Cole/Donnell Jones event, she said, *Not at all. In fact, they're not tickets at all. It's a guest-list issue. I have two **more** spots if you need them.*

"No, just two is fine," I told her. And she told me to bring my ID to show it to whoever was handling the VIP list at the club.

## STACY

I got to the point in my life where I didn't care what people thought of my past. My thing is, I had to do what I had to do to survive. *Period*. And if you gonna judge me, then you need to judge *you* first. Nobody was there to help me when I had it hard. Nobody was there when my uncle—

I don't even wanna go there. I'm just try'na move forward with my life. I'm just try'na make somethin' of my life; the first in my family to do so. Okay, yeah, I'm a little twisted in the head. A little *tick-tick-boom* at times. But what woman isn't? And as far as this whole *if you need to talk to me about anything* conversation, I fail to understand what Danté's talkin' about. I'm sayin' what does he need me to talk about other than *I'm that bitch that rocks his world*. What more does he need but a real *ride or die* bitch who can do all the domestic stuff and *still* be his superwoman. That's right: a lady in the streets, and a slut in the bedroom—that's me all day. And as long as he does right by me, I'm gonna be that chick that sucks his dick to the very last drop.

UP UNTIL now, I hadn't been to any big celebrity events in New York. Plenty of 'em go down in ATL: the Velvet Room. Verve. e.s.s.o. But most of what we got is celebs from *the dirty*, all of 'em doin' much of the same, somehow keepin' it crunk in hip-hop or clothes, or porn, or all of the above. It gets boring for a chick like me after a while. But on any given night you could come down to my 'hood and see the new chicks all lined up at the club, on account of some glossy, colorful handouts with sexual overtones that were handed out in the weeks before. And of course there were always some popular names printed as "special invited guests," or commercial attachments that are supposed to catch the eyes and, I guess, seduce potential club-goers. It got to a point where a girl didn't know what flyers to believe and which ones to throw away. And if I'm lucky enough to get to a real party, guaranteed to be jam-packed with ballers, I'm more than likely to see police *everywhere*, all of 'em starin' at me in my skimpy dresses. And of course the best of us are wearin' as little as possible, no matter how cold the weather is, just so we can catch ourselves a baller. And the ballers know what it is, 'cuz they come to the clubs, spend thousands of dollars on bottles and VIP treatment, and they show out and show off their jewels and rings and medallions for the very same reasons.

But this New York scene was different, at least the one Danté was takin' me to. First off the sidewalk was wall-to-wall people when we got there, with the whole red-carpet treatment out in front and someone to check our names on a guest list. I gotta say that I was feelin' special already—not the showpiece hangin' on a man's arm and him hittin' off a club promoter with a few bills for the favor. There was no impressive exhibition of police around, and no cocky thugs broadcasting what they had on their necks and wrists.

So, I immediately told myself *wow* when they flipped through so many pages of names and pointed out Danté's name. I had never done this before (the red-carpet bit) and I was already feeling out of place. But when the hostess signaled the club security to let us in through the velvet ropes, the rush was awesome from that instant.

Inside, the music was already intoxicating, and it went well with all the photographers snapping away at (I guess) celebrities walking across the red carpet. I say that because Danté and I were among those to cross through, and I *know*

I'm not no celebrity. Not *yet*, anyways. There was a huge white banner that served as a backdrop to all the action, complete with a number of sponsors branded all over it. Most of the people we saw had on after-work attire, dresses and a drink in hand, so to fit in we just needed to hit the bar.

"Hey, Danté, no pictures with the paparazzi?"

"Nah. I'm not really into the whole picture bit," he told me.

"Aw, come on, baby? Can I feel special for just this once?"

I noticed him inhaling and was about to change my mind, but before I did he agreed. And ever briefly we stepped into the spotlights that were focused on the red carpet while photographers took their shots at us. Oh my God, this felt so incredible! I felt like Beyoncé or Halle for a minute there. I had to get copies of these pictures, and found myself pulled in the direction of the photographers to exchange information. Danté eventually tugged at me and in a snap we were finally at the bar.

"You got Georgia Peach?" I asked the bartender.

"No, ma'am, it's Rémy night. Only Rémy is being served from now until."

"Until when?" I asked for my own information.

"Ahh, until we run out," said the bartender. Next thing I know, my lover and I are toasting with Rémy Red in hand.

"To this *incredible* new relationship," said Danté.

And we locked wrists as we sipped at our drinks. I could've floated away on the thick cloud of passion between us. It was like a dream.

"Aww, you guys are too cute," someone said in an effeminate voice to our right. When I looked around, a guy who stood about a foot shorter than Danté had already spun away.

"Hey, I *know* that guy from somewhere," Danté said. But he just as soon shrugged it off as we made our way deeper into the club. Thumping music, laughter, and dancing. DJ Enuf on the ones and twos. "Now *this* is a party!" I said, more into the swing of things. In the meantime, the two of us seemed to be following a train of folks that snaked through the crowd until we were practically *snug* in the thickness of people, the official and superficial fun being had, and the decor of Keyshia and Donnell posters taped and clipped all over the place. We negotiated a spot up in the VIP area (or so it seemed), where a second-floor railing seemed to be vacant and also would offer a greater view of the stage once the show began.

Danté whispered to me, "I think we should post up here because it's a mob scene up near the stage and we can see everything from right here. Trust me."

I nodded, but I felt my eyes sparkling at the lively crowd of partiers in our midst, but more so into Danté's eyes. *You are really suckin' me in, man. Really.*

Eventually, the same guy from the bar—*aww, you guys are too cute*—joined the group and I got a much better look at him.

"Hey, you know what? Now I know where I've seen him! That's the guy from the movie *Con Air*! Remember the flaming fag?"

"Oh, *Danté*," I scolded.

"Well, what do you expect me to call him? What's the *politically correct* way to describe him? That's the role he played, right? And look at him; that's him *all day long*."

I just wagged my head. But I also couldn't keep from looking in the direction of the actor. And I wondered if I wasn't being too obviously attracted to what was going on within this group. It didn't take long for me to trade smiles and then to work my way over to them. I befriended the actor, drank with them, and took pictures with them. I was so caught up I nearly forgot I had a date! And when I gazed over at Danté he gave me this look: *go ahead, girl. Do your thing!* And I was like, *okay.* And I shot a smile his way. But why in those pearly eyes of his did I see a question mark? I know he wasn't hatin' on my social skills? And by the way, is there somethin' wrong with me being a fanatic for a minute? I mean, after all, it was Danté who warned me earlier, *There will be celebrities there.* So was he saying that just to get me to come? And if he was, well then, like Master P said: *It ain't my fault!*

# DANTÉ

The drinks had clearly taken effect as Stacy got to dancing with her new group of friends, but also with me. I wasn't dancing, just standing there near the railing, sort of holding down our staked claim for when the show began. However, Stacy didn't mind winding her body in front of me, grinding her ass up against my groin, and provoking all types of attention with her sexual overtones. There came a point when one of the women in the group nearby approached Stacy and asked that she not dance that way because (I overheard) *our organization is a respectable one and yada, yada, yada.*

Knowing what I know about New York and the crowd we were blending with, I might've intervened and said something harsh like, *Mind your business, you prude.* But Stacy immediately agreed and didn't have a problem with the request. And we were left to wait for the miniconcert to begin. In the meantime, I was piecing this new piece into the Stacy puzzle: *yes, she's aggressive, she's a go-getter, a vixen, and (maybe) she has some sort of sleep disorder. But to that I could also add exhibitionist!*

DONNELL WAS okay. But Keyshia Cole had the crowd in stitches when she sang, and *man* did she *sang.*

> *Ohhh Looooove! Never knew what I was missin'*
> *I fouw-ouw-ouwed, I found you!*

Admittedly, up until that moment, I had not paid attention to Keyshia's song, mainly because they played it *to death* on the radio all damn day long; and I'm always suspicious of songs that get that *extra* radio play, all day long, when there are so many good songs out there to be enjoyed. But that's my personal issue. The reality now is that I'm a die-hard Keyshia Cole fan, and most anything she sings I want to get my ears on!

IN THE truck on our way back to Park Chester, Stacy got more vocal than I'd seen her. And I couldn't help knowing the Rémy Red had a lot to do with it.

"That was *soooooooooo* hot! Danté, you gotta, gotta, *gotta* let me know when there's another party like that. Oh my GOD! I actually met a real live actor!"

I was about to tell Stacy, *I get invites to that stuff all the time*. But it didn't make sense to me to open up *that* can of worms, especially knowing how busy my days are, and how few our exclusive nights are. I'd be cutting into my own social life. And yet, even without my response, Stacy rambled on and on about the party, the girls there, her sexy dance, and how she was gonna get the new Keyshia Cole CD for me. I could hear (and smell) the Rémy in her voice because this (so far as I'd learned) was not the Stacy I knew. Loud. Slurred speech. Redundant like a scratched record.

For real, my head was starting to pound from all the loud music, and I wanted to say, *Would you shut the fuck up?*

And, like a cue card was shown to her, Stacy snuggled closer to me in the truck with her Rémy-rich breath.

"Baby, *please* can we go to another party like that? I just loved that party. *Please*."

Now, Stacy was annoying me. I turned up the radio some as we cruised up Broadway, and I tried to let her high die off with time. It seemed to work because (at least in *my* mind) her loud overtures turned to mumbles. And soon I was ignoring her altogether.

"Well, if you won't take me to a party then I'ma just hafta start a party of my own," said Stacy.

I don't know if the two drinks I had were fueling my annoyance, and I don't know where it came from or why I had this sudden outburst, but out of nowhere I said, "Yeah, go ahead and *suck it* so you can *shut the fuck up*."

Stacy didn't even address my harsh tongue. She just

pulled out my limp dick and began her steady routine of convincing. Thing is, I really wasn't in the mood. I became half stiff, and in no shape to be her willing participant. Somewhere near Seventy-fifth Street, just twenty minutes into our drive up Broadway, Stacy came up for air from the weak-ass, unsatisfying head, and she got loud: "You don't really love me! If you did, you would give me what I want! You don't know what it's like!"

"What? What're you talkin' about? I don't know what *what's* like?"

"You don't know what it's like to lose your life and your home and your family!" Stacy said that so she could be heard over the music on Power 105, and she emphasized the *life*, *home*, and *family* with fists pounding on my dashboard.

To say the least, I was stuck on stupid. How we got from a conversation about partying to this, I'll never know. What I did know is that this was *obviously* a different woman than the one I thought I knew; different from the one I was making love to and a *world* away from the woman who I was ready to sign my life away to—at least that might've been the case in my mind, I guess. So, needless to say, my brain put the brakes on all those ideas.

AT THE red light I turned down Lil Wayne's groggy, whining voice and said to myself, *Wow*. And wow *again*. I was in a trance. It was just like my Pop always said, only it was playing itself in real time, in living color, right before my very eyes: *if it don't come out in the wash, it'll come out in the rinse.*

I was dumbfounded by the sudden explosion from Stacy. And before I had a chance to digest even that, she was sobbing in helpless, pain-felt wails, choking on her words, and struggling for air. *Is this the woman I'm falling madly in love with? Is this the woman who I bought flowers for yesterday and proclaimed her as the woman of my dreams? The same woman who sleeps in my bed, who I trust with—*

My thoughts rambled, causing my head to pound some more; the banging headache that had started ten minutes earlier was growing stronger. But there was obviously compassion needed here. Her cry for help and the tears that streamed down her face seemed very real. This young woman needed my help and I just couldn't say no. I couldn't turn my back on her.

I pulled over to the nearest parking space. Instinct told me that I was facing Columbus Avenue, on Seventy-eighth Street. Her sobbing slowed, but the impact of it all still had me confused. I could've been in Texas somewhere and it wouldn't have mattered, because Stacy was on this next chapter of blowing my mind and challenging me to a bout with delirium.

"You wanna talk about it?" I asked calmly. But nothing was calm about my heartbeat and the curiosity that was swelling in my head. Her words were still fresh in my mind, as though someone branded them on my brain with a red-hot branding iron meant for a steer. *You don't know what it's like to lose your life and your home and your family!*

Again, me with the silent *wow*.

"No. I don't wanna talk about it," she said. And that just left me stumped. We sat there in the car with the radio off, the silent chill of the AC keeping us comfortable from the

terrible heat outdoors. Meanwhile, as the temperature outdoors was near ninety, I guessed that the mental heat inside
Stacy had to be overwhelmingly hotter. She had apparently
been through some real tragedy that was lingering on her
mind all this time; even while our relationship seemed to
be normal (relatively), Stacy's mind was certainly *not* in order. I found myself rewinding the incidents: the rainy night
when we first hooked up outside the bowling alley. The
sudden outburst in the bedroom. And now *this*. But apparently the most unpredictable was yet to come.

"They shot him," Stacy sighed. And I watched her,
stunned, as the tears began streaming, this time without
the sobbing. "They shot him while I was right there in the
car. And that changed my *whole* life." I was the one to shut
up now, as Stacy's voice trembled. The fear that embraced
her words was very real and there was no point in interfering while she was on a roll. And every word was taking her
story, her past, and perhaps her future to another level.

"I ran for my life. They shot at me and I thought I was
dead. But I kept running. I kept *running*. Then I fell into a
ditch. And I could hear them still running. They were shouting and looking for me. I was quiet." Stacy continued her
story in short spurts with her voice dropping to a whisper.
At this point, I'm thinking, *What the fuck, Stacy. Why you
whispering? Nobody's after you now!* But she was so into her
story, and her stuttering was causing my own heart to beat,
and a series of chills ran through *my* body as I listened. I
began to feed into her fear and anxiety. At the same time,
the anticipation around us was thick. On one hand, I couldn't
wait to learn what happened next, while on the other, she
couldn't wait to express herself. And sure enough, as soon

as I thought about it, everything began to spill out—her story *and* the food and drink for the evening.

"Oh *shit*," I blurted. "Open the door—the *door*!"

Thank God Stacy was alert enough to open the door and she poked her head out just in time to let the vomit spew out and onto the street. I handed her a bottle of water from the stash I always keep on the backseat, so that was convenient, regardless of how warm the water was. I encouraged her to take some in and spit. She did. And now, more than ever, I felt ashamed for the previous half hour, the way I had talked to her, treated her, and the lack of caring I'd exhibited. I could only avoid eye contact to keep her from seeing my pitiful expression. Nevertheless, Stacy apparently wanted to get her story out.

"I WAS left out there in the woods, near the expressway, and I had to hitchhike home with just my torn blouse, and my leg and hip was hurtin' real bad. But I'm not really carin' about that 'cause I was just glad to be alive, you know? And as *soon* as I got home the police came and picked me up, like *I'm* the one who shot Darrell."

I was left to fill in the blanks here, guessing that "him" referred to a past boyfriend. And "they" were obviously upset enough to *shoot* her ex-boyfriend? But was the "they" she spoke of referring to the police? She continued and I kept my yap shut, trying to pull the pieces together.

"They had me in the police station for like twenty hours or something. Wouldn't even give me a ride home. Plus, my purse was lost somewhere back where they shot Darrell, so I had no money. . . ."

*Okay. So Darrell must be her ex.*

"But I swear I never said a word to the police 'bout the shooter, or nobody. I *ain't* no *snitch!*"

*Alrighty then*, I told myself in response to her convictions. Wondering what *that* had to do with the picture. And then, even *that* question was answered.

"So why the hell *his* people gotta come after *me*? I mean, I ain't do *nothin'* but *love* that man. I gave him the *best of me*. And, I mean, I can understand he dead and all, but *dag*, cain't they go after the *real shootahs*?" Stacy's slang was slipping here and there, and it reminded me of when we first met in the elevator. *I'm from down south—just outside of downtown 'Lanta. But I'm stayin' up here with Auntie for a while.*

And so much had transpired since then: how she grew on me, how we shared the most intimate moments of my life, exploring areas, positions, and other things that I'd rather not think about, especially now. And we came this far to finally land where? *Here?* Someone who shot her boyfriend in *'Lanta?* I felt like I'd been bamboozled; introduced to this woman's *representative* who initially put on a good show and introduced me to something so incredible. But now that I suddenly found out so much more, I felt as if I had reached square one. I had overlooked all the red flags and warnings just because (on the surface) this woman seemed so amazing. And now I'd come to find that there was so much more pain to bare. And then I realized I spoke to soon. She was still spitting up the story. . . .

"But, his sisters 'n' them came to my house with weapons. I *knowed* they had weapons 'cuz you don't just roll up on somebody's house like that, 'cuz *they* might have a gun layin' somewhere. So I went out. I mean, ain't nobody gonna threaten me and my children—"

And there it was: the *next* level of the hot ghetto mess, southern-style. Stacy had a life somewhere in Georgia with a boyfriend, kids— *Oh my God*, I thought. And I was coincidentally trying to swallow how deep this all had gotten. Meanwhile she's droppin' all these revelations on me and I'm thinking how I'd become *so* comfortable with Stacy that I had stopped using a rubber when we fucked. *Damn.* I had surrendered that safety measure after considering how close we'd become and how *into her* I was—as if I wanted to *prove* my commitment to her, or something. But now, as it turned out, there was nothing comfortable about us at all. We were a lie? No. Maybe *she* was a lie, because (for the most part) I kept it real. Expressed my true feelings. I thought about how we'd met and how quickly we'd lain together. I thought about her spontaneity, never questioning how a girl so young could know so much and know how to make a man feel so *damn good*. Thing is, I never questioned it because I was always in the heat of the moment. I wasn't thinking about possible diseases because the image Stacy projected was so picture-perfect. Her look, the way she kept herself; from her toes to the hair on her head seemed to be in perfect order. Her body was *bangin'*, and her face was so beautifully sculpted. And here I was, on my daily grind, minding my own business, and she just walks into my life, into my house, and into the kitchen, where she had full access to the cookie jar, and my cookies.

*Jesus. And I gave her that real dick, too. Not some one-night-stand dick.*

I remembered how I'd surrendered to this woman and

held nothing back. I remembered how perfect we had fit, me inside her, her in my embrace. Even when she cried on those occasions during sex, it encouraged the determination in me to be thorough and memorable and intense. And now that I knew better, I wondered just how thorough I was to *not* check this woman's background. How intense could I be to let her in my house without securing my valuables. And how ultimately memorable was it of me to be so fucking *blind*! Was it *really* that Mrs. Singletary was over-protective of her niece, trying to protect her virginity? Or was it more the truth that her aunt was hiding her and protecting her from certain attack?

And I could not help but remember when I served her breakfast in bed, and that moment when she put on the whole Sweet Polly Purebread act—*can a lil' ol' girl like me offer you an apology? You just came and scooped lil' ol' me up off the big bad streets of Haah-lem, and I'm ever so grateful. . . . So, you mind, Mista Garrett, if I just show you how grateful I am?*

But, now that the pieces of Stacy's puzzle were coming together, I felt like *I* was the one who was *scooped up*. And that *I* was the *sweet* one, and *just like she mentioned: a sucka*. Thought I found me a jar of candy, and come to find out that it might all be poisoned except for the ones at the top.

I felt I needed to say something at this point, to interrupt her flow, because she was encouraging me to jump out of my *own* car and to make a run for it.

CONTINUING WITH her drama, Stacy rattled off the details.

"So I come out to the porch and Darrell's sisters and I are talkin, 'cuz they wanna know if I set him up. I'm like, *no, I loved Darrell,* and I know deep down they *knew it.* But them heffas was lookin' for a scapegoat 'cuz, one, they ain't got no idea who done it, and *two, I ain't no snitch.* Then the short one starts talkin' shit, like she was gonna beat my ass even if I *didn't* set they brotha up. And she already got a beer in her hand and she throws that shit at me. Her big sista like three hundred pounds or somethin', so she's holdin' shorty back. At the same time, I already got my razor ready, so *whateva.* And then I blacked out."

The curiosity showed on my face, and Stacy went on explaining.

"One'a they brothas was behind me and I didn't know. The doctors said I got hit with somethin' hard. *See?*"

*Wow. And there's that next level.* Stacy dipped her head and parted the top of her hair to show me a three-inch scar. The hair had grown back where the scar was, but I could sure see that there were once stitches.

"The doctors said I came *this* close to dyin'. And I prayed to God that my neighbors came by to check on my kids, 'cuz—" At some point during this rapid-fire explanation, Stacy's tears had dried up, and that empowered me some. I wasn't feeling as sorry as I had. But when she got to the part about the neighbors and her kids, Stacy's tears streamed again. And through her hoarse cry she proclaimed, "Danté, I *love them children with all my heart. I swear on a stack'a Bibles I'd do anything for my children. Any-thing!"* She reached out and put her arms around me and I accepted.

"It's gonna be alright, baby. Calm down. It's gonna be fine," I said, unsure how deep in trouble she was or what the solutions might be. I just knew that holding her and supporting her at this moment was important for her sanity and well-being. Still, hugging her felt a whole lot different than it had hours earlier, for sure.

"*I swear on a stack'a Bibles, Danté.*" Stacy's cries were muffled against my chest and her tears soaked into my shirt.

"Where did all this take place, Stacy?"

"Down in 'Lanta. And after I came out the hospital I heard the city come and got my children. And plus, I couldn't make no money on account'a my injuries, so I was losin' my house. I had like forty thousand in equity that I built up over two years. But they don't care. Them banks will put you out quick down there if you're even thirty days late. . . ."

*Damn.* I thought about all the stories up in the Bronx, all the tenant issues and the whole mess with evictions and marshals and landlord blues. I knew of at least one tenant, some lady who I'll never forget, played the system *lovely* and managed to live rent-free for a year. I know all about it since I was the one called in to do the cleanup after they finally threw her ass out. It was nice pay for me since I had to do everything from trash removal to removing the nicotine from the walls and a whole bunch of other stuff she neglected, almost ruining the residence. But such was the life in Park Chester: you had your good ones and your bad ones. I just know if I ever own property, I'll be looking *hard* and thinking twice before renting to anyone.

". . . And while they doin' the foreclosure, I'm steady fightin' the city, try'na get my children back. *Plus*, them bitches still try'na bring drama, sendin' messages around town how they lookin' for me, and how if they find me they gonna *body* me. And then"—Stacy's tears stopped again, hitting me with the realization that there was some kind of off/on switch in her brain—"to add to that, I got a message that them dudes that actually *shot* Darrell was lookin' for me. So I was just the most-wanted bitch in 'Lanta, *knowwhatI'msayin*? But the courts and the social workers and them finally agreed to let my children go if I had somebody to help. So that's where they at now: with my momma. She got a *nice* house up in Lawrenceville. They would *never* think to look there. Too far up north, away from the 'hood."

"So, why didn't you just live with your moms?"

There was a pause and Stacy's mind seemed to wander for a time.

Then she said, "Momma don't love me. Momma don't want me. Ever since I was in my late teens she said I was *fast*, and that I didn't listen. She prob'ly right. But, still, you don't throw away your *daughter*. You gotta give people a chance to grow and mature; and everybody don't get wise all at once."

*Well, we will definitely make that a quotable from Stacy, the sociologist.*

"*Still*, I could *never-ever* throw away my children. I love 'em too much. And the only reason why Momma got 'em now is 'cuz *she* love 'em, too. She just don't love *me* no more."

I got to thinking about the time Stacy and I had together and how she'd pull away now and again to "use the bathroom." For a time, I thought she might have a weak bladder or something. But now I realized she was probably either on the phone with her children or conducting some sort of business with her ATL ties.

*Children.*

"Ahh, Stacy? You never told me you had kids."

"Okay, *yeah*. You're *right*. But keep it real, Danté. You would've never gave me a second look if I told you that."

"How can you assume *that*?"

"You and I both know that niggas ain't feelin' women who are tied down with kids. I done been down that road before. And I don't blame you, really. If I was in your shoes I wouldn't want a chick with kids, either. But, you're a winner, Danté. I never met a guy like you that is so hardworkin' and ain't try'na take shortcuts in life. Everybody I knew down there, at least the people I ran with, was slick about shit, and hustling somethin' or try'na git over. You? Look at-cha. Gotcha own business, your own clients who love you—like Ms. *Thomas*. Didn't think I knew about her, did ya?"

Before I got a chance to defend myself, or even to be upset or feel violated, Stacy smoothed her hand along the side of my face.

"None of that bothers me, Danté. What I'm attracted to is the man right here in front of me." Her hand was on my chest now, where my heart was beating like a DJ Premier hip-hop track. "Danté, in *here* is where the *real* man is. He's caring. He's compassionate. And he *says* he loves everything about me. So, do you expect a perfect Barbie Doll out of life? You want a *waif*, Danté? Or do you want a woman with some roots 'n' some backbone? A woman who has your back like you have hers?"

I was lost for words. But Stacy didn't mind filling in the empty air.

"It was better the way I did it, since now you got to know me better, without my *so-called* luggage. You proclaimed your love for me with the whole, *Stacy, I'm so glad you came into my life and this-that and the third, plus I done sucked you off, fucked ya' raw, and, as you say, turned your whole life around—*"

Damn, how she laid it all out felt like a progress report from the last two months. And I was frozen there behind the steering wheel, trying to weigh my options: *the nearest police station? Bellevue Hospital? Mt. Sinai? Did she leave anything at my apartment that would require us returning there?* What's more important was my health, and I was counting down the hours until my emergency visit to the local doctor's. I had to get my AIDS test, my urine and blood work, and any other kinda test they could think up— I was ready to *take them all*!

But something about Stacy was so real and grassroots that I couldn't just let her go. And it wasn't that she had kids, it was that she had never *told me* about them. Sure, in court that might not be a lie; there'd be no handcuffs or convictions. But in the court of *human events*, not telling something as big as being a mother of two is just as good as a lie. Deception at its best. And these were the things we disagreed on, right there in my parked vehicle.

"So, you gonna leave me?" she asked. And I know myself *so good* that I can say her question was the smartest thing she ever did. However, I *refuse* to believe that Stacy knew me so well. I refused to believe that she was so much smarter than me that she had me all figured out and knew what buttons to push and which questions to ask. But, in the words of the immortal Sammy Davis Jr.: *What kind of fool am I!*

## [ F O U R ]

MAYBE BEING A helpless romantic isn't so bad. After all, we were made to naturally interact with the opposite sex, so somewhere along the line (whether or not we decide to accept the fact) we need to choose *someone* to spend our sex with, to kiss and hold, to laugh and cry with, and to cohabitate with. Yes, animals might spend their leisure time hunting and fucking and procreating, but in the same fashion, humans spend their time sending e-mails and text messages and fucking. Shopping and fucking. Going out to the movies and fucking. Holding down a nine-to-five and fucking. If you're lucky enough, and you have the energy, you're *always* fucking. If you're more than lucky, and if you're planning for a future, you're doing all that under one roof *and* making babies. But the bottom line is, and I don't care if you're Oprah or Bill Gates, you accept, deny, live for, work around, and entirely support the hard or soft concept of *fucking*.

So then, to find someone you feel is a convenient, willing, and able-bodied partner would be a bonus, I would think. And not that I was all philosophical about my relationship with Stacy, but you'd have to agree that a decision was in order. In other words, a brother definitely had to *weigh his options.*

Things slowed down for us after that night of shocking revelations. We didn't stop seeing each other, but for the next few weeks we just took more time in getting to know each other, as opposed to having sex and everything else coming second. We both agreed that we had rushed into things, that we fell head over heels for each other, and that this could be the *big deal*—the relationship that we both longed for. But we first had to work our way through things we did *not* see coming, like the petty bickering we engaged in, and the silent spells that sometimes came with an attitude. We had to build up on the positives and try to do away with as many negatives as we could. Naturally, being the progressive, business-minded thinker that I am (and I'm not saying I'm the greatest), but I'm accustomed to being an optimist, and to seeing the cup half full, instead of half empty. Stacy, however, had been through some challenging, life-altering events that threatened her well-being, her children's well-being, and more. So, there was a lot more work to do in convincing Stacy that "the light is at the end of the tunnel," or the "tough times never last, but tough people do," or "you are what you believe you are." All of those positive affirmations might look like hot air to her (or, at least, brand new), while they're ideas that are painted up on my mental wall, inspiring me to work harder and strive and persist toward my goals in life. My new friend, on the other hand, with this ghetto drama down in Atlanta, and her children being so distant, with access to her by voice alone, was a real tragedy in itself. And now that I knew way more about them, Stacy didn't mind bringing them up in conversation now and again.

The other thing that I had to cope with was the feeling deep down inside that I wasn't supportive enough. I mean, here we were, supposed to be a couple, and I wasn't anything more than her shoulder to lean on. I wouldn't be considered the man that "had her back" with all the drama that was going on in her life. Maybe it was because we were so new and that it was way too much weight to take on all at once. Or, maybe (somewhere deep inside) I didn't feel that it was any of my business. Either way, it was a burden to even think about. But, drama or no drama, I knew I'd have to get to know the kids one day. Naturally, that came along with the package—the bigger picture.

In the meantime, I was still dealing with Stacy's occasionally whimpering in her sleep, and there were instances when she'd jump up screaming. Once when she jumped up, she wobbled into my kitchen and grabbed a steak knife. It took me a half hour to calm her down and to convince her that it wasn't me—*I'm not your enemy, Stacy!*

And here I was, thinking that there was only the bat to deal with. I have to say that *knowing* who your enemy is has to be comforting; because here I am lying in bed with a woman I see as my best friend, and she wilds out with a steak knife? That evening in my apartment, it was Stacy's decision to finally see a psychologist. And we both agreed that the visits would help with those demons in her past, demons that sent her into awful crying spells by day, and (sometimes) turned her into an unpredictable rebel at night.

AT TIMES I really *did* need to talk to Pastor Bishop, otherwise I'd be the one needing the psychologist.

ONE DAY, it got to a point when I was about to throw in
the towel (again). It was a stupid argument, really, about
her overuse of paper towels. Stacy used paper towels like
they were leaves falling off trees—in other words, free for
the taking. And it's not like I'm poor and can't afford them.
It's just that I *don't want to.* My thing is, keep a hand towel
nearby. Even the dishcloths tend to be dry on occasion, and
she'd pass those up just to get her hands on some more paper towels. Now, maybe if my family owned the company
or something, then I'd use paper towels with pride. But, a
wasteful person I am not. I like to conserve, especially in
*my* home.

"SO THEN you're gonna have to stop acting like it's a vacation cruise," said Pastor Bishop when I sat down to have a
talk with him. "You two need to find some other things to
do when you're together, other than, I'm guessing, the obvious. How about mapping out a strategy, a plan of action
as to how you will live your lives, how you will spend your
money, and how you will feel fulfilled. And, Danté?"

"Yes, Preach?

"Figure out what your contribution in life will be. You
are two healthy human beings. So there must be something
you can do that is beneficial to others around you."

"I think I do enough of that for the *both* of us, Preach."

"Well, I'd imagine you're speaking about your work, right?"

*"Exactly,"* I said, my mind focused on the workday ahead.

"But, young Danté, my question to you is, would you do that job, fix those windows and caulk those cracks in people's bathrooms, if it didn't pay you?" He waited for a response, but I was stumped, as though this were a *trick* question. "And that's my point, young man. You don't have to address this now, because it's *supposed* to require deep thought and evaluation. But just consider it from time to time: what would you do in life that was so fulfilling to you that you wouldn't care to get paid for it?"

"Alright. I gotcha, Preach. Glad I stopped by. You always help me to keep things in proper perspective."

"It might also serve you well to stop by this Sunday. Maybe you'll bring a—umm, *friend?*"

"You're one funny man, Preach. I can't promise, but I'll try."

"I know you will."

WHEN I got home that day, I was surprised to find Stacy waiting for me outside on one of the benches that leads to the building entrance. That threw me off for a second because she had the key to my apartment. So, I'm immediately guessing that she lost the key, or—

"What's wrong? You lock y'self out?

Stacy rose to give me a hug, wagging her head.

Muffled in my embrace, she said, "Just couldn't wait to see you."

I exhaled my relief, but I can't lie, it was good to feel the hug after a long day.

"Did you eat? Why don't we hit Uno's tonight?" I suggested.

"That's a plan," said Stacy.

After a shower and a change of clothes, Stacy and I walked arm in arm through the park, along Wood Avenue, over to the oval and Uno's restaurant, where it was very likely that I would see a resident, a neighbor or two. By this time—honestly—*I didn't give a shit.*

Once we were seated I said, "So I was thinking about what you said last night."

"Which part? We talked about a lot last night."

"The part about your children, and getting us a house down in Atlanta. And I say, let's check into it. I'm kinda tired of the same old grind, and it's been a little miserable since my dad and gramps passed. So, *yeah*. Let's check it out. It might just be the change I need."

Stacy got up, although we had just been seated. She shot around the table and nearly tackled me on my side of the booth.

"Oh GOD! Are you serious?! *Really!?*"

"Yup. I'm serious. I can't stay in one place forever. And besides, you make me very happy. So wherever we need to lay our heads to be together, I'm with it. I also did some numbers, checked my credit, and I even spoke with a couple brokers from down there. And it's entirely feasible—if I can clear my schedule and my workload—that we can shoot down there by August first."

Stacy uttered an eerie, crying scream that *had* to arouse just about everyone in the restaurant. I turned to face those who were closest to us, assuring them that all was okay and that *she's just a little happy*.

In timely fashion, our waitress came over and asked, "I hear you need drinks over here?"

In a most joyful voice, Stacy said "YES! Oh, God. He's gettin' me, I mean *us*, a house! Isn't that *great*!?" Stacy was teary-eyed, with her arms draped around my shoulders. She pulled herself in and snuggled her face into the crook of my neck and uttered appreciative sobs. I couldn't stop her. I just had to let the moment be. But my face said it all, how Stacy took my one little mention of a visit all the way to the real estate closing within seconds. What an *imagination*! Or, better yet, what weight she loved to put on my shoulders!

The waitress seemed to feel a little out of place, as if this wasn't her excitement to experience. To help things along, I ordered drinks for both of us: strawberry daiquiris.

"And please hurry. Before we have our first child," I told her and at the same time rolled my eyes.

While Stacy was sitting on my lap, so elated from the news I'd brought, I couldn't help feeling uncomfortable, the two of us all squeezed into this confined space.

She was all smooches and kisses, and then she suddenly let up and focused her big, beautiful eyes on mine.

"Wait a minute. Did you just say *our first child*?"

Before she screamed again, I held my hand over her mouth.

"Okay, let's not go too far. That was something of a joke—an answer to you saying *he's gonna buy me a house*. Stacy, you move entirely too fast. But, like Tupac says, *I'm not mad atcha*. That's the energy I love about you: that spontaneity. And I want you to change none of that. I'm inspired by you, the craziness—the whole nine. Now if you don't mind, I'd like some *breathing* room?"

We chuckled about how silly we looked all squished like we were. But, before Stacy shifted back around to her seat, she asked me, "So, when did you finally decide?"

"I didn't *decide* anything, Stacy. I'm just taking a trip down with you and *speculating on some real estate*, that's all. And besides, I think seeing your children will be a plus and maybe it will heal whatever you're going through. So, if the only thing that's stopping you is having somebody by your side that will have your back, I'll be there. I ain't gonna let nothin' happen to you. And, for the record, you can't go through life being afraid. You do what you gotta do. For you and for your children. Remember that most people are cowards. Hot air and tough talk. Nobody's livin' like a cowboy today."

Stacy looked at me like *I* was crazy.

"I mean, like back in the day they used to wear their guns on their waist and they used to challenge each other to a duel out in the middle of town, in the middle of the streets. Ain't you ever stopped to take a look at some of those old movies on cable?"

"Ahh, *nooo?*" she said with a hint of sarcasm.

"Well, *I have*. And things ain't what they use to be. People are held accountable today for their actions. Plus, everywhere you look, Big Brother is watching."

"Big Brother?"

I nodded and said, "Yup. The cameras in the streets, in the parking lots, on top of buildings, in the sky. You just can't hide from *shit* anymore."

"Sounds like you're upset about that," said Stacy.

"Very funny. But, hardly."

Then she said, *"Never mind all that,* I got some good news, too."

"And what would that be?" I asked this in a sarcastic way, but I was genuinely curious as to what good news she had.

In a singsong voice she said, *"I got a credit card. I got a credit card!"*

"Wow. That's great. But be careful. That's the trap. They put a little bit of money out there for you to spend, and then you owe interest for life."

She shrugged that off and showed me a black-and-platinum card.

"Ain't no way I gotta worry about *that,* with *this.*"

I took hold of the card. "Damn. They're making these offers look more and more appealing every day. Maybe I need to get me a card. So what are they offerin' you, a thousand?"

"Um, *excuse* me, but this is way past *offer.* This is the actual card. And it's not a *thousand,* mister-I-got-it-goin'-on."

"How much they approve you for?"

"Well, the paper says a hundred thousand."

*"What*?! Show me the paper."

Stacy pulled out an envelope from her purse. The paper was ripped, except for the part about the approval.

"Shit! And I thought *I* was doin' something. Girl, you betta count your blessings. 'Cuz in this economy, they don't come up off of this much credit for just *anybody.*"

"Whatchu try'na say? I'm not *worthy*?"

"No-no-no, I'm not sayin' that. I don't really know much

about your money situation." *That is, if you don't count your tellin' me about banks, losing your house, and foreclosure.* "You never shared any of that with me. But I'm just sayin', watch out. Spend it wisely. Don't take out what you know you can't put back. That's all."

Stacy made a face of acceptance and I knew I was suddenly off the hook. But I couldn't help thinking she wasn't all the way worthy of that card, especially the way she carried herself. No job. Living with her auntie (and me), and a whole lot of free time on her hands.

*I guess the banks up here are more lenient? That, or she has an angel or something on her side.*

I HAD other things to think about if I was gonna take this much-needed vacation by August. I had a short list of things to fix and clients to see. I'd have to get someone dependable to stand in, in case one of my regulars had an emergency. Not that there would be one, but it's always better to be safe than sorry. I also planned on paying my bills forward for two months. That way, when I got back I wouldn't be stressed to handle that. And it's not like I'm stressin', with over $70K in the bank—thanks in part to Pop's insurance policy. However, I'm something of a workaholic. I just need to keep stackin' paper like a squirrel or something.

In the meantime, using Pastor Bishop's advice was already feeling good. He had asked why I didn't take "a leap of faith" if I was really serious about making the relationship work. He had asked why I was treating Stacy like a Happy Meal and not a three-course dinner at a five-star restaurant. I thought the way he said it was funny, but later

on it really made sense. The quickies in the car *had to stop*.
The falling asleep after a long day's work *had to stop*. As for
my falling asleep, I'd just have to make adjustments on my
workload—get up earlier or something—so that I could
devote quality time (and energy) to my boo. My boo: that
was another thing. I had to change my language from what
might be looked upon as a teenage crush, and I had to start
recognizing that this was *my lady*, especially if she was
that. And I didn't say anything to *her* about this, but there
were a couple of times that Stacy just impulsively dropped
to her knees and straight-up *emptied* me. *That* had to stop,
*too*. I couldn't look at my lover as a freak or a vixen. I had to
get that out of my brain—literally. I had to think of her as
my love *first*, and everything else would be coincidental to
that.

"IT'S ME," Stacy proclaimed over my shoulder in that
singsong voice (the side of her I liked most). I was brushing
my teeth at the time, nude and watching the mirror as she
approached. It was at moments like these that I'd reflect,
and for all the reasons I could recall, I was proud of my
choice. At that moment Stacy was so innocent and predictable. I could see she just wanted love, like I did. I could see
she was just a naked human being, like me, and she merely
wanted the warmth of a trusted, caring man. I could see
there in the mirror how (despite her flaws) she could easily
fit in as the other half of me. However, who was I to haggle?
Sure, all my faults were not open to the public or explained
in rants, but nevertheless I knew I had them. After all, mil-
lionaire or miser, who among us is perfect?

Here in the mirror, I could also see through all the bullshit; all that thug shit she tried to throw at me during our squabbles. When she was angry or picking a fight (maybe while she was on or approaching her period), she transformed into more of the male side of herself—if that makes sense. She'd talk tough, her walk changed some, and her facial expression held solid as a rock. It was something of a transformation, the way she moved in and out of bliss, straight into some hostile rage, cursing in every other sentence. *Mothafucka this, mothafucka that.* Sometimes I'd just sit and listen to her just to see how far she'd go, how much she'd ramble until she ran out of things to say, or people to curse. But then there were these heavenly times when—

*"yeah, it's you, my love"*

—she was so soft and pink, and manageable. She was a child wanting to be molded. She didn't seem to have a care in the world beside me, her man.

STACY STOOD there behind me, holding me as I got rid of a mouthful of sloppy tooth scrub, and after a couple of rinses I turned to pull her into my embrace and took the opportunity to enter the "silly season" we always remembered from Barack Obama's comment.

"Girl, you know it's true . . . Ooo, ooo, ooo, I love *youuuuuu*."

"Now *that* was gay," she said in the voice of Riley, our favorite Boondocks character.

The nerve of her to go *there* while I had her in the most compromising position, able to tickle her until she—

"I'm sorry, I'm sorry! *I take it back! I take it back!*" She screamed bloody murder, but playfully so.

My teeth clenched, my face knotted up, and my strong GI Joe grip on her body was not letting up. I held on tight as Stacy tried every which way she could to get loose. With her naked in my arms, I felt like I had claimed the catch of the day and that she was the big fish flappin' this way and that.

*"I take it back! I take it baaaaaaaaaaaack!"*

"Okay. Jesus. You don't hafta scream," I eventually said. But I still had her in my arms. It had been so long since we'd been here—not necessarily naked together, but naked, at peace, and in sync with each other. Even if this feeling *was* a result of the conversation we had earlier at Uno. Even if a vacation *was* planned for the near future, and that the relationship between us was expected to move to the next level; still, this was what life was about. This was why I put long hours in and enjoyed short hours of my own. This was why I stacked paper and focused on doing the job right each and every time. This was the reason for all of that, and I didn't even see it coming. I had just been preparing for it all along. And I'm so glad I did!

And now that I was a nose apart from Stacy, I could appreciate the scent of her exhales, and her freshly bathed body. Damn, how my senses so easily stirred in her presence. The touch of her fingertips (along with the sight of her beautiful face) was a sensation that stimulated my nerves and encouraged my deep breathing. All these signals inevitably inspired my skin to tingle and my dick to get hard. And if that wasn't the signal to turn off the lights, to carry my baby out of the bathroom and to my bed, then water ain't wet.

The one thing that I always heard from girlfriends was how great I kissed. And although I never really paid it much attention, with life moving forward the way it has, that "skill" has become more and more my anchor—something the rest of my body had to catch up with before it was too late. *Hey, Mr. Tongue, meet my friends, the fingers. Fingers, you already know Mr. Left and Mr. Right from the Hand family. And, of course, all of you know my friend Foreplay. So everyone make yourselves at home. Get to know one another! I'm sure you all have so much in common! Oh! Look who came through the door! It's Dick! Hey, Dick, I really need to introduce you to my new friend over here. He's chillin' in the corner, but he's a very important cat. Dick, meet Patience.*

## STACY

With a certain finesse, Danté laid me down on the bed as he would a suit that he didn't want to get wrinkled before the big day. He did this delicately, affectionately, and purposefully, as though this was about to be our first time together—*and he maybe wanna make a good impression on me.* But then that meant this couldn't be another typical romp in the bed. And not that I was thinking that way, just that the way this was all going down felt so *different.* I could even feel myself constrained to keep with a certain tempo in a PG-17 kinda manner. I don't know how to explain my body and my actions and how I was caught up in this total surrender, as though this time—more than any other—was the moment of all moments. The way he looked into my eyes. The way his fingers teased my skin. The kisses he planted. What was happening here was some other kind of agenda or procedure that must've been explored by every sexual scientist and every other sex therapist. Except, I never once studied, practiced, or took notes from any of those sources. So then, what was guiding this man to start at my toes? *Aargh!* I could've screamed! He was massaging and kissing and licking them all at once. And what in the world was encouraging him to touch and caress and care for my ankles, calves, the backs of my knees and thighs like he did? What was urging him to bury his face *right there* between my legs, the one place where he had never gone before? I was right there at the tipping point *already*! And I felt my abandon and began to feel myself in harmony with whatever absolute intentions he had. He grabbed hold of my breasts like he didn't wanna let go until they were one with his hands; until they were satisfied by his licking and nibbling. And what was it that eventually caused us to glue ourselves into the twisted knot we became, with our tongues, hands, and muscles realizing what was already so familiar?

Was this his *curriculum*? My eyes rolled back in my face at the thought.

Foreplay was but his freshman activity. Administration, orientation, and making himself at home with me, as if this was the first time we met. He explored the school, curious, fascinated, and necessary all at once. There were some challenges posed, and some mandatory things he had to adhere to, but nothing he couldn't take on. He apparently knew he had to make the right choices and not move too fast, too aggressively, or *get out of line*. (Not yet, anyway.) But that was the easy task, since he had been here so many times, even if only in my dreams. As the hour progressed, Danté became a sophomore, indulging in pleasures with which he was already familiar. More than comfortable now, he revisited those areas that he'd already satisfied, and which seemed to also satisfy *him*. By the swelling between his legs, his intentions appeared to grow with a greater urgency. And naturally, the urge inside of me was wanton and inspired as well. To be honest here, I (his *education*) was permissive in every way. Without saying so, I wanted him to learn me, even if the friction belonged to both of us, along with the giving and taking and nervous breathing. Not to be mistaken, "educating" and "being educated" was what this was about, *wasn't it?* And he was clearly striving and driven to be educated within the walls and halls of my institution, *wasn't he?*

There was trouble near the end of Danté's sophomore term, when I tested his staying power. Maybe I was going too far, considering the look on his face, as though he was finding it hard to breathe; or, at least his breathing was stifled. Maybe it was how I grabbed him and yanked at him within my own craving for him to fill me. My hunger for him was *crazy*! And I felt like he was on the verge, trying to hold back everything inside of him; a buildup that was just so great that I could feel it pulsating inside of me; like he was ready to explode with energy unexplained. But that was something of a frustration that, I guess, every student had to go through. Still, Danté didn't complete his mission there. I could see that mind-over-matter look in his eyes.

And then it was clear that he *was* in control and that he *wouldn't* end this so soon. My *God* this felt so good. So *amazing*! There was more deep breathing between the two of us and I continued to enjoy the wet and wild and wonderful feelings I was going through. I could've cried out louder if not for the fact that I could hardly speak—too entrapped, too engaged, and right at the threshold of that point of no return. So, I merely sighed and cried and held on to him. I noticed he was doing some of the same.

"You okay?" I asked once he came up for air; once we both got a moment to breathe.

Danté said, "Oh-h-h-oh . . . I'm *good. Reeeeal good.*" Without regard for his response, I felt somewhat obliged to go down on him some more. Taking my pupil in and out of my classroom, schooling him through every angle and test I could think up. Inevitably, I processed him for the next phase—the junior level of my passions.

By this time, subtlety was tossed by the wayside, and along with that his discipline. No longer could he merely be patient and wait for an assembly or a schedule as to when and where. Danté was a junior now! He had run the entire length of this blessed facility more times than anyone else—or so it appeared. His grades were strong and his confidence was stronger, and the world he had adopted was more accepting with a greater embrace of the man he was. He was on *top* of his lessons, *pushing* his way in, but *still gently*, until it was understood that he was here to give *as well* as take. And he seemed to be so sure of himself that all who had come before him came for the purpose of only *taking.* And obviously I was already familiar with this practice, and maybe that was familiar and satisfying in itself.

But the *giving* apparently satisfied *him*. It provoked a lot of noise down the hallway, and also in the front office. But he didn't concern himself. He simply came here to learn and to get the most out of this education process.

There was a dance. And, like many of the other school activities, this was meant to provide a form of release; a chance to become familiar with a bigger picture, and that it's not all black-and-white, cut-and-dried. This was leisure and harmony between two people who could move together and find a synchronicity unlike in the classroom. This was also a license for Danté to become more active and demanding all at once. He could really dance! He could gyrate and thrust and drive and bounce up and down, and I appreciated him in my cries and my joyful noise. When he pushed, I gladly received, and I embraced him evermore with a want for as much as he could give me. And yet, that would be premature just now, since his agenda would be to become a senior and to officially graduate.

And that's what this was all about, reaching the highest level of satisfaction. For Danté was overcome with achievement—the entrepreneur that he is. Only, in this case, it was the achievement of love fulfilled. There was a purpose in his eyes, to give. To receive was coincidental. As for me, I wanted more than an A-student in my classroom. I wanted Danté to be the honors student that shined above and beyond anything in my history. I expected him to show me that education had a whole different meaning after he graduated. And the diploma on the wall would be the ultimate achievement, the reason why we came together in the first place.

And hopefully he had his eyes set on that (even if they

were closed). Everything about this time together and our movements spelled out harmony, and that we were meant to be. This felt nothing like any man I had ever laid with. It was even different than when he and I had made love in the past months. My sounds were endorsements of what Danté meant in my life. And the feelings I experienced were convictions that I was right all along. And that feeling further encouraged me to take more of him, and how he pressed on, muscling into my body with thorough and sometimes possessive measures. My cries were at times loud and hoarse, a combination of pleasure and pain as one—pain, for the long, challenging road that I braved to get to this point, and pleasure, in the pure carnal enjoyment Danté delivered.

"Oh, Danté. Oh, Danté! *Oh, Danté*!!!" And that was *all she wrote*. You coulda stuck a fork in me, 'cuz I was *done*. The warm juices inside of me flowed. The friction between us suddenly got slippery and hot and wetter—if there's such a thing. That, and my fingernails clawing into his sweaty back. That, and my trembling, and hyperventilating in his ear.

"Don't you leave me, *Danté*? *Pleease* don't leave *meee*." I could feel myself losing it over and over again. One, two, and three orgasms. This was the deepest submission I'd ever felt. And I couldn't even control the words that were coming out of my mouth.

## DANTÉ

*Wow.* It sort of threw a damper on such a completely incredible encounter together.

"Don't you leave me, *Danté? Pleease* don't leave *meee*." The words poured out like some woman's final dying statement. They were without power, and so desperate.

But I wasn't gonna let it get to me. I pushed it *way* back in my mind and held on tight. We held each other, mumbling back and forth our testimonies and commitments. We kissed and caressed and molded into each other's embrace, until very early in the morning, when I found us stuck together, again with our own brand of glue.

# [ F I V E ]

THE FIRST WEEK of August couldn't have come soon enough. I took care of all the last-minute odds and ends, clients on my list, and bills paid forward. *Whew!* You'd think I was goin' to the islands or on a cruise or something. Just headin' down south, for goodness' sakes. But just as much as I was going down to speculate on things, I also needed a vacation. Long hours, stress, and a crazy-ass girlfriend will do that to you every time.

IT WAS more economical for us to drive, so we took my Blazer, loaded up with some snacks, and headed for 95 south. Somewhere along the way, I-95 would turn into I-85, and (according to Google maps) it would be a straight shot right into Lawrenceville, Georgia, where Stacy's mom lived. It was a cinch to follow. Our problem wouldn't be the trip as much as it was our time spent together on the trip. From the moment we left, Stacy was that *other* person. And I didn't realize it until I jumped in the driver's seat.

"Did you mail those letters I—*oh*, I didn't realize you were on the phone," I said, hating how Stacy wore that damn earpiece as if it were another organ on her body. And, listening in, I realized the phone call she was on was just setting things off *real* nice—arguing about her cell-phone bill and why it was so high. So high, in fact, that they had disconnected her service the night before without warning. Shit, I guess I'd be mad, too, if Sprint cut me off without my knowing. And couldn't they check her credit to see that she just got approved for $100 grand? I mean, credibility should *definitely* be there. I say that now, but at the time I didn't try to understand. I just knew that every-thing seemed so *peaceful* the night before! Furthermore, even while she's on the phone, she stops to say:

"Stop on One hundred thirty-sixth Street."

My face twisted, because that wasn't part of any agenda that *I* was familiar with. In response, her hand muffling the receiver, she said, "We're having company for the trip."

*Whoa. Really.*

And, real quickly, I'm putting two plus two together. Stacy's brother was living down in Atlanta. Her brother's children (that would be her nieces) were living up in Har-lem. One of his daughters had a newborn, while the other was clearly working on her first baby. Either that, or she was just—

*Never mind.*

"Um . . . company, as in *one person*?" I asked.

"No. Company as in *two* people. We're picking up my brother's daughters. Is that gonna be a problem?" Stacy looked as if she wanted to direct her dispute with Sprint in my direction, and I was just tryin' *not* to hear that shit.

Obviously, my answer relating to the additional travelers was a real defining moment here. After all, her brother and her brother's children *were* family—family that I'd have to accept as my own one way or another. And, considering the vows Stacy and I were committing to, such as our *oneness*, that would make her family my family. And vice versa. I suppose it all just came so suddenly, so unexpectedly, especially since I've been a loner for a minute. Hell, even when Pop and Grandpop were alive, I had a lot of my own space. My "alone time." The girlfriends I had weren't live-ins (such as Stacy was becoming), and frankly I had been enjoying my island called "Danté." I didn't have to answer to anybody. I had no responsibilities except for the ones I've created. And (pardon my French, but) *fuck everybody else. Really.* People bring problems. Less people, less problems. Shit, Biggie shoulda rapped about *that* shit, for real. *Mo' people, mo' problems.*

And to keep it *all the way real*, I had a damn hard time accepting Stacy so close to me. And if it wasn't for the total package she presented, I just might be that same, single nigga today. But the reality is what it is. And this was the woman I fell for, and I was goin' for broke.

*See?* I said I wasn't perfect.

As I'm driving, I'm tryin' to keep her calm, but she's gettin' real nasty with the customer-service rep, as if the rep has a personal grudge against Stacy. Before you know it, she takes things to the *next* level.

"Oh, really? Lemme speak to your supervisor."

I reached over and put my hand on Stacy's knee to try to calm her. But she shot me that look—*why are you interrupting me?* And so I looked back toward the road, telling myself this was useless.

ONCE WE arrived in Harlem, we had a rack of other issues to face. Number one: Stacy's mention of two people
suddenly turned to two and a half; I wasn't aware we'd
have a newborn baby on board. Immediately I know I'm in
for some trip. A car full of women, and the only other male
in the car can't speak. So, I already know I'm gonna be
speechless for the trip. Even I'm smart enough to know
that one false move from a man in a pool of estrogen can be
fatal. Number two: when we pulled up to their place on
136th Street, the sidewalk was filled with at least three
suitcases, a bassinet, a stroller, a fold-up crib, miscellaneous
bags, and what appeared to be a cooler.

*You're kidding*, I told myself once I realized that this
wasn't a heap of trash set out on the sidewalk for pickup.
The next hour was spent with Jazmine and Chloe trying to
downsize their load, sorting through things to figure out
what they could and what they could not take for the trip.
Of course, Stacy explained to them (for me) that this was a
matter of convenience and that they weren't using this trip
(and my truck) to move *all* their goddamn belongings cross-
country. And as I stood back, watching and listening to
laughter and the nonsense that fit in perfectly here—*but
the baby needs that . . . that's my hair dryer! That's a gift
we got for Aunt Lee Lee . . . But those are my party dresses!
[laughter] . . .* —I honestly tried to see these ladies (and
their child) as family. But, we'd just met. The trip hadn't
even begun yet and I was already having major doubts. Add
to that, I didn't get out to help them one bit with the pack-

ing, so no doubt I was on Stacy's shit list, right next to the Sprint customer-service rep.

Along 95, Stacy had to wait an hour or so for the Sprint issue to be corrected, and for her phone to come back on. So she was still frustrated enough to keep quiet, her face turned toward the passenger's-side window while Chloe toyed with the child. Meanwhile, Jazmine chatted it up on the phone, arguing with her boyfriend as to why he should or shouldn't be staying home instead of going out while she was away.

ALL THE while, I'm sayin', *What the fuck? My girl got an attitude, I got the goo-goo-gaa-gaa and the boyfriend issues in my ear. I wonder what the good pastor would say about this. He would surely use the Happy Meal scenario to remind me that her problems were my problems, and yada yada yada. But, Jesus, Joseph, and Mary. That was all easier said than done, especially when you're right in the center of it all—the seat where I was currently sitting.*

Add to all of that, I was starting to get weary behind the wheel. Stacy didn't say anything for a while, and I tried like hell to hold it down for a while longer. But once we got deep into a dark Pennsylvania portion of the turnpike, she turned gangsta.

"Pull over the next exit." There was no *darling, baby, sugah-pie*; just *pull over*. And if that phone call hadn't been so long ago, and if we hadn't had the young ladies in the car, I'm thinkin' the words *nigga* and *fuck* would've surely come from her mouth.

"I'm okay," I said, part lie and part good intention.

"But *I'm* not. *Next exit*," Stacy said with that determined tone of hers. And she began to gather her things from where she sat in the passenger seat, tossing things into her handbag and carryall. She made arrangements with the stack of CDs she'd brought so that (I figured) her music would be right for her turn behind the wheel.

It didn't take much for me to read between the lines. The next thing you know I'm in the bathroom at the next service station, relieving myself and praying that God had this trip on his agenda of Events to Watch.

We filled the tank, I got myself a cappuccino and espresso mixed, and we were back on the road. Stacy at the wheel. Me cranked back for a nap. And Mary J. Blige singing grown-folks music. In the backseat, Chloe was snoring over her wide-eyed, newborn son, while Jazmine was still negotiating with her (she hoped) stay-home boyfriend, trying to be controlling on a cell phone with (she said) less than one bar left. As I dozed off, I remembered praying that the girl had forgotten her charger.

IT WAS our first movie together. A theater far and away from the comfortable home I had, the wife, the kids, and the whole family unit. But I wasn't there at home where I was supposed to be. I was out looking for that thrill with a new girl. *Fresh flesh*. The movie was even irrelevant, since all I wanted, regardless of how cavalier a show I put on, was to tap this piece of ass. She was cute. She had a cute, lanky body. And when I got through with her I probably wouldn't even remember her name. But that was beside the point.

The point now was how I was acting in the theater. She was playing hard to get, but I had a trick or two up my sleeve. I started with the touching: at the popcorn counter, escorting her to our seats, and in the casual conversation we had during the twenty minutes of previews preceding the movie. Usually, I get real upset if I miss *any* of *The 20*. But that didn't even matter this evening. I just wanted this babe to surrender. And, so far, my plan was going as expected.

Somewhere during the first hour, I reached for her leg and cupped her knee with my hand.

She said, "*Stop,*" like a little whining bitch. However, I knew that wouldn't last. I snuggled up close and began to peck at her neck until she stopped pulling away. Until I was so soft with my pecks that they no longer tickled, but instead served as soothing bouts of pleasure. *Now*, it was on to the legs, and there was no argument this time. A girl has got to play hard to get in the beginning. That's the way most of them have been taught from their moms, their aunts, and their big sisters. Hell, they even update them in school programs now. *Shit.* No free meals for the playas on the set.

But those things that girls were taught were nothing but hurdles for men to overcome. Nothing but prevention measures for us to circumvent just because the hurdle is there. So, my mind was set on one thing, and that goal was getting closer as the movie progressed. My hands eventually reached pay dirt; no, not between her legs. That *already belonged to me* as far as I was concerned. I could almost count down the hours until I got that ass right where I wanted it. But, where my hands were headed was the ankles. The feet. Those hardworking and less-appreciated heels, insoles, and toes. Momma said if I could please a woman's feet, just about everything else could be called mine.

So, in the theater I massaged my date's feet one at a time. I paid extra special attention to the areas that made her cringe. And she don't think I know she cringed when I know *exactly* when she cringed. She tried to hide that shit; *but not from a playa!* Now. I never, never, never *ever* do this with a first date, but I felt adventurous tonight. I felt this cutie was so transparent that I could go to just about any extent, so why not? And I took her bare foot to my lips. I tongue-kissed her toes one at a time. I lapped at the balls of her feet and saw her try to conceal her giggle. And somewhere into my appreciation toward her other foot, the movie ended.

RIGHT THERE is when I act like I've been caught. I've been a *bad boy* and I don't deserve a date like her. I pretend the date is over. I pretend I'm just gonna take her home and *may*be call her for another date. And my date is so coy, but feeling so hot, bothered, and unsatisfied. I know these things.

"Can you pull over?" she says. And in the back of my head I know what's next. It's the fantasy all guys have. It's gonna be head in the car. It's gonna be in the front seat, the backseat, or she'll be kneeling on the raw earth while I'm sitting in the driver's seat, door open, legs open, zipper down. So, of course I'm gonna pull over the first chance I get; the first dead, dark spot along I-75.

"Wait a minute," she says. And she pulls out a mini-bottle of vodka. She swigs at it twice, like some champion getting her confidence up so she can ride a bull in a rodeo. Meanwhile, I step out of the truck and slip in the back door. I make preparations back there, moving whatever is in the way because it's *about to go down*. In a side pocket there in the back of the truck is a miniflashlight, and I'm already playing with it, shining its light on and off her face.

"Come on back here, you *pretty mothafucka*."

And in ghetto fashion, she doesn't step out of the truck and in through the back door. No, she climbs over and through the seats until she makes it safe.

I waste no time. I'm already at her neck.

I'm urging her to kiss me in the mouth, but she says, "I don't kiss in the mouth."

But then, there are so *many* things she won't do until I change all that. Did she forget she said *no* in the theater to my hand on her legs? *Hmmm. How soon we forget. Just a matter of time.*

It's about midnight now. *Let's move this a little faster,* I'm thinking as headlights from other vehicles pass us nearby. The reflections are merely hints of that passing traffic, but it turns the inside of the truck into a mysterious labyrinth, however confined. And the kissing turned to fondling. The fondling turned to my hand in the crotch of her shorts, feeling the wetness she built up, even as she swigged at some more vodka and eventually licked my fingers clean.

Her shorts were easily removed. At that point I had her put on a show for me.

"Play with yourself," I told her. And my tiny flashlight was right on time, showing me the juicy-wet folds of my demands and her obedience. "Play with it. That's right; just like that. Get into it, girl." And I watched her moan and groan and even eat at her own sloppy fingers. No more direction needed from me. She was on a roll—autopilot. Meanwhile, I'm already pulling my jeans down over my own "greatness."

No lie: the show she's putting on is *off the hook*. I never expected her to take it to this extreme. But since she did, hell, I might as well go the distance.

Something tells me *no penetration*, like maybe this woman is unsafe? Maybe she does this all the time? These questions enter my head at the damnedest time, but *a nigga gotta do what a nigga gotta do*. I grab a chunk of her hair and pull her toward me. But she stops me—

"Hold up," she says. And she reaches into her purse in the front seat; ass up near my face. From the purse she pulls out her brand-new black and platinum MasterCard. That's when she says, "Hold *this*, while I suck *this*."

I didn't understand where she was going with this. I didn't care, either, not while I was throbbing and snug in her mouth. I slipped the card into my shirt pocket and, as the saying goes, I *go with the flow*. She's on her own now, moving at an engrossing pace. And sooner than later she's working on my meat like a marathon is going on and that she might be judged by her performance. At the same time, my back is against the inside of the truck, praying that this might never end. And she's still sucking me and stroking me and playing with herself and moaning all the while. It's already hot in the truck. Windows are fogged and there's no visibility. I dropped that flashlight at least a half hour ago, but I didn't need to see this. I needed to *feel* it. And it was lifting me higher. And the blood in my head was rushing. And just when I'm feeling a surge pushing through me, my sweat-dripping brow is stimulated by a cool breeze. I'm startled, even as my body is convulsing. I open my eyes and see Stacy's overworked face lifting up from my lap. The door of my truck is open. Two black guys are out there in the dark, on the shoulder of the road. One is pulling Stacy out of the truck, while the other has a long-barreled revolver pointed at my head.

"Good night, playa." The gunman levels the pistol so that it's farther down, close to my heart; right where I put the black and platinum MasterCard. Then I hear the blast.

*"Boom!"*

The pain doesn't affect me as fast as the shock. But it's there nevertheless. And I convulse again, this time from the impact of the blast. The blast from me; the blast from a stranger's gun out there on the shoulder of I-75—together they shook me from my sleep. But I also let out a yell. And within seconds I had a Blazer full of women laughing their asses off at me.

"Where are we?" I asked, wide awake now, but in a disgruntled voice.

The laughter fell off into chuckles.

"Virginia," said Stacy. "And you better not get too loud, 'r else the boogeyman's gonna getcha." And Stacy impersonated me and my recent nightmare scream.

"Don't start. I need to get to a bathroom," I said, careful not to show signs of discomfort on account of what craziness was lurking in my drawers.

"We could do the next exit," said Stacy.

*"Please,"* was all I could blurt out.

---

THESE STOPS along the throughway can be challenging. And I'm not talking about the huge visitor centers where Starbucks and Wendy's and Cinnabon have vested interests. I'm talkin' about the smaller mom-and-pop gas stations (the ones that brave the dangerous nights without bulletproof enclosures) that are all illuminated like Hollywood sets and set up to be more convenience stores than gas stations. They have just about every emergency item in existence, there to satisfy your every whim. Of course, everything is marked up to the hilt, from novelties to first-aid kits. DVDs and NoDoz pills. Sweaters to sunglasses and even electronic slot machines. All of them, for convenience purposes, have bathrooms. Some for men and some for women. Others just have one toilet that can be shared. Still others are no more than the back storage rooms where the mops and cleaning supplies are kept. Almost always, these bathrooms are not the best kept, since they're *always* in use.

I went into the storeroom-slash-bathroom with a washcloth, a fresh pair of underwear, jeans, and a T-shirt that I fished out of my suitcase, and I emerged with a plastic bag of soiled clothes. A coffee this time. And while Chloe took charge of gassing up the car, Stacy took a moment to approach me.

"You okay?" I asked her. "Need me to drive?"

"I'm fine. The question is, are *you* okay?" she asked. And I knew I had been removed from her shit list.

After a pause, I said, "I got a funny feelin' about Atlanta."

"How so?"

"You remember when you told me all about the shooting, the ex-boyfriend in the truck on the side of the road?

How he had a family at home, the movie y'all went to, and all that?"

Stacy didn't say anything, just gave me a look to remind me how I was the one to suggest she forget all that.

"Well, I just had a nightmare about that shit. It was the craziest dream. But, I'm hopin' it's not some kind of a signal. I mean, you use to wake up screamin', and now it's *me*. I mean, what type of voodoo shit is *this*? I'm dreamin' that I'm *another* man? A *family* man, at that? I'm even speaking his language and doing the things the *he* does. And I'm out cheating on my wife with *you*. And then, *bang*! I get shot. *What the fuck*, Stacy."

Stacy put her hand to the back of my head and caressed it. It was the most soothing, most appreciated gesture a woman could do for me. Besides the affection that comes with it, I'd say that caressing my scalp is almost as orgasmic as I could come next to sex itself. Seriously. And thank God Stacy realized that and came to my rescue. At least she lost that attitude somewhere along the way, probably at my expense.

"I'm sorry," said Stacy, "for bringin' so much strife into your life."

"It's not your fault, boo. Please. Don't take the blame for shit I'm dreamin'. I guess I'm just buggin'. Overreacting." I pulled her into my embrace. "I just wish we can stop all this arguing and bickering back and forth. Can we try that for at least one week straight, no matter what?"

Stacy smiled as if that was *her* idea. Then she said, "That's a plan."

———

I MADE small talk with Chloe and Jazmine in hopes of fixing things, and maybe creating some kind of rapport between us. The laughter at my outburst earlier helped to repair the attitude *I* had for the first part of the trip, and things were loosened some more once we passed through Virginia and when I got to asking the girls about themselves. I was already familiar with Chloe's situation and that she was a single stay-at-home mom. Most times you had to be when you were dependent on welfare and without a job or support from family to care for the child while you worked. What I *didn't* know was that her boyfriend (the baby's father) had been called off to serve in the war in Iraq. Naturally, I had sympathy for the situation, not left to assume that hers was just another case of welfare fraud. Jazmine, on the other hand, was a little evasive about where she worked and what she was doing with her life. But, during our conversation, Stacy was still going strong behind the wheel; alert enough to shoot me a look that said, *Stay out of her business*. That's when I vaguely recalled hearing that Jazmine was a stripper at Sin City in the Bronx. Maybe not a profession to be proud of, at least not here and now. But you could be sure I was curious to know the details on that issue—something Stacy was sure to share with me later.

The next morning I found myself waking up at a service station. We were parked with the air conditioner on blast, R. Kelly had been bumped by Keyshia Cole, I was still in the passenger's seat, and Stacy was sound asleep behind the steering wheel. I looked in the backseat to see that the girls were also sound asleep. The baby, however, had his eyes wide open and was playing with a plastic teething toy.

In baby talk, I said to him, "Don't you ever sleep. Huh?" And I reached back to let him hold my finger to try to build some rapport. Moments later I had to encourage everyone to rise and shine so we could get some food.


IF THERE isn't a Waffle House near every gas station along I-75, then my name ain't Danté from the Bronx. And there was no sense in my asking for eggs because I don't eat pork. And these cooks (just about all of them) use the same utensils for the pork that they use for the home fries and eggs. So, what's the point? Why not just throw the eggs, the pork bacon, and the home fries in one pile, mix it all up, and call it pork eggs and potatoes?

"No, thanks. I'll just have a coffee and a waffle. Unless you have turkey bacon?" I'm no prude when it comes to food, I just *don't* like pork with my eggs. Now, take me to IHOP, and the story would be different.

Stacy made a face since I got particular about my breakfast.

*I don't have to tell her whose body this is, do I?*

Of course, the girls had pork bacon, eggs, waffles, and— *Who the hell is paying for all this?* Naturally, I bitched and moaned to myself, but I knew I'd be carrying the weight when all was said and done, and I picked up the bill before I left the girls (and the baby) to finish up their food.

While I had my "alone time," I spent some money in the coin toss, one of those machines where you drop your quarters through a slot and a metal bar continues to move back and forth, hopefully pushing your quarter into an abundance of other quarters that were already positioned to tip over the edge, where they'd fall into a tray as your winnings. Why I always fall for this trap, I don't know. Maybe I'm just greedy and don't see that this is too good to be true? The winnings look to be guaranteed: the quarters are all piled up in a landslide. All the odds seem to point in my direction. There's the tease, when two or three quarters drop (after you've already put ten or fifteen in!). And then you might get lucky and a chunk of change falls, but it still either matches your input or falls short. I froze there in front of the coin slot for a time; some sixth-sense moment threw me into an out-of-body experience. It was as if a voice was talking to me:

*Isn't this coin-operated gamble similar to the risk you're taking right now?*

What do you mean? What gamble?

*I think you know what gamble I mean. And it begins with an S and ends with a Y.*

You should shut up. I know what I'm doin'. And since when does true love, out of nowhere, come and share the elevator with you.

*Just remember I told you so.*

Of course, the moment I had with the inner conversation just happened to piggyback the nightmare I had in the car. And now I had to live with second-guessing and thinking about life's "what ifs." How convenient.

I NOTICED changes in the scenery as the morning grew warmer. Stacy let me drive, and I was wide awake on coffee. So, I figured I'd let the girls indulge in some niggeritis while I did some sightseeing. We were deep, deep, deep

into Virginia and I was beginning to see signs of the Caroli-
nas. A lot of farm land, trees along the interstate, and more
deer and muskrats and raccoons lying along the sides of the
roads than I cared to count. Not only that, but the windshield of my truck needed some serious treatment with all
the buzzards slamming up against the glass all night and
day. This one big *nasty* insect was so large, and splattered
so much against the window, that I swore it was a bird.

Surprising myself, I actually held up good for the re-
mainder of the trip, focusing on my goals and dreams, taking it all the way into Atlanta. I could already feel the
down-home atmosphere. Whether it was the increase of
pickup trucks on the road or how spacious land and properties were—I can't say. Either way, it didn't feel like this
would ever be the type of place where I needed to brace
myself for nightly, random gunfire from rooftops or for air
pollution. An added bonus was the real hospitable, friendly,
and helpful rest-stop attendants always ready with guid-
ance. Even at the fast-food franchises the servers were bubbly and courteous. So much different than what we're use
to in the Bronx.

We made a stop at Walmart, just one of many that we
saw along the way, and I secretly wondered who was profit-
ing off all these hundreds of stores. Whoever it was—I'm
sure—was sitting pretty without a care in the world. Wish
I was in their place. But then I caught myself, because no
matter *how* much money you have, it doesn't ensure good
health or well-being in such unpredictable times.

*Note to self: suggest my vegetarian lifestyle to Chloe and
Jazmine.* Ha-ha. Sure.

In Walmart we picked up a few things that we'd need to

eat, as well as those last-minute items that were forgotten back in the Bronx. I knew Stacy's nieces didn't need *shit*, with all the belongings they'd dragged down the interstate interfering with my rearview the entire trip. Damn good thing they were staying awhile and that I wouldn't have to be responsible for getting them back to New York. *I know. So cruel.* But, shit; people will impose themselves all the time, and they'll never realize who is picking up *their* slack until they're forced to pick it up themselves. *Hello!* And, another thing: I honestly never heard the names Chloe and Jazmine in the few months I've known Stacy. But all of a sudden they show up as tagalongs and I'm supposed to recognize them as if they're part of the daily conversation? *Jeesh.*

When we were in line to pay, we had to listen to a preacher using the crowded Walmart checkout as his makeshift pulpit. The whole bit about *working together as a Christian community, each one-teach one, and we must have TOTAL support for this to grow and mature.* I don't have anything against anyone getting their hustle on, but a brother had been driving for hours, and I wasn't really trying to hear a whole bunch of preaching. Especially when you're holding up the line behind you. After another minute of watching him hand out his flyers and invite everyone to his sermon, we finally checked out and headed for the Blazer. The funny face the cashier made when the preacher left said it all: *everybody got a hustle.* What really made the encounter most memorable was how in this *huge* parking lot, we had to be parked a few spaces away from the preacher. And *no he didn't just get behind the wheel of a taxi*! I told myself, *Out here it must also be* hard for a pimp.

ARRIVING IN Lawrenceville made my day. Fourteen hours on the road and we were finally pulling into a community called Endeavor, where most of the homes were worn by maybe eight years (my guess), but well kept just the same. And the houses were not what you call *climbing* on top of one another, either—not like in the Bronx, where many of the row houses are so close you can hear a cat's meow, or where a domestic dispute can easily spill over into your "zone" and screw up a pleasant dinner. Have the nerve to yell *shut up!* and see if somebody's ex-Marine doesn't come knocking on your door to look for trouble. Shoot *him* in the chest and see if the rest of his family, and their families, don't start a race war right in your front yard. Before you know it, everyone's on the six-o'clock news wondering what the fuck happened. But even that's not news enough because the president is in town, he's managed to shut down a quarter of Manhattan just so he can get to sightsee, and suddenly your ghetto drama is *forgotten* drama on the six-o'clock news—*two dead and twelve injured.* Next story.

ASSESSING THE surroundings and considering that many of these communities have neighborhood-watch groups, tennis courts, pools, lakes, and other amenities to pamper their residents, I recognized nothing but peace and serenity in Lawrenceville. And I am *so* not mad at that. In the meantime, as we rolled up to Stacy's mom's home, the front door swung open before I threw the truck into park. Next thing

I see is another young thing in short shorts and a cut-off tee charging out toward us.

"Brianna! Brianna! Ohmy*Gawd*, she got so *big*!" The yelling that was killing my ears in the truck eventually spilled out onto the driveway. A few more family members pranced out of the house so that everyone was hovering over Chloe's newborn baby. I could see who Stacy's mom was because the two practically ignored each other for a time. No hugs exchanged.

Eventually, Stacy said, "Hi, Ma."

Her mother mumbled something back, but then went *right* back to smiling over the baby, as if to keep herself occupied.

To intervene in any of this conflict of interest before it included me, I set out to introduce myself to Mrs. Singletary.

"His name *Soldier*," Chloe announced to everyone.

"I'm Danté. I run a company called Mister Fix-It, up in the Bronx. I do a lot of work for your sister. Yvonne, is it? I only know her as Mrs. Singletary, though." Meanwhile, as the touching and the hype over the baby continued, Stacy broke away to hug this big, chunky dude who was three shades lighter than her and three times bigger than me. She wasted no time in pulling me away from her mom and said, "Rory, this is *my* soldier, Danté. Danté, this is my big brother I told you so much about."

The homeboy handshakes, the brief buddy hug, and an eye-to-eye exchange transpired (that understanding between brother and boyfriend), right before the big man and I grabbed up as many of the suitcases and bags as we could and carried them into the house. Instinctively, I wondered where Stacy's children were—it was the beginning of August, school was out, unless—

"They at summer camp," I overheard from the little crowd of women behind us. In the meantime, I was impressed with the amount of space there was in the Singletary home. But crazier than that, there was just about *one* piece of furniture in the home: a couch in the living-room area, just to the right of the doorway. Most of the first floor, but for the entryway, was carpeted, worn down (I imagined) from so much traffic. And as I stepped farther through the hallway I gazed around at the kitchen. Very well-decorated yellow walls and marble countertops, but the dining-room table definitely didn't fit in. Essentially, the house was bare, and I didn't find out until later, while I was taking a nap, what exactly happened and why the house looked so unlived-in.

"Girl, you don't know the half," said Brianna. Her slang was cute, but not so different that I couldn't pick up every word, even half asleep. "Momma took me to Hollywood, try'na pursue my acting. We put everything out in the yard a week before we left. We sold *everything*. I mean, the beds, the stereo, the couches. Momma even sold the dishes out the cabinets."

"Say word," one of the girls replied. I was too tired to try to figure out who, what, when, or where. I just needed a place to lay my head for now. Chatter on, ladies . . .

"And she rented the car *and* the house to this fool-ass nigga who was fakin' like he was big-time, but he was so big-time he couldn't pay his rent. So basically, we had to shut down the whole Hollywood dream just to save Momma's credit. 'Cuz he wasn't payin' nothin' after a while. Momma said he owed'd us like five thousand dollahs. And if she ain't come back here to straighten his ass out, we'd'a lost the house."

*Damn*, I said in my sleep. I had questions, but my mouth wasn't moving as fast as my brain was; and my brain was moving *real* slow right now. And the other thing fuckin' with my head was how heavy Stacy's southern drawl had grown all of a sudden.

*When in Rome, do as the Romans do.*

"So he paid her the money?"

"Yup. But Momma had to get crunk on that nigga. She found out he falsified some shit with the mortgage company, *plus* that nigga was on some federal probation. And that's when Momma went to *work* on that ass. She even put a call in to his probation officer and all they needed was her affidavit, and that nigga woulda got locked the fuck up."

"But even so, that money was for mortgage. Y'all sold all your shit? *Dayum*. If that woulda happened to me, I'da lost my mind." I knew that was Stacy's voice. Especially when those *next* words came out.

"Well, I'ma tell you what. Momma and I ain't the tightest, but I'ma do y'all a solid 'cuz I ain't fittin' to see y'all sittin' and sleepin' on the floor. Plus, how the kids been handlin' all this? She got my kids sleepin' on the floor, too? 'Cuz y'all wanna do the Hollywood shuffle?"

Brianna intervened before Stacy went into a tirade.

"Sis, the babies got a nice comfortable situation. We got 'em some sleepin' bags, and they *lovin'* it. Every night they pretendin' they on a campin' trip. Playin' hide and seek 'er somethin'. Them kids got no problems in the world, girl."

Stacy dug deeper: "Where were they when you all was on your trip?"

"At Uncle Willy's place. Him and Rory still stay together over in Gwinnett County, and the kids stayed with them for six months while we caught the blues in Hollywood."

"What were y'all there for, a movie or somethin'?"

"Sis, I hit you up on MySpace with *all* that. Ain't you check *anythin'* I sent you?"

"Lil' sis. Life been crazy, crazy, *crazy* ever since I left here. I hardly go up on the computer. And when I do, it's just to get an e-mail or somethin'. Plus, if you ain't know, I gotta *man* now. So I'm steady helpin' him grow his business, 'cuz one day, *guuurl!* we gonna hit it *big*. I could just *feel* it."

I'm listening to all this, and I guess they figured me to be knocked out and unreceptive, but even dead, inanimate, lifeless sponges absorb things. And that was me: lifeless, sucking in every word. Every Ebonic-laden word. I could feel the anticipation and the energy building up in Stacy. I could sense some of what was about to come out of her mouth and I wanted to jump up and snatch her to the side for a chat, but she was already too far gone.

"*Guurl*, I just got me a big ol' investment to do *whateva* I wanna do with it. So, ain't no sense livin' like paupers. Let's go and get us some furniture. My kids gonna have them a nice surprise when they get home."

*Oh Lord.*

# [ SIX ]

## STACY

YOU DIN' HAFTA tell me another word. 'Cuz if I got a dolla, my kids gonna get ninety cent of it if it's gonna make them comfortable. And if I ain't got nothin'? I'ma shoot me a rooster 'r sumpthin' so they could eat. I put that on everything I love. So, me with a hundred-thousand-dollar credit card in my hands? And my kids are sleeping in bags on the floor? What? Are they serious?

Our first stop was IKEA. And the shopping spree was off to a running start. We filled up four shopping carts, and that's *not* including the beds, the sofas, and some other furniture that wouldn't fit in the car. We really rushed through our first stop just so we could hit a used-car lot, but my eyes were on their like-new cars. After all, if I'm gonna be ballin', I might as well look the part, *right*? Anyway, I wasn't gonna buy the car right away, just wanted to check it out for future purchase. I knew Danté would kill me if I came back with all the furniture *and* a new ride. Not like he was the boss of me or nothin'; I just know how he is. So I just figured I'd take it easy. After the dealership visit, we stopped

by the mall, where I picked up some Victoria's Secret linge-
rie for me and my sis, and we went by Foot Locker, where I
got sneakers for the whole family—even Mom. It felt so
good to come to the rescue of my family, with my knight in
shining armor by my side. And I rode that high into the evening as we shopped at Publix for a month's worth of grocer-
ies, and after that we stopped by Wendy's for fast food.

We were makin' a whole lotta noise on the way home
with the radio blastin' Q-102, and I had a buzz because I
couldn't wait to pop one of the bottles of wine we bought.
It felt like Christmas Eve and we were headed home to open
all the gifts early. Only thing I could think about was cele-
brating with my man. The fast food could wait for later.

## DANTÉ

By 8:00 p.m., some five hours later, the house was still
quiet and I was at peace. Truth is, the peace and quiet was
*probably* what woke me, since I'm not at all used to living
like this. For all my life, I can remember sirens, loud music,
and teenagers hanging out in groups at unreasonable hours,
shouting and starting senseless fights with one another. If it
wasn't the teenagers, the traffic, or the domestic disputes
right there in the street, there'd be gunshots fired from the
top of someone's building. It was that same reckless, irre-
sponsible attitude that hung in the air, so thick it could
create a funk; so thick it could be considered loud. And
sometimes, so deadly that you either surrendered or became
vigilant. So, for the life of me, as I took a walk inside and
out of the Singletary home, it was hard to see how Stacy

had the opportunity to get involved with the violent esca-
pade she had talked about, the one that had virtually chased
her out of town. And then I somehow recalled something
she'd said about the jurisdiction of her mom's house in respect to where all the drama took place. Suburbia, versus
the congested city.

*She got a nice house up in Lawrenceville. They would never
think to look there. Too far up north, away from the 'hood.*

So then maybe that was the reason why the Singletary
home seemed like some kind of a safe haven for her kids.
Or, at least, that was the vision I was left with. Still, I found
myself looking (and listening) closely at the home security
system. Every time someone came in or left the house
you'd hear:

"Garage door, *open.*"

"Back door, *open.*"

"Front door, *open.*"

The system seemed to cover everything, but all the
while I'm thinking, *So? And if someone decides to kick in the
door? "Front door, open" ain't gonna help a damn bit.* And I
gathered that this was the reason for the aluminum bat I
had noticed in the pantry. *In the pantry?*

The rest of the house was more or less predictable:
"cookie-cutter specials," we HG Channel fans call them.
You stomp on the floor and you can hear the basement
door rattle. You pull the front door closed hard enough and
the impact can be felt throughout the dwelling. Same old
fixtures and utilities and appliances in the bathrooms, the
kitchen, and the laundry room. Same old chandeliers, ceiling
fans, and moldings that come standard when the house is
built. And, of course, central heat and AC throughout, all

of it (I'm informed) payable through one power, gas, and light company. Again, someone, somewhere, is sittin' pretty getting all of *that* money.

The overwhelming plus I noticed was the space in the house. The square footage had to be over twenty-five hundred. A far cry from the thousand square feet I had to manage up in the BX.

*Noises outside. Nine p.m.*

Lord have *mercy*. Sounded like a party showed up, already in progress.

There was the car that her brother, Rory, drove, there was my Blazer, and another white truck behind them with the words IKEA FURNITURE WAREHOUSE branded across its side. A caravan had just arrived, for sure. And everyone that went for the ride was apparently full of joy. If I didn't know better, Stacy bought everyone something with her new black and platinum MasterCard. *Jesus.*


AFTER AN hour (at least) of moving all the purchased goods into the house, I got a better look at things: the his-and-hers beds for Stacy's kids, Jason and Jackie, the sectional and dining-room set, the mattress set for her sister (the bed she wanted had to be ordered); there was also a large-screen TV, a desktop, and a laptop computer, a whole bunch of kitchen stuff, more food than a family could eat in a month, and master beds for the guest room and (of all people) Stacy's mom. Everybody had new sneakers on and you could smell that new-sneaker freshness in the air. And as I'm towing things through the house, and helping Rory assemble the furniture in the living room (where there was the most space), I'm looking over at Stacy spending time with her kids. I can't get her attention, but my subliminal messages are shooting over at her like a machine gun.

*How much did you spend? How are you gonna pay it back? I told you earlier you had to be careful.*

But my inaudible conversation was going nowhere. After a time, I just said, *What the hell.* And I stuck it in the back of my mind. I was just happy to see *her* happy. No sense in messing that up. She had her kids in her arms, which was the reason we had come to Atlanta in the first place. Not only that, she had apparently cleared things up with her moms, which seemed like a good thing as well. I just couldn't help thinking that all this was a pipe dream, empty happiness that was produced thanks to the little plastic card she got. *The card.* Wow. How much different things felt when you could spend money. How many smiles and how much contentment and how many relationships repaired when you can spend money. I wondered if I had a million dollars, could I buy happiness in all the people around me? Clearly, she was doing it with less than $100 grand. That is, I *hope* it was *waaaay* less than $100 grand. But I also *knew* that no matter how much money she had, purchased happiness doesn't last long; not even as long as the money lasts.

AFTER A hefty, late dinner, most of us got niggeritis and fell asleep in our respective areas of the house. Stacy had her one-year-old, Jackie, sleeping between us. Jason was almost six years old, and I knew it was way past his bedtime to be playing with his new video game all night. I could hear the TV real clear through these cookie-cutter walls. And I was sure the rest of the house could as well. So, I got myself out of bed and went to the room next door, where Jason and Rory shared the space. Rory was snoring like a horse, dead tired and slumped on a blow-up mattress on the floor, while Jason was lying on his new bed, facing his new TV and flipping the controller like a pro.

"You think it might be time to catch up on some sleep, young man?" I said this, but I also went to sit on the bed and see what he was up to on TV.

"Play," he offered. And he tried handing me the controller for player number two—one of the two he had been using. Jason, boy genius, was playing Red Faction, where the players and guns you choose shoot up one another during a prescribed time limit.

"Okay, Jason. I'll play, only if you do two things for me."

"Okay—what?"

"First of all, we gotta turn this down some. People are trying to sleep," I said. Then, under my breath, I said, "*Not that you care.* Also, if I win, you have to put the game up, and get some sleep. You got day camp tomorrow, bright and early, *right?*"

"But it's mandatory swim tomorrow. I *hate* mandatory swim."

"Okay. Well, you can't be a tough guy and shoot everybody up in Red Faction and in the morning be a scaredy-cat for mandatory swim, now can you?"

Jason made that confused face that I'm sure child psychologists see every day. But I went on with my proposal.

"So, you gotta *promise*, Jason. You promise?"

"Yeah," he said with that disgruntled look. And I imitated the whole Muhammed Ali look, like I was gonna kick his little ass within five minutes, and then lights out. That was around midnight. By 3:00 a.m. I still hadn't beaten Jason. But we played until we both fell off to sleep on his bed. Stacy came in and woke me.

"Y'all look so cute. Come on."

More than half asleep, I allowed myself to be pulled up from the bed. Stacy tucked her son in and we held hands leaving the room. The image of that peaceful little genius stuck in my mind as we did.

"I put the baby to sleep. You need to shower."

I made a face, but she was right. I dragged myself into the shower and when I came out, Stacy was in a fuck-me negligee.

Again, me with the curious expression. *"In your mother's house?"*

Stacy sucked her teeth. "Don't worry about her. I own that bitch." She said that and handed me a glass of·Alizé. We toasted.

"To the best of times," she went on.

"Is that a Jay-Z quote? Or Charles Dickens?"

After twisting her lips to the side, she said, "Another one of your smart-aleck comments?"

After my first sip, I tried to ask her about money. She put her hand to my mouth.

"Don't steal my joy," she said. And I hushed up. Next thing I know, Stacy dropped to her knees and opened the towel I had around my waist until it fell to my feet. Now, in my mind, the pastor's influence was overshadowing all this, with his usual speech about the Happy Meal standing out in bright neon lights. *I know. I know, Pastor.* But maybe just this one more time.

My head back and my hands on my hips, I realized more of those amazing feelings that Stacy always pleasured me with. She did this *so* well, engaged herself as if she were on a mission; and she made it so I didn't have to feel guilty for not immediately returning the favor. She made it seem as though she *liked* to give head. And I guess, with my guilty conscience, I was left to wonder what pleasure she got out of this. But every time I think with the whole conscious-black-man side of my brain, it's precisely at *this* time when I'm being selfish and when she's blowing my mind. And I conveniently forget. Besides, today seemed *so different.* Today seemed to be some kind of redemption for Stacy. She achieved her goal, and then some. She's back with her kids, back in her 'hood, secured by a strong line of credit, and now she's got a pulsating man-size muscle working across her tongue and gums. And damned if this wasn't just turning me on, encouraging me to give love in return.

I grabbed a chunk of Stacy's hair, pulled her and her sloppy gums off me, and I swung her around so that she was bent over the new bed. Seconds later I was bending over and kissing her ever so lovingly. I loved it when she shaved down there, all prepared for me to slick my tongue along the smooth skin of her sensitive sex. And only when she began pulling away from me, at the moment her body became stiff as a board, unable to take any more, I shifted gears and went for the routine driving in and out, in and out. And her sighs grew to the point that I had to cover her mouth with my hand. *Damn cookie-cutter house.* At the same time, my other hand was securing her waist and I just went for it. It was fast and furious, and then it was slow and gradual and methodic and reaching for the deepest Stacy possible.

# STACY

This was a time to celebrate. I was back home, back with my family, and my man was here. Plus, I was happy as a pig in shit after the lil' shopping spree we came from. So I was tryin' not to hear anything about my spending and all that conscious-consumer stuff Danté be talkin' about. I just wanted to be supported 150 percent. And now that we were in the bedroom alone, I felt so obliged to give this man pleasures from out of this world.

Somethin' about my mouth and Danté's dick works so perfectly. It fits so snug, I'm comfortable workin' with it. And when I look up to see his eyes roll back, I feel as if there's no greater ecstasy for a man. Plus, somebody spoiled this man before I got to him. Because he never said *no* to my lips and tongue lovin' him like they do. And I've had straight-up prudes stop me from goin' down on them— which was a *trip* 'cuz I thought all men liked head. So, in my mind I'm like, *Whatever, man. Your loss.* But Danté's lovin' it. And I love this man to death, so he can get it *whenever*. The thing that's so different about Danté from most every other man I been with is that he will give me pleasure in return. He won't make me feel used and left unsatisfied. He will hold and caress me, and I always feel comforted within his embrace. And, as my ladies out there know, ain't *nothing* like that feeling and bein' hooked up with the right one. For me, Danté *is* that right one. He will give it to me in a smooth, romantic rhythm, and he can be rough with it, too. The thing is *balance*, and not overdoing it so that it gets ordinary or boring. One thing I don't think will *ever* get boring is Danté givin' *me* head. The attention he devotes, the pace that he brings with his tongue game, is *crazy*. How can I explain how it feels except that it's *electrifying*! He sends chills through me and my body just goes into the jolts and spasms and I wanna pull out my weave. And all of that comes *before* the oceanic orgasm that pushes through me. My toes are curlin'. My eyes are all over the place. I'm pullin' the bed sheets off and we're eventually sliding off the bed and onto the floor. I cannot control myself when Danté really puts his work in. There are the quick wham-bam-thank-you-ma'am encounters we have. But then there are those thorough, passionate times that he forever surprises me, and sensations shoot up inside of me like some kinda lightning bolt. Wow. And just when I think I've had it all, I find myself beggin' him to give me more. I need his dick inside of me and I don't mind placing my direct order. *Give it to me, Danté. Fuck me.* From there on in, I know not what I'm saying. My mouth, my hands, and the rest of my body—everything has a mind of its own.

## DANTÉ

I had to pull out quick and step away from her limp, frustrated body. I wanted this to last, and if that was gonna be the case I needed to cool it. I went to gulp down the rest of the Alizé, then I walked around the room like some naked

Adonis, taking deep breaths so that I could simmer down. This was something I had to teach myself so that (no matter how excited I was) I wouldn't cum too quick. Most times it worked. And when it didn't, the worst case was that things got messy. But thank God I never had a mishap where I got a woman pregnant. Stacy says she can't get pregnant because of some IUD she has in. I don't know about all that. I just know to *wear a rubber or withdraw*. And still, after all those revelations and all that we'd been through, Stacy and I were still not using the rubber.

"COME HERE," I directed. And Stacy made her way across the room and assumed a doggy-style position on the floor. Right there I became a beast for a few minutes, grabbing at her hair, snatching her head back, and feeding her dick from behind, over and over again. That was the whole object of pulling out, so I could start all over again from scratch.

More noise from Stacy. Then again, with my hand covering her mouth. Again I pulled out; but now I directed her to the corner of the room where I stood with my back against the wall. Since she was so obedient, and since the activity was driving my ego through the roof, I just followed my carnal urges.

"Kneel down. *Suck it.*" I could feel myself becoming that raunchy, careless monster—that man in the nightmare, that bloody dream I had on the trip down to Atlanta. But, by all indications, Stacy was going with the flow. She was loving this and willing to oblige. So who was I to poop a party?

Sloppy and wet and ready, I leveraged our bodies so that

she could continue to blow me, but now we were moving to the floor, with Stacy on her back and me hovering over her, working in and out of her mouth—her second pussy. In my mind, I guess, this was a *new* missionary position.

Although I was on the edge of orgasm, my intention was not to end up this way. And, with the little senses I had left, I pulled my baby up from the floor and carried her to the bed. Now was the time for the *real* missionary work. A shame how I was manipulating her like this, but (I promise) there was a heavy connection between us. In her eyes, her breathing, and the convictions she voiced over and over, Stacy was lovin' every minute of this. And so it was no problem to throw her onto the bed and to then dive easily on top of her. It was no problem to grab her legs and order her to hold them so that her knees were rubbing at her ears and so that she'd allow absolute access to every inch of her. And that's what I took. I took it over and again, my face flush against hers and hugging her so that our bodies molded as one. And now it didn't matter who heard. It didn't matter that the walls were paper thin. If the whole world heard that we were making love, then maybe they *should* know. Maybe they should part the sea and allow us to come through just like we were both cumming now. Her flexible body going through spasms, and my stiff body shivering with the absolute release.

IN THE morning, I had enough energy to wake the kids and make breakfast for nine people (three of them *little* people), then we ushered the kids off to day camp. On the way back to the Singletary house, Stacy wanted to stop and get some *knickknacks* that she said she forgot the night before.

Her idea of knickknacks was a DVD player for her brother, a new playpen for Jackie, and a whole line of Victoria's Secret thongs and panties and bras for herself. *Didn't she already go to Victoria's Secret?*

As if she needed an excuse for me, she said, *"Well?* You do want me to be beautiful *and* look good, *right?"* She said this in front of the cashier, as she whipped out that credit card, and then hugged up on me and kissed me with those lips that had worked long and hard the night before. How could I argue?

She didn't stop there. Proactiv System's skin care for the two of us—she got that from one of those impulse kiosks you always see along the walkway in the mall. Never mind that this spending wasn't part of the *knickknacks* Stacy wanted. Then there were a number of designer suits for me. Our favorite video collection of Boondocks (because she left hers at home—*my* home, that is). And then were the sneakers—three pairs of them—and the jackets, the new his and hers Mogul cell phones from Sprint (her favorite service provider), and finally a few cases of wine from the local Publix supermarket. In my head I counted all of seven thousand dollars that she had spent before we finally made it home. But add that to the furniture, electronics, and other household items from the day before, and I'd say she had to be close to $40 or $50 grand, easy. Without a doubt, this woman's spending was untouchable. And she did it like such a pro. But for me to say anything to her, I'd get that same old sad-eyed response: *don't steal my joy.*

I KNOW a friend, who knows a friend, who knows a friend. As usual, it's a client-related connection. So Stacy and I went to a Sunday-night dinner engagement, featuring superstar Kool DJ Red Alert. As the coincidence goes, he had just moved down to Atlanta and set up shop where he performed live each week at a restaurant and nightclub called Flambeaux in Stone Mountain, Georgia. Of course, Stacy might not be all that familiar, but me, Bronx boy that I is, was entirely familiar with Red Alert's importance in New York City radio. He had continued to be a staple in radio and in hip-hop culture for as long as I could remember. So, I thought we'd take the trip to the Sunday-night event and chill with Red.

"RED IS cool," said Stacy.

"That he is. The *Kooooool DJ Red Alert*," I said, imitating how I always remembered him saying it on New York radio. "Did you dig that old-school jam he played?"

"Old school? *Everything* he played was old-school."

"Okay. I know that. But that disco-lady song was *smoking.* I ain't heard that in a *looooong* time."

Stacy flatly replied, "I ain't heard that *ever.*"

I wasn't gonna let Stacy's little sarcasm spoil the night. I just wanted to always remember that look in her eyes when we were inside the club; how she was all dreamy-eyed and in love. And now that we were outside for some air, and holding on to my arm like she did just continued the romance. I couldn't remember ever taking a walk with her, I mean one of those romantic walks under the moon and stars. And with every step we took through the restaurant parking lot, that became more and more a good idea. The moon was full. There was a clearing across the street—basically more parking area and uneven land. So I suggested we go for a stroll. Maybe walk off some of the alcohol we'd drunk, however casual our indulgence. Stacy was pointing at stores in the Mall at Stonecrest, explaining that this was one of Georgia's largest shopping experiences. But, without being too abrupt, I changed the subject from shopping. I'm sure that to her, talking about shopping was a complete thrill. For me, it was a complete waste of time.

Maybe it was just me, but this just seemed like a time for reflection. Our stomachs were fed, our buzz was minimal, and our hormonal imbalances had been satisfied (and then some!) the night before. So, this seemed as good a time as any to get deep.

"So what do you want out of life, Stacy?"

Without hesitation, she said, "Well, of course I want my kids to be happy. But more than that, I don't want them to have to go through the same hurdles and challenges I had to."

"Life is *always* gonna give us that, no matter who we are," I told her.

"Yeah, but the *unnecessary* stuff, Danté. The silly stuff that we get into? I really don't want that kind of struggle in my space. I want *peace*. I've earned that by sacrificing. But besides the kids' being happy, *I wanna be happy*, Danté. And I'll do what I have to to get that, by any means necessary. But I'ma also *give* what I have to get there. I want a house, but I'ma make it a home for a king to come back to after a hard day's work. And, Danté, I'm thinkin' that king is you." Stacy sure had me quiet with that testimony. We kissed and hugged for an extended period of time.

Stacy further said, "I never really wanted no *superstar* life. I mean, it would be nice to experience. That whole red-carpet bit in New York was like a fantasy, and I know I was trippin' a little, but I'm just fine with someone I love, and someone who loves my kids. If I can get that, I'll give you the world. I'll cook and clean and wash your dirty drawers. It's *whateva*, Danté."

"Damn, baby. All of that *and* the way you put it on me in the bed? You make a man wanna say woo-woo-*woo*!" I hugged Stacy and we kissed there under the moon like we were the only two brand-new people on earth. Yeah, I was aware that cars were gliding past and that people were hopping into and out of their parked cars; some owners were there to more or less show off their rides and blast their music in the nearby parking lot. But right this second, nothing else mattered.

"What was that?"

"What was *what*?"

"Stacy, that was a *wolf*."

"Yeah, we got them out here."

"Yeah, we—*what*?" I pulled Stacy back toward the club parking lot. "Girl, you must be crazy, talkin' like it's *okay* to hang out near a wolf."

Stacy laughed. "Really. It's okay, baby. I been seein' them wheneva I'm *outside* of the city. But it's just *not* that serious. They don't have news flashes all up on the TV talkin' about *wolf bite, wolf bite*." She laughed again, but that was irrelevant because right now we were crossing the street at *my* pace. The stroll down lovers' lane was *over*.

"Well, shit. Don't make *me* no difference, 'cause I'm back in my truck and headed back to Lawrenceville in a few seconds."

"Don't they be bustin' shots off in the Bronx, right near where you live?" Stacy asked.

"But that's the Bronx. By the looks of things here, your bullets are *wolves*."

"You funny."

"Okay, but nevertheless, if I have my choice, I don't wanna deal with either—bullets *or* wolves. How about that?"


JUST AS we made it across the street, just as we stepped into the parking lot, a tricked-out, fire-engine-red Chevy convertible, with its reggae music blasting, pulled up to a sudden stop in front of us. And all four of the guys in the vehicle had sunglasses on. Not that I cared, but that didn't make a bit of sense because it was close to 11:00 p.m. The driver had a brimmed red baseball cap on, the kind meant for profiling, not for the baseball field. Of course, the hat had the requisite *A* embroidered in white. *Atlanta? Or Asshole?*

By the looks of things, these guys were up to no good, so I pulled at Stacy to move to the right. But the Chevy backed up abruptly and blocked us. When we went the opposite way, the Chevy jerked forward, blocking us again.

"Hey, yo, we don't want no trouble. Y'all go 'head and have a good night now."

The driver threw the vehicle into park and sat up high in his seat—high enough for his ass to be where a head should be.

"Yo, don't be *rude, dude*. Me waan' talk to dah pretty

lady, dass all." He pulled down his shades and his eyes crossed as he trumpeted his abrupt response. *"We don't want no trouble,* you say? Well, we don't waan' no trouble *eeeder,* playboy." Even I could've laughed at the horrible impersonation he did of me. But there was nothing funny about this. The guys with him were also sitting up now, all of them grittin' on me with their various head ties of black, red, and green-mixed shreds, more or less daring me to rebel. One of them had a half head of hair braided with the other half in an Afro blow out. He also had a patch over one eye. No sense in me trying to figure out *that* fad.

A couple of the troublemakers were smoking weed out in the open air. One was very muscled and had his arms folded as some sign of strength. I ain't no master in martial arts or no boxing specialist, but if the shit hit the fan, I wasn't a gunslinger. First thing I'm gonna do is kick the biggest guy in the nuts right before I pull Stacy along to try to make a break for it. Ain't no way to beat four guys intent on causing some harm. So, the solution here was to kick it out, or talk it out.

What was strange to me was Stacy. She had her face turned away from the Chevy, and she was mumbling into her cell phone. I was hoping hers was not a 911 call, because, so far, these guys were harmless. So far.

"Hey, lil' momma. What's good?" asked the driver.

"Yo, that *is* her!" one of the guys with the weed pronounced. And now *he too* was making a cell-phone call, as if there might be some consequence here. *Fuckin' world according to cell phones.*

The driver seemed to take that as a cue, and he said,

"You know when they find out that's yo' ass, right?" I twisted my face, wondering what the hell he was talking about. By then I realized he wasn't talking to me.

Stacy, still half on and half off her phone call, swung her head around and the ghetto (all of it) poured out of her mouth like the dam had just broken.

"Nigga WHAT. **Fuck** you, **and** THEM!" My whole *body* froze as I watched Stacy transform before my very eyes. I had seen some parts of *this* personality in a couple of our arguments, but never this aggressive. She was loud enough to be heard by half the parking lot. And, given the circumstances, a few witnesses might be *just* what the doctor ordered. Hell, we were outnumbered and, the worst-case scenario, outgunned.

All the while, Stacy's head was wagging, her neck cranking, and her arms flailing.

"You need to get a *fuckin'* life, that's what you need to do. Come on, Danté." It was a direct order from Stacy, and the way she cursed at them, with the drawl in the words, seemed to make it that much more poisonous. Shit, she had *me* scared, and I'm the man loving this woman. Now she was pulling me away from these cats like this had come to an end. But it seemed that hers was a perfect response to their bullshit because they didn't push the issue. The car didn't block us again.

I couldn't help but think, *Damn, I love this woman!* But I didn't wanna speak too soon, because (as they say) *it ain't over till it's over.* After a tongue-lashing like that, there was no telling where this would lead or what in God's name brought all this to *my* face. It was when I looked back over my shoulder to see one of the weed smokers (the one on the cell phone, with the two-way hairstyle) make a gesture in our direction that I realized this might be just another page in a short story. I couldn't tell whether it was directed at me, at Stacy, or at both of us. Either way, I smelled trouble.

"Stacy? You looked like you were ready to go toe-to-toe with those guys."

"Well, wasn't it *you* tellin' me I shouldn't be afraid? *Ahem?* I sort of remember *somebody* sayin', 'You can't go through life being afraid. You do what you gotta do. For you, and for your children.'"

*Damn. This woman has total recall like a mafucka.*

"You don't let anything get by you, do you?" She wagged her head in that no-nonsense way. I went on to say, "I'm not suggesting that you be afraid, Stacy. What I *am* suggesting is that you avoid any *unnecessary* confrontations, especially when we're outnumbered two to one. I mean, *okay* if you *want* that, I guess I'll hafta fight and yell, and swing and dig somebody's eyes out until I'm lying in a hospital bed wishin' and prayin' and healin'. But I'd *rather not* if I *don't* have to." I knew better than to let her get a word in, otherwise she'd inevitably talk her way into an argument. She'd be angry at me, or else spiral into a mood swing, which often resulted when it was clear that I was right and she was wrong. Of course, the last plate on that menu was no sex, maybe for a week. Any way you sliced it, I could not win.

When we got back to Momma's house, I circled the Blazer to let Stacy out, and she no sooner took me into her embrace.

"I'm sorry to bring you so much trouble, Danté. It's just—"

I hugged her back, loving how she had just laid all her burdens on me at a moment's notice.

"What is it, Stacy?" I asked this and noticed a tear falling.

"One of them: the one with the patch eye."

"The crazy hair?"

She nodded against my chest. "That's him. That's who shot my ex. His name is Theo. But we was in the same school. I know his name is Theodore Jefferson Barnes."

Wagging my head, unable to make sense out of anything, I said, "You think you have a problem with him? You think he's comin' after you?"

Stacy was sobbing now. "It's just all twisted, Danté. How he gonna shoot my man and then the same girls he rollin' wit' gon' come at me 'n' claim I set 'em up." Stacy was a mess, mascara running from her eyes and weak at the knees as I held on.

There was no smooth way to do this, but I had to try to change the subject quickly. I had watched this woman digress and spiral in the past and I knew she *wanted* to experience this drama. I knew that she was *comfortable* revisiting these moments, these people, and the emotions that went with them. The trick was to pull her out of this quick so that she wouldn't fall so deep that I couldn't retrieve her. *Wow. What I go through to love a woman.*


"BABY, NOT that this has anything to do with what happened back there, but I was wondering if there's an agenda for the week. I mean, are we gonna relax? Are we gonna do some sightseeing? Maybe take the kids to the movies or an indoor amusement park or something?" I was *so* desperate trying to brush that whole bit from our minds; trying to get Stacy's mind on something else, using her children as the bait. Yes, it was desperate, but necessary.

Stacy seemed to be stuck. Her eyes cleared up, but she was clearly confused by the change in subject. There was concern in her eyes and then she cocked her head to the side some; *really* confused. I knew, though, that the mention of her children would throw her off. But not to the point that she'd do what she was doing now, staring at me like I was a bad habit.

A WHOLE week went by since the altercation (if I can call it that) near the parking lot of the Red Alert event at Flambeaux. During the week I got more familiar with Jason and Jackie. Jason was kicking my butt less and less with the Red Faction—but of course, all the butt whoopings he was dishing out added up—while little Jackie got comfortable holding my big finger with her miniature hand. Her hand was so soft, and her smile so cute, that I couldn't help wondering where their daddy was. Somebody, somewhere, was missing out on all this good love from the little people. *His* little people.

Besides the kids, Stacy and I did at least four to five different restaurants, we caught a couple of movies, and I got to do some real-estate research. Wow. Everywhere I looked they were building brand-new communities; brand-new spacious homes that could be purchased for cheap. Cheap meant two to three hundred thousand dollars. The buyer wouldn't have to put any money down if his or her credit score was in the 600 range. Not only that: the developers of these homes were (across the board) picking up the closing costs. That *really* made it easy and affordable for home buyers. And *cookie-cutter special or not*, a two-hundred-thousand-dollar home here in Atlanta, if repositioned most anywhere in New York, could be a nine-hundred-thousand-dollar home. Even a million-dollar home. Just the mere *idea* of the incredible difference in the value placed on a home was attractive. And the house wasn't built with materials that were cheaper or less expensive—that wasn't it. Even I knew the price of a two-by-four in New York and how the cost wasn't much different down in Atlanta. It was all about location, location, location. And the availability of land was minimal in Manhattan and its surrounding boroughs. So, naturally, real-estate sellers or owners in the suburbs try to squeeze every cent out of potential buyers just because of the proximity to New York City, where all the jobs seemed to be. Atlanta, on the other hand, was rich in jobs if you went *downtown*. There were also remote jobs at factories and corporations like Coca-Cola, Quaker Oats, CNN, and so many others that planted themselves along industrial parks and so forth; but even those are limited positions when you weigh them against the population in Atlanta and how it's grown by the millions over the past decades. So, needless to say, to get to and from any of these good jobs, you gotta have a car. And if you happen to live an hour out of the city, you just might run into traffic troubles and even relationship troubles, since a lot of your at-home time will be absorbed by I-85, or I-285 and its ridiculous rush-hour mess.

---

DESPITE THE challenges, ATL is still (in my view) a hot spot, and *the place to be*. And it's not just *anybody* who's finding their home here: it's celebrities, businessmen, and little people like *me*. *Black* people are calling Atlanta the *New Mecca* or the *Modern-day Harlem*. I wasn't so sure about that. With wolves, frogs, and snakes making their presence known in and out of the woods, maybe a better name for Atlanta might be the *Rural Harlem*. Still, I'd rather negotiate with wild animals than live bullets any day.

Another thing is, Atlanta residents aren't afraid to support and vote black mayors into office. And now that it's happened for more than a few terms, it's become normal to see a black mayor. Even a black *woman* as mayor. Try that in the Hamptons, or South Beach, Florida, or Palm Springs, California. In fact, Atlanta's airport is the biggest in the world, and is run mostly by black employees. One of the restaurants Stacy and I went to was at the airport, and the restaurant was operated by mostly blacks. After a while, as an outsider looking at all this for the first time, you'd think that white folks might feel a little displaced, or even irrelevant. But then that might just be good old-fashioned redemption? And I don't know about most others, but I *love* myself. And loving myself means loving other people who are a lot like me. *Self-affirmation* is what I've heard it called. And I suppose that's why so many people who like to cook buy cooking magazines or watch the cooking channels. I suppose that's why people who practice the same religion then eat together, socialize, and picnic with one another and support one another through cooperative economics. So, too, are the folks in Atlanta supporting one another, even if its black managers run white-owned franchises; it

still serves to put checks in folks' pockets and food on the
tables of many families. And socializing together and shar-
ing time and space together. Sure, you have your bad ap-
ples; but that's the case everywhere you go. I'm not saying
that I'm gonna all of a sudden up and move down here, especially considering the consistency and the roots my family has developed in New York. I just realize that *Atlanta
has it goin' on*. And even if I'm not living here, I would at
least like to consider scooping up one of these properties so
that I, too, can watch my money grow.


WEEK TWO, and I was doing more fixing than sightseeing
and vacationing. By that, I mean, Mrs. Singletary's home
had some issues I couldn't help working on. The banister
(leading from the first floor to the second) was loose. Part
two of the two-car garage door was stuck, and so for a while
there was only parking for one car. And whoever had their
car outside in the notorious Atlanta heat got their ass fried
the moment they got in the driver's seat. Mrs. Singletary
also had an ant problem, so I played exterminator, went
down to Home Depot, and out of my *own* pocket I purchased what was necessary to get rid of the insect issue.
And, that wouldn't be the end of it because the ants would
surface again in the future. You just had to maintain the
practice of taking care of shit, something I *knew* I wouldn't
be around to do. But all along I'm thinking it's a nice gesture to do this for them. After all, I do it for her sister up
north. And thinking about that got me laughing while I
was working, telling myself I could easily identify Mrs.
Singletary in the Bronx by calling her Singletary North,

and in Lawrenceville, the sister would be Singletary South. *Danté, the name butcher.* Meanwhile, besides exterminator and fix-it man, I also grabbed some paint and spackle from Home Depot and I filled in those nicks and scars that decorated the walls in most of the house. And to do things *really* right, I knew the interior walls had to be painted throughout; but to myself I'm saying, *I'm only fucking your daughter, we're not married yet. Shit, I'm still a free man!*

The laughter was keeping me sane because my ass was *not* supposed to be working. But then again, I felt right at home and relaxed doing just what I loved. So, call me crazy, but this is me.

While I'm doing some last-minute cleanup, the house is about to get noisy again. I was sure the honking horn outside was Stacy and the girls returning home. They'd been gone all day, like they were most weekdays, running the kids to and from day camp, dropping Mrs. Singletary off to work, and doing *I guess* whatever it is that girls do when they group together. I didn't mind. The spare time did me good; I got to correct some issues at the house, and (I hate to think this way, but) sometimes Stacy and I could use the distance. We were still working on having that entire month with absolutely no arguing. I figure, if we could get a month in, we could get six months in. If we could do it for six months, then we could manage a year. If we could practice being happy for a year, then it would surely be a joy to live together.

I had just been promising myself that I'd get some sleep—the opportunity to rest. But that's when I heard the honking. And honking was unusual in this quiet neighborhood so I stepped lively toward the front of the house to see what was up.

*I think I'm getting a migraine.* And it was just so sudden, the moment I set my eyes on the girls all hopping out of the new car in the driveway.

*No more,* I huffed.

# [ S E V E N ]

## S T A C Y

I COULD TELL Danté was in the shower because he always leaves his clothes lying around like a trail to a pot of gold. It was like he was leaving me clues to come and find him, and maybe jump in the shower with him. A part of me was hoping that Danté hadn't heard our noise and maybe copped an attitude to be softened by a cold shower. I thought this might be the case since I noticed the blinds moving inside the house. And if it was, then the bathroom was *right* where we needed to be for this argument about to go down. No way this man (good lover, or not) was gonna tell me how to spend my money. We were doing good, too—going strong for about a week and a half without argument. But I could feel the shit about to hit the fan.

"Baby, *I got a surprise*," I said as I entered the bathroom.

I could see parts of Danté through the shower door, and it made me remember how long it had been since we had a rendezvous in the shower. As happy as I was, I was ready to get it on right *now*.

"I'm sure you do. And you've had surprises for me just about every day this week, haven't you."

I wasn't about to answer that bullshit.

"Stacy, didn't we have this talk already about the spending? Didn't we talk about *not* spending if you couldn't repay? *Hey!* Where you goin'?" I saw Danté about to poke his head out from the shower as I made a break for the door.

I could hear him even in the hallway. "Come 'ere, Stacy. Why can't we talk like two grown-ass adults? I thought you were supposed to be so *h'wurd*."

*Man, I wanna kick his ass right now.*

# DANTÉ

I impressed myself at that moment, how I fed her the *h'wurd* instead of *hard*. It was part of the slang in the South, how words like *is* and *scared* and *cared* were pronounced (by many) as *ee'yah* and *sc'rred* and *c'rrred*. Of course, in New York, that kind of Ebonics is something of a novelty. But in the South, folks are real serious about their slang.

For a split second, Stacy stopped to say something before she left the bathroom, but then she slammed the door behind her. So, here we were again, in the land of digress. I already knew the routine: we wouldn't talk to each other, she'd bury herself into her kids or her nieces, and there wouldn't be a chance of getting any coochie. *That* shit, I was trying not to hear, since I had just finished a long day's work at *her momma's house*, of all places. So, to say the least, I was fed up. And really, all that talk from the good pastor about how to treat a woman and all my affirmations about the future sometimes don't hold up against a nigga with an attitude. Okay, so women get emotional: that's expected. *But when does the guy get to vent? How much of this shit do I need to hold in before I start yellin' and cursin', until I'm on the brink of self-destruction? When?*

I can't be the strong one all the time, can I? Holding my tongue and letting this woman (or *any* woman) just treat me like they damn well please. Sometimes *I'm* tired of the disrespect, as if what I say isn't important. Shit, I had just managed to hold my own after two family deaths in a row, *plus* I held the family business in check the whole time. So, again: *how much of this bullshit must I take?*

If I said it, I meant it: Stacy and I needed some separating at certain times, otherwise we'd be killing each other. So, without hesitation, I threw the few belongings I had into the backseat of the Blazer, and I sped off from the Singletary home. It broke my heart to leave Jason, Jackie, and the others without saying something, but this was about me. And if I didn't think of me, who else would?


THANK GOD for the GPS system I bought before leaving the Bronx. This little gadget, once plugged into the lighter, was the magic wand that got us all the way to Atlanta without a glitch. I didn't realize it, but thinking I can follow I-95 all the way down to I-85 was a damn trick! Sometimes you're driving on the road for a very long time without any indication that you're still on track. Then the blue, white, and red signs start changing to green, and then there are bypasses; it really gets confusing at times, especially if you haven't made this trip a whole lot. But we made it.

Nevertheless, the GPS didn't help much when we went out to look at a lot of the new real-estate developments because many of the streets were brand new, etched out of what once was wooded area and brush. Many of these new developments were so fresh that a tracking system couldn't pull up their street names; they hadn't been registered yet. So I always had to enter a nearby address that had been established for a while longer.

Nevertheless, since I was looking for a hotel (not a motel), it was easy to tap the hotel icon on the GPS and find myself a bed for the night (or two). I wasn't trying to go high, but the Best Western sounded like a good deal for under a hundred dollars per night. And when I punched in the nearest location, I was directed to downtown Atlanta, about a half hour south of Lawrenceville. Either way, I didn't mind. I had wanted to see the big city anyway.

BORED AND tired, I decided to take a moment to turn on my cell phone. I had purposely turned it off the minute we left the Bronx, trying to stay with the *vacation* plans. But since I had a bunch more spare time on my hands, I was curious to see who might've called. In the back of my mind I was hoping that Stacy might've left a message: *baby, I'm sorry. I love you. Please come back and make love to me.* But while that had happened at least three times in our brief history together, something told me that this time would be different. In the Bronx, it was just me, Stacy, and her aunt hovering over her, playing sergeant major. Therefore, there was little else for her to focus on except me, the business that I ran, and the social life we were trying to maintain. However, she was home now, with plenty of people to claim their love for her (especially with all that *shit* she'd bought for them). But, more important, she had those children to hug. And no matter how much of an *ass* she becomes, however spontaneously, those children deserve the best. They didn't do nothin' to receive *my* hate. And I don't even hate their mom; she just gets on my *last* nerve sometimes!

My first missed call was from an 800 number. Nothing familiar, so I wrote it off as a sales call. Sometimes these companies can become a nuisance, trying every desperate measure to get some money out of you. Another call was from Sprint, trying to get a survey done: *"This call won't cost you anything. We're just asking for a moment of your time to rate our performance on your last call."* That would be in response to the call I made to pay my bill up until September. But I was glad the voice mail caught the call, because I really don't have the time to respond to the nonsense; except for now, that is, with me sitting in a hotel room catching up on my voice mails.

I erased that one; then played the next message. "This is an important matter from Chase Bank. Please call us at 800-935-9935. Use reference number—"

My face tightened for a second, wondering what *that* call might've been about. Number one, I bank with Bank of America. Number two, I don't have any dealings with Chase, for loans, accounts, credit—nothing. So, I figured not to get stirred up. It was an electronic voice anyway, not that companies using such mechanisms weren't about their business, just that with real people you tend to feel more comfortable. *Press one, press five, please hold, arrrgh!*

*"Erased. Next message . . ."* This next call had come in a week earlier. There was nothing but some scrambling on the next recording, like someone was fiddling with the phone. I was about to delete it, but then someone said, *"Sounds like a voice mail, not a machine. We might just hafta go . . . him."* The voice had faded out for a half second, but I could swear the last words I heard were *go get him.* I figured it to be someone reaching the wrong number. But there was no way to tell since the call had come from an undisclosed phone number.

Next recorded message, the line went dead.

"What the fuck, is my voice mail Grand Central Station all of a sudden?"

Then there was this: *"Mr. Garrett? Hi, this is Marlene at Wells Realty. I thought I'd call you in person to find out about your August payment? We haven't received it and I wanted to give you this courtesy call 'cuz I know you're always on time. How's everything going? Well, this is still too early for any action. Please call me back. I'll leave this issue aside so Mr. Wells won't know a thing. Hope all is—"* Although there were other messages to check, I hung up the phone before Marlene's message ended. I immediately dialed Wells Realty. But then, as the phone kept ringing, I realized it was ten o'clock at night. *Shit. Hafta call her in the—*

I got to wondering why they hadn't received my payment, and my first notion was to call Bank of America. But they'd be closed, too. And there was no way I was going through all that automated mess—*press one, press two, press sixteen.*

So, I organized a few things in my room and went down

to the lobby, where I'd noticed a computer when I had registered at the front desk. Someone was using it currently, so I just waited my turn. I had noticed this over the years, how it was a hotel courtesy to have one or two computers handy for its guests. After a moment or so I noticed that the old lady who was using the computer was jerking her head from side to side. At first, I thought she was going through a seizure. But when I got a better look I realized she was playing a *video game*! And of all the games to play, Granny was fuckin' with Grand Theft Auto!

WAGGING MY head at the senselessness of it all, I found myself roaming out of the hotel for some air. Before you knew it, I was wandering up Peachtree Street, giving myself a personal tour of downtown Atlanta. I eventually ended up at the CNN Center trying to get a seat for some dinner at this somewhat elegant, somewhat relaxed spot called McCormick & Schmick's. The maître d' was very nice, even as she delivered me the bad news.

"We stopped serving at ten." But then this pretty woman went way out of her way. "Let me see if they're still serving down at Ruth's Chris." And although I was urging her not to bother, she insisted and proceeded to look up a number behind her cute little podium by the entrance. Then, in speedy fashion, she called the restaurant, confirmed that they were still serving, made the reservation for one, and got me a cab to take me *straight* there. I felt like I was an e-mail that had been shuffled, recategorized, and appropriately filed and flagged for priority purposes. It was efficient and convenient, but also a little uncomfortable to be treated so well by a perfect stranger all of a sudden becoming my personal assistant! Now, *that* was hospitality.

Within ten minutes I was welcomed into the posh Ruth's Chris. I couldn't imagine what a restaurant with two first names had to offer me. But once I was seated and served and fed, *wow*. I wanted to go back and thank that woman for going out of her way. It was that special touch that made my night, and made me forget everything else that was going on in my life. I just felt that escape and I ran with it. And the bottle of champagne I ordered didn't hurt my wanting to escape. After dinner, I waxed off one more glass of bubbly, enough to feel a nice buzz.

"Sir, can I call you a cab?"

"Nah, *I'm good*."

"Sir, I'm afraid I must insist," said the restaurant manager. "It's just policy."

"Alright. No sense in goin' against"—I put my fingers up to symbolize quotation marks before I said—"*policy*."

He said he didn't mind if I waited outside. But I could just about *feel* him looking through the window, keeping an eye on me.

The taxi pulled up as if he were a fare chaser waiting around the corner for the call.

I jumped in and waved at the manager of Ruth's Chris.

"Olympic Park," I told the driver.

"That's just three blocks up the way," said the driver.

"Okay?" I responded, but the taxi didn't move. "Listen, if it's money you're worried about, I got you."

"There's a flat rate for—"

"Dude, whatever it is, I said *I got you.*"

Finally the cab pulled away from the restaurant.

MINUTES LATER, I was strolling again, this time through Olympic Park, at the well-kept center of downtown Atlanta. Even so late at night, this felt real good. The weather allowed for a slight wind, and that made things that much more perfect, especially in the Atlanta heat. The sky was dark, with no warning signs of a thunderstorm, like the week before. I had so much room to breathe—I'm not talking about the whole *inhale-exhale* bit, but my *mind* got a chance to breathe. This was the first time in the months since my loss that I could step back and look at things differently. I wasn't in a rush to get to work in the morning. I wasn't pressured or anticipating or anxious or spent. I simply found myself suspended here in this beautiful place in the universe. The planet, the environment around me, and no other people existed here. *This* was peace. *This* was tranquility. And somehow, no matter how much I tried, I didn't think I'd ever get that with Stacy.

I DIDN'T realize it, but I had left my cell phone on. I had been heading back up Marietta toward Peachtree Street (just about my only measure of things in the downtown area) and now the damn thing was chirping in my pocket. But it wasn't my ringer, it was an indication that a text message was waiting.

Immediately, I could see who sent the text and I wondered if she'd had a change of heart. But even if she hadn't, there was no sense in *me* harboring any of *her* anger.

Stacy: So whats da plan *now*?

Me: Good evening to u too. Isn't it a beautiful night?

Stacy: Depends whos askin & whos bein asked.

Me: So then your purpose behind the text was what?

Stacy: The plan?

Me: The plan dear is to find me some fucking PEACE!

The phone started to ring. But instead of answering it, I got fed up and went from one extreme *right* into another. There was a bridge where I was walking, and in the distance was a large parking lot that was empty, otherwise used for the big arena in the area. And then I blacked out. Somehow, the phone I had in my hand was the only connection to Stacy and her drama, Stacy and her financial mismanagement; Stacy and her fuckin' *big mouth*! So, as if to get rid of anything and everything having to do with Stacy, I just followed my gut feeling and threw the cell phone so far into the distance that even if I tried I wouldn't find it. At the same time I let out this hoarse holler, and I didn't care who heard it. I just needed to release some of my pent-up rage to nobody and everybody all at once. And just to think, a few moments earlier I was at peace with the world.

NOT A block away from the Best Western, some thumping music eased up behind me, coming up the street, same direction as I was headed. It was so loud I couldn't help turning to look. I almost wanted to curse at how the music was ringing in my ears—in my *head*. But once I did, I quickly turned it back. *Oh shit*.

It was that same fire-engine-red Chevy that had crossed our path that Sunday night at the Red Alert function at Flambeaux in Stone Mountain. You couldn't miss this car with its sparkling rims, and especially the goons it was filled with.

All I had to hear was, *"Yo, wait! That's him! That's her man!"*

Then another dude said, *"Git 'im."*

Tipsy or not, I was no fool. And I definitely wasn't about to stand around to get a beat-down by some troublemakers in a town where I wasn't necessarily welcome; not by my looks, not by my New York accent, and definitely not in the tipsy condition I was in. Another thing—when Stacy and I talked ourselves out of harm's way last time, one of these dudes made a gesture as if he was aiming a gun at us. So, it was clear to me that they (1) had guns and were accustomed to using them, or (2) had access to guns, and were fakin' the funk. Whichever was true, I wasn't interested in findin' out, and I moved faster, trying my best to ignore but also stay away from the doom that lurked. I could see that the vehicle had slowed some and that two of them had hopped out. That was my chance to cut in front of the Chevy, and I crossed the street, climbed over the island dividing the two directions of traffic. Once I made my way to the other side of the street, the Chevy surged forward, its wheels burned rubber on the pavement, and within seconds I was surrounded. Two coming at me in the car and two on foot. One of those on foot was patch-eyed with half his head braided and the other half in a 'fro. I couldn't be mistaken: this was the same guy who had been in the car at Flambeaux. But I wasn't tripping about that; it was clear that this was that same crew. What I wasn't expecting was what happened next.

One of the government buildings that lines Marrieta Street was positioned directly in front of me. And right there on the sidewalk they had installed a series of four-foot-long, thick-as-hell cement pillars. But these were meant to be barricades, in the wake of all the terrorism in the country. They were meant to obstruct a vehicle that might be loaded with a bomb, so that it wouldn't reach the foundation of the building like what happened with the first bombing attempt on New York's World Trade Center. But I was certain that these barriers were not positioned to be an obstruction to a fast-forward pedestrian like me.

I wasn't paying attention to where I was going and my upper thigh slammed into one of these barriers. In fact, the impact of the obstacle was gut-wrenching, provoking a beastly grunt that pushed out of my mouth. Next thing I know, I found myself breathless and somehow thrown forward into a semiflip, face-first into one of the planters positioned at incremental spots between the pillars. All I could feel was this punishing pain in my abdomen. Plus, my body was suddenly stiff everywhere. But all of that was just the segue to what I'm told happened next. They say my head slammed into the sidewalk. And when I hear that, all I can imagine is the worst pain ever. But I can't say I even felt that pain; if I did, it was probably short and sweet. It was enough to leave a scar, I know that much. Other than that, I couldn't remember *jack*. And everything else, like Stacy, Lawrenceville, and the assholes who drove me to nearly kill myself, I could honestly say I couldn't remember.

# OPHELIA

Walking down the hospital corridor with that daggon IV stand made me feel worse than I already did. Add to that, the dizziness that first put me in the hospital was outdone by the pains in my stomach. I wondered what *that* was about, and could only hope it was just my body needing some real food. One of Momma's home-cooked meals would do it. And truth be told, sure couldn't wait to fall in Momma's lap; she'd know just what to do with me. She'd know how to get me better with one of her special remedies, and before you know it I'd be a little girl again. I hate to be actin' like a momma's girl but I guess I'm guilty, even at age forty-six.

"Mrs. King? Are you alright?"

"That's *Ms.* King. And I sure am alright. Can you do me a favor and contact my doctor to find out how I can get some real food in here?"

"Well, whaddaya like, Ms. King? I can sure help ya with that."

I could sense that this young woman had maybe heard this complaint before, since the food was just—well, I won't put the food down; I'll just say that it's nothing like Momma's. And ain't *no way* it compares to a Delta dish, honey.

I leaned in closer to the young lady, pulling my hospital gown together at the same time.

"Excuse me, what's your name, sweetie?"

"I'm JiJi," she replied proudly.

"Well, alright, JiJi. Um, I just hope by *real food* you're not talkin' about those Chick-fil-A and Blimpie shops downstairs."

"No, ma'am. Head nurse says we need to take *real* good care a you. She says you're one of 'Lanta's top attorneys. So your wish is my command, ma'am. Any particular dish you like?"

Beyond the flattery, I was thinking about my stomach and what it might be able to bear after all the hoopla with the ambulance ride, the tests in the emergency room, and whatnot.

"Anyway, I can get a mixed-greens salad?"

"Coming up, one mixed-greens salad fit for a king. Or, er, a *queen*?"

I chuckled at this young lady's tact before asking, "What's your name, sweetheart?"

"JiJi," she replied, as if she wasn't all-the-way sure.

"Well, JiJi, ain't you just the cutest thing. You have a real nice energy about you. And if you keep that up, I promise you will go far."

"Thank you, ma'am. I'll be right back with your food. Room 219, right?"

"Uhh, right," I assumed. And then I continued on my stroll down the corridor. I felt so sluggish, and really out of place in the hospital. Usually when I'm here, it's because I'm representing an accident victim or even a patient on their death bed. Never am I here as the daggon *patient*. Made me ill just thinking about it. And I know this could've been avoided if I'd just taken better care of myself. But the workload was heavy, and I knew I was slippin'; quick meals, skippin' my workouts, and lack of sleep will do it every time. And this case I'm workin' for the past two months has been taxin' my butt real *good*. Add to that all the meetings, the phone calls, the trips in and out of town, there's a lot of driving, and somewhere in the mix I get to spend some quality time with my boyfriend, the new love of my life. To say the very least, I got a full plate. Plus, my brain and my cell phone both work overtime. Thank God they both operate on their own and need very little maintenance; otherwise I'd be SOL. Really. I can't operate without my brain. But I *definitely* can't operate without my cell phone.

"What's his deal?" I asked a nurse who stood near the doorway of the room immediately next to mine. I was being nosy, like I used to do when I did my share of ambulance chasin'. Finding out about a patient was as easy as conversation and relationships with the nurses and doctors. Before long, it was as if I myself was a hospital staff member, knowing all that I know. Except, I hadn't been in a hospital for this many hours in quite a long time. And maybe my conversation with the nurse was my wanting to know if I still had what it took.

"Oh. You caught me. He's such a work of art, Mrs. King."

"That's Ms. King, Sandra."

"Oh. Right. Okay. Well, I just *love* me some perfection, Ms. King." Sandra uttered an appreciative exhale and sighed. She was the student nurse I'd been in a conversation with earlier, when I arrived at Atlanta Medical Center. We hit it off real good, talking about how much Atlanta had changed, what life might be like with a black president, and (of course) men versus boys—my favorite conversation to have with college students.

I pushed up a doubtful sound from my belly and reached my head in to take a look at the new exhibit. Then I said,

"Perfection, huh? Wow, you young ladies see everything so *differently*. So footloose and fancy-free. Not a problem in the world. All men are Adonis, huh? Ahhhhh, to be young again," I said as I got a last peek.

Sandra giggled. "You're kidding, right? I—I really hope you're kidding, Ms. King. You are *gorgeous*! I'd give my right arm for your beauty and wisdom."

"Thanks, Sandra. Wish I could cash that compliment in for a favorable court judgment."

"Huh?"

I wagged my head, not intending to get this young woman caught up in my complex court case.

"So, what's his diagnosis?"

"He's in a coma, Ms. King. Had some type of accident in the street and he's been lights-out ever since."

My concern grew as I took a more important gaze.

"Wow. How long?"

"Well, I think he's goin' on ten weeks now."

"Oh, my."

Sandra was wagging her head. "I know. And not a lick of family has come to check on him."

"Really? Who's carrying the bill for his care?"

"Uhh, I don't know, really. I don't really get those details, Ms. King. I'm just a lowly nurse's aide. A lot to learn, but in the meantime just doin' God's will."

My eyes peered into Sandra's. So proud of our young people when they were doin' the right thing.

"What's his name?"

"Aw." Her expression soured, and then the head wagging again. "That's another thing. Had no ID on him. His chart is marked as John Doe."

The compassion immediately kicked in. And even though I was weak and my tummy ached, I wasn't as dizzy as I was earlier; and I was definitely competent enough to see a problem here. In fact, this little puzzle, if anything, gave me *more* energy. I guess it's the practice I'm accustomed to, always coming to the rescue in one way or another.

"You mind?"

Sandra ushered me farther into the patient's room and closed the door behind us before handing me the patient's clipboard.

"You know they'd have my *behind* for doin' this."

"The hospital administrator is a family friend. Don't worry your little head; I gotcha," I said with the most significance I could muster under the circumstances. Sandra helped me with my IV stand and we approached the bedside of John Doe. It didn't take long for me to recognize how right she was. He *was* gorgeous. Perfection. Why all men couldn't—

I felt myself digressing as I held my tongue and looked over the charts. I have seen more than enough of these charts in the ten years I'd been studying and practicing law, first as a paralegal for the billionaire attorney BJ Worth, and then in my own firm, where medical-malpractice and personal-injury cases were my specialty.

"Ten weeks, huh?"

"I believe so," Sandra replied.

Now I was waggin' my head, then looking at this young man clinging to life. He was still filled with a spirit and an energy, but somehow unable to move or to open his eyes. It was tragic to see this and to know that there was the possibility that he might not return to normal. Comas were like that: a crossroads of a sort that didn't guarantee you 100 percent normalcy. For a moment I froze in the reality before me, but to be honest, no sooner did I shake it off. It was easy for me to recall so many others who I'd seen in this very same condition; maybe not in a coma, but certainly bedridden. And, although it's not a pretty sight and that I'm compassionate about it all, I couldn't help that it all kind of plays in my head as one big blur of images and names and circumstances. To say I'm jaded is an understatement. I've just seen *so much* during my career as a lawyer. They call this "the practice," but it's not just because we go through so much to learn and to obtain and then to *maintain* what we've learned; it's also the sum total of all our experience that comes along with the territory. The activities and people and challenges *outside* the courtroom and the office tend to take a toll on us as well. I could be standing in a hospital room over a cop clinging to a life-support system on one day, and the next I could be in a local jail across a table from a client who couldn't care less about his future, and *way* less about mine. I'm in court one day, negotiating with a nerd of a district attorney, and the next I'm with a forensic specialist learning about the unique qualities of different-caliber bullets. It all comes with the territory, keeps life unpredictable, and really amounts to a wealth of connectivity from every which way. And sure there's opportunity and resources and immeasurable amounts of money to be earned, but sometimes I just need to put the brakes on. My paralegal, Angela, is just one of those protective shields, taking a lot of my calls and weeding out a lot of the nonsense that can interrupt my flow. If it's not Angela to provide that insulation, it's me just leaving my phone alone for a while to go and work out in the gym, or to relax in my private Jacuzzi. Fortunately, everything (my office, the gym, the Jacuzzi, and my beauty salon) is all under one roof. And then the *absolute* rule for me is to shut my phone off at ten o'clock every night. So, thank God I get *some* relaxation. But, otherwise, this profession is a *grind*. It's got its pros and cons just like every other business. The thing is, the workload gets so heavy that I sometimes need to pull back, but the moment I wanna take a vacation there's always another priority in store. Always another client in need.

I can't lie. I tend to bring much of the weight on myself because I have such a kind heart (my mom's side of me) and a I'm no-nonsense (my dad's side of me). So, if I see a person in trouble, my heart reaches out sort of unconditionally—the kindness in me. And yet, I'm diligent in troubleshooting to the heart of the issue. So, in the case of John Doe, he clearly needed an advocate to find out more about his family and other vital statistics. Chances are he might've been robbed or left his wallet at home. But ten weeks of coma is *crazy*. It wasn't a crime but a miscommunication that needed to be addressed at once. And, most likely, police officers have shoved this man's case to the side. Not good.

"Has anyone at all come to see him?"

Sandra shrugged and her eyes turned weird all at once.

"The police, every now and then. But that's all I seen."

*Of course*, I told myself. And with that, I headed back to my room, the IV rack rolling alongside me as though it were my mascot. And although my body needed some healing, some therapy, and some rest and relaxation, my mind was already in overdrive.

## [ EIGHT ]

IT HAS BEEN a blessed life for me, I have to say, when I look at where I came from, and where it's landed me today. Along with the enormous income I pull down from securing contracts for entertainers, churches, and corporations, I currently have partnerships in a few Atlanta nightclubs, a nice chunk of stock in Comcast cable, and two commercial properties in downtown Atlanta. I now live in a twenty-two-room mansion on two acres in Cascade. I keep just two vehicles, and a motorcycle that I sometimes feel adventurous enough to drive. And I can even claim all that through my hard work ethic. It wasn't given to me by my parents and I didn't inherit from a rich uncle. Well, *correction*: I had to repossess the motorcycle from a client who was lunching on his bill. But *everything* else, I assure you, was earned fair and square.

The thing is, I tend to feel like an angel a lot of times, protected and blessed by the Most High. I've never had any major tragedies in my life, I've never been to the bottom of the well in terms of my finances or my living arrangements,

and only up until recently could I say the same for my
health. It's all been pretty much peaches and cream the
whole way. I won't say there weren't challenges, 'cause that
would be a lie. Yes, the breakup with my husband was horrible. He was my first boyfriend, my first true love. And the
loss took a toll on me mentally. I was in the most unlikely
situation, trapped by single parenthood. Something I *never,
ever* expected for myself. Here I was, playing the good girl
all through my teenage years, never steppin' out on my
man; and never did I consider any alternatives. I was that
*ride-or-die* chick that you always hear about in the hip-hop
community. Then, from left field, here came Darius, home
after what was supposed to be a long day at work; I'll never
forget the words:

"*Baby. I don't know how to tell you this, but I'm leaving
you.*"

The words threw me into a spell, and they echoed in my
head for so many months thereafter. I thought about us as
teenagers and how I had to sneak in and out of our back
door just to see Darius, back when my dad would threaten:
*I'll shoot him dead if I catch him in my house!* I thought about
school and being a cheerleader, and Darius running all over
the football field like some superjock, maybe trying to win
my approval. But he didn't need to go that far; I was sold
from the day he enrolled in our school. He was such a
champion in my eyes with his tall, athletic build and his
GQ facial features. He was the type of hunk who a girl just
wanted to *touch*, much less have as a first love. He was the
type of guy who you wanted everyone to know was yours,
especially all the jealous girls in my classes who just couldn't

keep up with me in grades. In the end, he was the type of guy you wanted to bring home to Momma, and eventually marry. And when I did just that, I can honestly say my dream came true. A fairy-tale life that was handed to me at age nineteen was the life I lived up until I was thirty. For eleven years.

Meanwhile, my daughter, Dancer, was, I guess, the greatest benefit from my relationship with Darius. That girl is my pride and joy; the spitting image of me. And no matter what I had to do to grow her into a strong, responsible woman, I was gonna do it. I intended to see that Dancer had the absolute best of everything. The best schools. The best clothes. The best childhood. And maybe it was a blessing that Darius and I went our separate ways, because I probably wouldn't have ventured into law if I was left to live as his kept housewife. I wouldn't have earned the Teflon-tough way of life I have, or the aggressive, no-nonsense attitude I bring to the courtroom. In fact, I wouldn't be involved in law *at all*.

Being a lawyer was a mere childhood dream. I would watch those cop and law TV shows, and I would imagine myself in those roles. I could always figure out who did what, and way before the truth was revealed. I did the same when I watched game shows, wishing they would *dare* call me one day to be a contestant. But I never took my dream any further. It was always my agenda to take care of Dancer, and my man. So, when the *my man* part of my life took a detour, I basically had to get over it. When I did, it was still early enough that I could attend college, study what I had to, and step up to the courthouse stairs. Ophelia King is *here*!

And not to brag or anything, but if nothing else, the timing was just right. There is the old law, there are the *new* laws, and then there's *Ophelia's Law*! And really that's nothing more than all the old-school stuff combined with the advent of technology. I just happen to be planted in law at the right time, right in the middle of that curve. I'm no stranger to e-mails and the Internet. I'm no stranger to law books and the ritual of reading. I was studying law at an age that was just right, if you asked me. I was also in school with those who were much younger than I. They were either fresh out of college or grad school, while I was more experienced in the ways of *life*. And now it was time to bring that to the world of law.

To quote one of my professors: *"The legal world needs Ophelia King."*

And so it was.

FROM MY point of view, the law is no different than reading *and* comprehending an entire shelf of encyclopedias. There's an enormous job of studying it all, and it's tough to recall. And I guess that's what makes lawyering such a prestigious trade, since not everyone can master it. What makes for that *specialty* that a lawyer embraces as their own is nothing more than (as with the encyclopedias) the *particular* area or subject matter or topic that he or she chooses to focus on. Constitutional law. Criminal law. Real-estate law. Tax law. Family law. Property law. Corporate law. Entertainment law. Federal. State. Municipal. Ordinances. There's *so much*. And, even if you do know *all* of that?

None of it would prepare you in the courtroom. In that arena, you nearly have to be a boxer, a scuba diver, and a football player. The thing is, by the time I learned how impossible the legal "ride" would be, I was already in too deep. I think if I'd known how difficult it would be to grasp, I might've gone a different route in life. But there was this article I read in *Upscale Magazine* about the legal giant named Johnny Cochran. Everyone knew who Johnny Cochran was. And who could miss his aggressive approaches in the OJ trial? Who could miss his many appearances on CNN and when he had his own show on Court TV, going head-to-head with that right-winger Nancy Grace? So, inspired by Johnny's godlike presence in national and international media, I stayed on my grind. It didn't matter *how* much work I had to do, or *what* I needed to study. *I was game!* And since I now had no partner in life, the *law* became my new first love and my life.

I had to learn that what they teach us in law school is more theory, and not necessarily the focus on any *one* type of law. More so, I learned how to *find* my way to answers that are favorable to my position and my case. And because the law is ever changing, I also had to determine and challenge situations based on new laws, decisions, and revelations in the Supreme Court. Such decisions must be accounted for. Certain appeals that are relevant must be researched. *Research* is really what law is; intelligent, surgical research that will bring hard conclusions to be affirmed in the courtroom, by a judge and/or jury of our peers. Add to all my studies that I was older and wiser than most anyone else in the class, remember I had also been an athlete, bouncing and flipping around as a cheerleader. Taking my turn at basketball and soccer and track. If a boy could do it, *Ophelia* could do it! So, I had that very same state of mind, that very same skill set as a resource in law. From being awarded medals and trophies in our debate teams to being voted valedictorian of my class, I was living my dream, all the way up to working at and then running Atlanta's biggest law firm.

# STACY

I was so fuckin' mad that Danté up and left me like he did. And his reasons were weak, just like his faith in me. One day I'm gonna find me a nigga who will ride with me, no matter what. And all of that stuff about how I spend money was not for him to say. I mean, he ain't the boss of me. I make my own rules, live by my own set of standards. And if he don't wanna be part of my equation, then to hell with him.

But I really do miss me some Danté dick. Plus, his tongue was a dream come true. I sometimes wish that, as women, we could cut the fat and have the dick without the big-mouth men that come along with it. Maybe some kinda switch can be invented?

"Stacy, what happened to that man of yours? He did a damn good job around this house. We need more men like him in the world. Hope you don't mess *that* good thing up."

Oooh, I could *kill* my mother for sayin' shit like that! As if I mess it up with *every* man. As if it was my fault for the last—*oooh, I could just KILL HER!*

And if it wasn't my no-good mother, it was my kid.

"Mommy, what happened to Danté?" My baby was asking me this question continuously for the weeks since Danté disappeared. I almost wanted to slap the shit out of him at one point. But something told me not to turn my aggression on my kids. It was *Danté* who I had the beef with. I really loved that man. I can't believe he'd break my heart like this. And, now that I think about it, I need to *tax* his ass for leavin' me *and* for stealin' my heart. There's no question who would have the last laugh when I'm through.

# DANTÉ

She was coming at me with some kind of weapon in her hand. I pretended not to notice, but just the same took a deep, relaxed breath. When she reached five feet and closing in, I could see from the corner of my eye that it was a knife she had snug in her palm. I turned casually, as though I might be easy prey, as if to accept a friendly greeting. But the truth is, I was waiting for her to swing her weapon. Little did *she* know, in my left hand was my *own* weapon, a short, heavy crowbar with a pointed edge. The crowbar was out of sight. And had more life (and history) than this woman was ready for. The first thing to come to mind was Dad's words: *never hit a woman*. But, so help me, *Dad*, this *particular* woman was about to catch it, *big time*. Although my weapon was bigger and more threatening than hers, I had an even *bigger* weapon, and that was the element of surprise.

Her distance from me was now three feet. *Strike.*

I wasn't about to wait another millisecond. If I did, there might not be a second chance. *Better to be judged by twelve than carried by six*, Grandpa use to say. I wonder if Grandpa and Dad agreed, and if this applied to women as well. No time to consider those options, I immediately pivoted, with my crowbar level with her face; in particular, I was trying to put an eye out. But I merely connected with her temple. Except, I didn't stop there. As she cried out and stumbled backward, and as the knife skittered across the concrete, her threat to me dropped to less than zero. I swung again, this time aiming for the knee. A louder scream, and now she folded to the floor. I would've gone for the knee first if she hadn't posed such a threat with the knife. But that didn't matter now because things were working in my favor. It was time to put my foot on her neck (so to speak) and finish this tramp. The thing is, I could finish her now and never have to worry about her again, or I could leave it at that, hoping the injuries would teach her a lesson to never fuck with me again.

Next thing I know, I'm kneeling at an altar, hands folded, eyes closed:

> *"Our Father, Who art in Heaven,*
> *Hallowed be Thy Name"*

The woman's face (the one who I'm defending myself against) is not recognizable to me; it's not as if I *know* her, and I can't see why she'd come after me or why she'd want to hurt me, but I have to say she's cute, with nice tits. And as usual, whenever I'm attempting to recall the possibilities, just when a clouded memory is starting to focus, an idea of

where I *might* know this woman from, the splitting headaches start again. I'm wincing and squeezing my fists tighter
than ever. I want to punch a wall, but I'm instead burying
my face in a pillow. I want to yell but the yell is trapped
deep down inside my belly. When I finally let it go, I realize
I'm in confined quarters. Soon, I'm looking at all this as an
outsider. There's a cargo van that says MISTER FIX-IT. As if I
have Superman's X-ray vision, I can see through the now-
transparent exterior of the van, where there's a man trapped
inside. He's banging on the walls—walls with posters and
pictures of that same psycho woman in the attack. The
man is rocking the van and trying to escape like some caged
animal. Upon closer look, the man in that van is no stranger.
That man is me.

These dreams have been consuming me for some time
now. Or for at least as long as I can recall, which is about
three weeks—I think. I'm told I was in an eleven-week
coma and that I barely made it out alive. But I honestly
don't remember any of that. All I know is these headaches
that come every so often, and these nightmares that haunt
me with some crazy woman always hunting me. And they're
driving me mad. On the other hand, my whole body's numb.
I'm feeling so stiff and my knees are killing me when I get
up to go to the bathroom.

*The bathroom.* That's another thing. I don't know where
the hell I am. They tell me this is Fulton County in Georgia. They tell me *Ophelia this, Ophelia that,* and I'm being
cared for by Ophelia. Something about her being in the
hospital at the same time I was. She supposedly was being
treated for some dizzy spells and was on the same emergency wing as me.

*Emergency? How'd I end up there?*

One thing led to another, and I guess she was my savior of some kind because they needed someone to step in and take responsibility because I *couldn't?* I still don't understand it all, but Lord knows I want to because this is all so strange, and I feel so out of place. I'm suddenly in another world, around people I don't know. But then, what about *my* family? I mean, this is all great to know these folks are out for my best interests, looking after me, and nursing me back to health. But I needed to call my dad. No doubt he'll be needing me for somebody's malfunctioning plumbing or an AC issue. And another thing: Grandpa can't do everything himself. I know he *acts* like he can, but Dad and I know better. We gotta look out for him because he sometimes takes on more than he can handle. He did it last spring, trying to carry some Sheetrock up three flights. The next day we found out he had back pains, and he was out of work for the rest of the week. But regardless of Dad needing me, and Grandpa pretending he doesn't, I miss both those dudes. *If I could just find their numbers.*

"You okay?"

My eyes were closed and I was rubbing my head when Toni peeked in. Toni is Ophelia's niece, directed by her auntie to look after me. She's probably twenty or twenty-one and (she says) tends to many of her auntie's personal tasks, including the cleaners, shopping, bills, and whatnot. Somehow, even though Toni has the position of handling the menial deeds of her aunt Ophelia, I get the strange feeling that she's too saditty to get her hands dirty. Maybe that's just my sixth sense at work. So, I find myself saying,

*I'm okay*, even if I'm not and I need something. It's just that I'm big on getting things done myself; not a welfare case. Now, on this occasion, it was probably obvious that I was lying. Toni probably heard me yelling on account of my latest nightmare, and now she still had her head reaching in the door of the guest room.

My response started as a stutter. "J-juss-just—" I could barely get a word out as Toni looked at me with that flat expression—the one that says, *I know you're lying, but I'll play along with you.* My head jerked a couple of times, and that probably spooked her. I was sitting up in the bed now, trying to make sense of this. That's when I blurted, "Is there any way I can make a phone call?"

"Uhh, *sure?*" She responded to me as if that option had always been there and I just hadn't taken advantage of it. "Phone's in the kitchen," Toni said. "Need me to get it for you?" True enough, the room I was in didn't have a phone, not even a dresser.

I wagged my head and tried to stand up to go get it myself.

*The knees. Ouch.*

It wasn't until I limped through the mansion's hallways, down the winding steps to the main level, and into the kitchen that I realized I had no numbers to call. I didn't have a wallet, a phone book, or even a cell phone where numbers were stored. And now that I was in the kitchen, smelling some freshly made pecan pie, the refrigerator was calling me like a long-lost friend. I got sidetracked altogether. Some coffee, some pecan pie, and some CNN helped to ease the pain in my knees; or maybe it was my sitting on the plush couch and just taking the weight off that did the trick. Either way, my attention was diverted to the current events around the world. So much was going on and so suddenly, like it was all hitting me at once. I hadn't seen a TV in what felt like years. And now that I had, it felt as though I'd been away, like on a spaceship, and a world of activities had come and gone before I returned to earth. I was surprised that Ms. Saditty had valid opinions and could hold a lengthy conversation about politics. I figured her age group was strictly music and movies and that's all. But she was on point, I must say.

We watched the news and talked for a time. It was the first time we spoke at length since she had explained the process of my recovery and how her aunt had virtually rescued me from oblivion. She explained how Ophelia was connected to the moon here in Atlanta and that she knew just about everybody and could get just about anything done with one phone call. She explained about the financial responsibilities left at the hospital and how her aunt *knew people* and was able to orchestrate things with the hospital administrators so that the various financial obligations were attended to, or at least put on hold for later. "This way the doctors and nurses could get you back to normal," Toni had explained a week or so earlier. And as I got to know her better, weighing in with my pros-and-cons judgments, the *bleep-bleep* sounded, signaling every level of the mansion that someone was entering the home. Moments later, all cheery and bubbly, the lady of the house walked in. This would be the first time we met face-to-face; the first time I could thank the woman who had cared for me when the hospital administrators had no next of kin to contact relating to me and my circumstances, my diagnosis, or my progress.

"So, I guess I'm forever in debt to you, Ms. *Ophelia King*." My announcement was animated, but my comments were a sincere and heartfelt introduction. And they were greeted with a smile that was enormous, even in its modesty. But, more than her smile, her eyes glistened so brilliantly, luring me into her warm hug.

"How ya doin'?" she asked in that rich, spirited southern drawl of hers. Her eyes danced in their sockets and sucked me in like an impressionable child.

"Not too bad, thanks to *you*, Ms. King. Except for my knees, that is. But I'm starting to get around a little. I would've thanked you sooner, but you've been in and out of town, I hear."

"Yes, I practice in Florida as well as Georgia. I'm working this case out there and it's really taxing me. Glad to see you're up and around. Oh, and you can call me Ophelia. You gonna be okay?" Ophelia caught me wincing and expressed a momma's concern.

I shook my head, knowing that her words were easier said than done; and again I backed off the complaining as an indication that this was nothing and that I could handle it.

Ophelia said, "Okay," in a *suit-yourself* sort of way. Then she asked, "Would you care to come down into my office?"

I half shrugged and half agreed, and we headed downstairs to the lower level of the home. I moved a lot slower than Ophelia, and for the first time that I could remember I felt inferior and handicapped. *Damn, my knees were hurting.*

When I finally reached the bottom floor, I was introduced to Ophelia's paralegal, Angela. Her first appraisal of me, I must admit, was offensive. I felt like a piece of real estate that she was appraising with her puny, speculative eyes. But I easily overlooked it, not judging the woman either way. After all, she was the paralegal for *the* Ophelia King.

The office was a combination family room, kitchenette, and reception area. And, following Ophelia back to her office, I was introduced to Ophelia's cousin Ray Ray.

"He's not as important as my Toni, but he—*well*, I s'pose he's existing for a reason, right, Ray Ray?"

"Yup. Just a fly on your wall, cousin."

The two relatives were crackin' me up, Ophelia with her sarcasm and Ray Ray playing her yes man.

I was shown the gym, Jacuzzi, and sauna, and even a beauty salon that was positioned next to her office. The office we stepped into had its own smoked-glass doors, and was prestigious like any attorney's office I'd seen on prime-time TV.

"Have a seat," she said with a jubilant energy.

I absorbed great pain in doing as suggested, but the expensive leather chair soothed my senses. "So how was your much-deserved vacation?"

"Oh, *great*. Now if I could just be on vacation *all the time*, life would be *perfect*. I'm so glad we're finally able to have this talk."

"Me, too, Ms.—er, *Ophelia*. I have to say I'm humbled and really grateful for your hospitality."

"I appreciate that, my friend, but this is really strange to sit with a man who doesn't know his name. Do you have *any recall* at *all*?"

I responded with silence, knowing that this was indeed embarrassing.

"My niece mentioned something about your dad? Your grandfather? Were you able to contact them? Do you have a name, at least? I can have a private investigator look into this. I have a couple on my payroll."

"My dad's name is Preston. And his father, the same."

"Okay! *See?* That's a start. And where are you from? What city? 'Cuz I *know* you don't come from these parts."

I squeezed my hand over my face as if this would help rub out the blank I was drawing.

"I only know repairs, Ms. Ophelia."

"Just Ophelia is fine. *Repairs?*"

"Yes. My dad and my grandpa and I run a business and we fix apartments. Plumbing. Electrical. We fix washers and dryers. 'You name it, we fix it. Mister Fix-It.'"

"Okaaaay. So, is that your motto? Is there a business name?"

"Not sure, ma'am. That's just the first thing that comes to mind when I think of my dad. *You name it, we fix it. Mister Fix-It.*"

"And Preston is your dad. You're sure about that?"

"As far as I know."

"Well, if your dad and your granddad are named Preston,

then I'm left to guess at the possibility that *your* name
might be Preston, too. *Ya think?*" Ophelia's smile was in-
fectious, and although I was drawing a blank, again, she
made me want to *agree* with her, no matter *what* she suggested. Grass is always red, isn't it, Preston? *Absolutely,
ma'am.*

After freezing up for a time, she said, "Well, I'm gonna
do some research and see what I can find out for you. In the
meantime, my home is your home. Don't you worry about
*anything.* I have a full gym, Jacuzzi, and sauna. My pool outside. *Whatever.* My house is up for sale and there may be a
broker or two coming through now and again, but otherwise, make yourself at home. I don't know what you know
about me, *Preston*, but I've been truly blessed with good
fortune. I have a growing successful law practice, I have
quite a track record in the courtrooms of Georgia, and I
have a number of investments that I can retire on. But, as
I've learned, *to whom much is given, much is required.* I believe that I was brought into your life, and that you were
brought into mine for a reason. And that brings me to another issue: do you remember *at all* what happened to you
and what landed you in the hospital? You had a pretty bad
head injury, and then there's—"

"What, Ms. Ophelia? What's *wrong* with me? Something I need to know?"

"The doctors say you have partial amnesia. There was
some kind of disruption on your blood-brain barrier caused
by the head trauma and subsequent coma. I don't know *all*
the particulars, but I do know that you're an accident victim of *some* kind. And that's what *I* do. I protect accident
victims, I try medical malpractice suits, and I've seen people

like you recover from neurological symptoms such as these sometimes within a few days. Only, your case is something special, Preston. You were in an eleven-week coma that you are lucky to return from, so say the doctors. And you seem to have all of your faculties except for—"

"Except for my *brain*?"

"Well, your memory. But I've met plenty of people who've been there, and I want to see you back to good health. And if there's someone to sue over this, then I'm gonna get you *that* money, too. Preston, I've worked with some of the biggest attorneys in Georgia, so *trust me*. If there's something amiss, I'm gonna find it."

I nodded.

"Toni tells me you're getting frequent headaches, and I checked with the doctors. *Here*."

She handed me a bottle of tablets. Thank God I could still read. Motrin. And the capsules were two hundred milligrams. "I'm told you should take two if the pain starts again. And if it gets really bad, take three, but *not* on an empty stomach."

I was willing to go along with whatever she wanted, as long as I could get rid of these headaches. But I couldn't help noticing how absolutely beautiful and together this woman was. She had to be at least ten years older than I was; if not, then I was not only absentminded but a numbskull. Ophelia was an achiever; that *was* clear. She was much further advanced in her life than I could *ever* claim to be. Especially now. And, to say the least, I was in total awe.

"Mom? I heard your voice." I heard the younger female voice before I got a look at the face. And then I eventually *did* see the person behind the voice. *Whoa.* It immediately hit me that this was a younger version of Ophelia. The facial features. The body. The energy.

All that seemed to double up on me once these two hugged.

"How was your trip back, Ma?"

"Good, baby. Did you meet our guest? Preston, this is my daughter, Dancer. And Dance—I call her *Dance*—just *happens* to be one of Atlanta's *hottest* female singers!" Ophelia's face lit up when she announced this. I could see the pride in her expression. I could also see the humble demeanor of Dancer. Wow, what a name.

Dancer seemed to have a lot to talk about with her mom, including some type of recording collaboration with a local rap artist, and some other business about being a featured act at Atlanta's Bronner Bros. Hair Show. I excused myself and began to back out of the office, but Ophelia help up her hand. *Wait.*

*Don't hafta tell me twice.*

"Dancer, why don't you show Preston the studio I built for you."

And so it was. Just a little farther down the hallway was a combination studio and living quarters that Dancer seemed to fit comfortably in. It felt as though the two women had shown this jewel to many a visitor. I hardly blinked before Dancer flipped a few switches and lit up the sound board, computer screens, the sound booth, and seconds later music began to play.

Ophelia immediately rocked her head to the tempo of the music. It was clear to see that she couldn't have heard this less than a thousand times. I didn't see STAGE MOM on Ophelia's forehead. But PROUD MOM was definitely broadcast from there.

"Nice," I said. And I wanted to hear more.

# [ N I N E ]

## O P H E L I A

TAKING CHARGE OF situations like these comes natural to me. I do it for so many others when they're caught out there on the short end of the stick, whether they're in accidents, disputes, or any of life's *other* challenges. I take care of the young and old, rich or poor. And they pay me handsomely. So, I'm thinking, *I'm blessed, so why don't I give back, help this guy, and ask for nothing in return? How could it hurt? He's harmless. He's injured. And he's clearly lost his way home. And besides, he's been very helpful around the house since his legs healed up and during his recuperation. And besides that, Dancer seems to like him. And if Dancer likes him, I guess I like him.*

I got Bo Humphrey on the case; he's my lead private investigator. I've sent him out to search and score for me on divorce cases, insurance claims, and especially when there's someone vital to a case who I can't find—he's the best at that. So, naturally I called him about Preston and gave him the limited information that I had regarding his dad, his business, and that he somehow migrated from up north. When he returned, Bo had come up with *zero*, and that was unlike him. I wondered if he wasn't losing his touch, or if something else was off track.

"There's fourteen hundred businesses with 'Mister Fix-It' in their name," Bo told me. "And that doesn't count all the books, videos on YouTube, and other associated Web presences that use the *Mister Fix-It* phrase. So, before I put my assistant on an all-day, all-night, year-long campaign to find what *might* be a lead, I have a suggestion."

"Shoot."

"Percival Culberson owes a favor for getting him out of that tax mess last year."

"Okay?"

"And he just got promoted."

"Really? At WAGA?"

"That's right. He's now the executive producer for the six-o'clock news."

"Hmmm. Now *that* is an interesting piece of news," I said to Bo. But in the back of my mind, I could already feel the gears in motion. I could already see the thing I imagined becoming reality.

Ray Ray, the cousin who grew up like a brother to me, also doubles as my driver—that is, when he can keep his driver's license straight. He's the last of the ghetto issues in my household; still with some of the baby-momma drama, the in-again, out-again jail record, and a few weed charges here and there. It's a burden sometimes to have to come in and clean up after Ray Ray all the time, but then I recall the good old days and all the fun times we had as children. I remember him being at so many family functions, triumphs, and ceremonies, and it sort of erases any of his current miseries; that is, whatever miseries he happens to be going through at the time.

To visit the news-anchor-turned-producer, I asked Ray Ray to play driver so that I'd be able to catch up on the motion I needed to submit at my next court appearance. We eventually found ourselves out in the parking lot, where I knew I'd catch him heading through the employee entrance at Atlanta's WAGA-TV. To be honest, I thought things might've changed in the months since we'd seen each other last; but my office was already in the area, and a busy rush hour was in sight, so I figured, even if we *didn't* get lucky, the worst-case scenario was that we'd miss some of that mess that always clutters up I-20.

"Ray Ray, would you mind keeping an eye out for this guy so I can focus on the work I'm doing?"

"No question, *'Felia.*"

"You still remember what he looks like?"

"I gotcha, cuz. Much as Toni be keepin' that dang news on e'ry night? That man's face is tattooed on my brains."

"That, and them dang Black & Mild cigarettes."

Ray Ray laughed, 'cuz he knew how I felt about his smoking and how that odor followed him everywhere he went—like in the kitchen and on the sofas in the living room. I gotta love my cousin, but I gotta give him the *tough* love, too. If I don't, who will?

# PLAINTIFF'S MOTION
# FOR BAIL

WHEREAS, the Defendant, Theodore Jefferson Barnes, requests that this Court establish bail . . .

AS I was putting together my motion, I couldn't help knowing that this was a clear case of wicked Atlanta politics. There was no doubt that Theodore Jefferson Barnes hangs among the wrong people. But the sweep these feds executed was a blind attempt to bust any- and everybody who might have some insight on The Bullet, and everybody who's anybody knows that The Bullet is untouchable. Everyone I know in law enforcement or in the court system is straight-up scared of that man. And all these people they picked up ain't gonna turn on him, either. They just shootin' in the dark, hopin' to hit somethin'. I've seen it all before, how law enforcement can't get hold of the big boy, so they try to squeeze and threaten and intimidate the low-level runners, their families, and *basically* anyone who is guilty by association. Thing is, that's none of my business. My client was at the nightclub when the bust went down. Period. End of story. The ounce of weed he had on him is coincidental to the bust. If the government wants to threaten probation or a suspended sentence, I'll talk it over with my client and urge him to entertain it. But for the prosecutor to play these games and threaten five years and a thousand-dollar fine is silliness at best. If the government thought he would become an informant on a known killer and reputed lord of the Atlanta underworld in return for a lenient judicial procedure, then they're sadly mistaken. I'd tell my client to *do the time*—all day long. And see, that's what's wrong with the system now: people always trying to take advantage of others. That's why it's so hard to trust Lady Justice. That's why I left *that side* of justice years ago, because of how unbalanced things were. If my client—or *any* client, for that matter—is not properly represented by someone who *gives a damn* then *everyone* might as well give up their rights and check in at their local lockup.

Ray Ray pulled the driver's door open. "Ain't that him, cuz?"

I shuffled my papers to the side and made my way out of my Benz. That was one thing I never got use to: the comfort of the backseat. I was always the aggressive one at the steering wheel. Hard to surrender that position. And although I appreciate luxury, I don't think I'd ever get comfortable like some pampered prima donna.

It didn't take much to catch up to my old college chum. "Congratulations, Percival!" I was maybe ten feet from the newscaster when I announced myself. He seemed startled. Percival Culberson was a go-getter in college. I knew of him only from a distance, when he would moderate the college debates we had between schools. Even then, he always seemed to have that TV-host personality goin' on. Not the cutest cookie in the jar, but sharp, with that whole perfect English-speaking way he had about him. And how could he miss the whippersnapper that I was? Any debate team *I* was on never lost a competition. And my name was always announced in the school papers as the future legal eagle that also played soccer, chess, and held down the cheerleading squad. And furthermore, I was *claiming* the valedictorian crown in my entire last year of school, as if it were *already* mine. Sure, that was a bit cocky of me to think that way, and I honestly *really am* a humble person. But whenever it came to *any* challenge, best believe that my family, my friends, and anyone at school knew Ophelia King would be giving it 1000 percent in that quest to become the winner who took all.

"Ophelia! What a surprise!"

We shared a gentle, unimposing hug and some small talk before I got down to the nitty-gritty.

"I need a favor, Percival." He looked at his watch, but I couldn't help thinking that whatever priority he had in mind would have to wait.

"Something relating to a case? You know legal gives us hell when—"

"No, Percival. This has nothing to do with any case, court proceedings, or any of that." I put a grip on his arm to try to get him to *listen* instead of prejudge. "I'm trying to help a friend. He's been in an accident, fell into a subsequent coma, and there's the amnesia now. Just *crazy*. Anyway, I need you to do a little feature or a brief story about his situation so that somebody out there will recognize his face and come forth. I'm hoping to get family, friends, co-workers to *claim* this man because right now he has no idea who he is, except for the father and grandfather he keeps mentioning."

Percival appeared to be thinking about my proposition. No doubt, so many others have come his way with the want for some news feature or TV exposure, to say nothing of the ideas and themes he and his co-workers come up with. But I was banking on my direct approach, as well as my track record and that he and I went to school together. The cards were definitely stacked in my favor here. It was something I learned soon after law school: get as many points, resources, and as much agreement as you can to back your claim or position. Get as close to a sure thing as you can. Even with, there's no guarantee that you'll win. But it's better to have than to have not.

"The thing here was *time*, Ophelia. I already like your story, and I know how far you and I go back. But I need to see what's on the table upstairs. Politics. Special interests. Tragedies. Economics. And now there's *Obama mania*. There are so many stories, concerns, and motives behind them all; and all of that changes from day to day."

"Sounds like you need my negotiation skills up there."

Percival chuckled and nodded at once. *Agreement.* "Already, before I walk in that door, there will be a stack of initiatives, a schedule to keep to, and so many hidden agendas underneath it all. I swear it's hard to know what's going on in people's minds and what their motives are. It's bizarre. But I will promise to get this onto my agenda."

I shot him my cute smile. "*Double* promise?" I pretended to hold him accountable for the commitment he'd given me, as if there'd be some critical, liberty-threatening legal repercussions weighing in.

"I gotcha, Ophelia. You've been a major impact in my life, and any way I can, I'd like to return the favor *tenfold*." With that, I handed him a folder with a photo of my houseguest, a description, and some other intelligent details I thought might be helpful.

———

AND THAT'S all it took. A little *resourcing*. A little encouraging. But I had no idea that my helping this perfect stranger would turn out to be the latest drama to reach my doorstep.

I RECEIVED an e-mail from Percival informing me of the forthcoming broadcast. Unfortunately, I only got to check e-mails into the early evening. I had been in court most of the morning and in the late afternoon I felt the need for a nap. And that's just what the doctors ordered, a nap when I felt overworked, *no matter what*. Well, a long drawn-out morning in the courtroom certainly qualifies as a *no-matter-what* occasion. And if I could get that to be my ritual, to get some rest after sitting through a morning of mostly other people's court appearances, then that's what it was gonna have to be.

By the time I got to read the e-mails, to learn about the broadcast I missed on WAGA, there were already voice-mail messages responding to the story. Ten of them. *Wow, that was fast.*

*"Hey there. I'm Chantelle. That man up on the TV is Carter. We been married for two years now, and he just up and disappeared a month ago. Could you tell him I'm waitin' for him to come home? I got some chores left undone."*

I was about to call the 404 phone number that Chantelle had left. I was already excited when the message started playing back. Except, there was this faint giggle at the end of the message. I had to rewind the message and listen to it again. Only on the second listen did I actually *hear* the "month ago" and the bit about "chores left undone." The notion of a husband missing for over a month, and for a wife to only be interested in *chores left undone* was amusing. And while I laughed at the idea, the next message was already playing.

"*This is Maxine. I don't know what made me call, 'cuz the truth is, I don't know this man from Adam. But you know they's a shortage a good men here, and that's one fiiiiine brother on that TV. Puleeeze call a sistah if he can't find his home, 'cuz I surely got a place for him!*"

I didn't need to hear any more of these messages to know what I was dealing with. The thirteen-to-one theory was playing itself out before my very eyes. That is, the ratio between men and women in Atlanta. For reasons that are many, good, single men are hard to come by here. And maybe this isn't merely an Atlanta thing and I just have tunnel vision. But I do know that whether it's men falling in and out of prison, in and out of marriage, drugs, or the gay lifestyle, a good man is hard to find in Atlanta. If not in those ways, black men are falling, period. AIDS. The murder rate. Partnering with white women. Black-on-black violence. Even induction into the military. For all those reasons, our black men are disappearing. *They're either taken, they're fakin', or they're mistaken*, as the saying goes. And black women, from the bottom up, are fed up with the statistics.

So, that's what I had to deal with—the thirteen-to-one ratio. Thirteen women to every man. And many of *those* men have even taken advantage of the situation so they can enjoy having their cake and eating it, too. In the end, it would make my job of screening inquiries that much more difficult. By midnight, there were over two hundred calls, and by the next morning over five hundred voice mails were backed up, with just as many messages in my office e-mail. I found myself saying, *Lawd have MERCY! Thank God I didn't use my personal e-mail.*

As if my life wasn't already a trip!

The next morning brought along with it a brand-new stack of revelations. I had planned on playing catch-up in my home office because Angela, my paralegal, has only been with me a few months. I trust her more now than I did when she started with me, but that's always a process. You never want to give the new people in your life access to everything, especially if you're not sure, or if the relationship is seasonal or for a lifetime. So, she doesn't yet do the personal stuff, the bills for the house and all my other commitments. Toni is supposed to be taking care of that stuff; that's the reason why I had her move in with me right after she finished college. However, even that has taken some time. Toni hasn't become all that efficient and responsible as I hope she'll become. So, in the meantime, I do my own personal bill-keeping, and as much as I try to stay on top of it all, I can digress at times. All-night cramming on a case, traveling to different districts in Georgia, and somehow making time to go and see Dancer at one performance or another can wear on a woman's ability to keep her game tight. Mail will start out on the kitchen counter, then it will shift to the dining-room table, and sometimes to my bedroom. At other times, it does follow some unspoken protocol and finds its way down to my office. But what we haven't yet established is that Angela should be taking care of it from start to finish.

"Hey, cuzin. You made the papers again." Ray Ray came through my doors while I was multitasking—writing checks and watching CNN. Usually, I would get on him for not knocking and I'd encourage him to use discretion—*never know when I have a client, Ray Ray.* But, did he not say I had made the papers?

## AMNESIA VICTIM LOST FOR 12 WEEKS
### by Terrell Weeks, Associated Press

ATLANTA (AP)—A man known only as "Preston" survived a terrible attack, or accident (authorities aren't sure which), in downtown Atlanta just 12 weeks ago and apparently had all data wiped from his brain's hard drive, including his very identity, and his home address.

For the first 11 weeks, Preston had been in a coma at Atlanta Medical Center, but he woke up with his new "blank" hard drive. He now calls Fulton County his home, where he is under the care of famed attorney Ophelia King, who rescued Preston from his circumstances once he woke from the coma a few weeks ago. Other than that he was a "handyman who worked alongside his father and grandfather," Preston is unable to remember his name, where he worked and what he did for a living, or where he's from. His new "friends" are hoping that Preston's real family will see the news and come forth to identify and welcome him back home.

Jonathan Farmer, director of the medical team that cared for Preston, says: "We felt that his intellect was still intact, and it seemed his survival skills were normal, and that it might be a matter of time until everything is back to normal."

Upon further investigation, this reporter found it unclear as to exactly how many others are afflicted with psychogenic fugues, or what the precise underlying causes are. Victims may lose all memory of themselves, family or friends, but otherwise seem to function normally and can perform routine tasks. Many experience an urge to move constantly from place to place. Most victims eventually regain their memories, though it can take weeks and sometimes years.

Psychogenic fugues can be triggered by stress or unresolved conflict, according to experts. But Dr. John Hart Jr., president of the behavioral neurology section of the American Academy of Neurology, says researchers are trying to determine why some people might be more susceptible than others. "It's among the rarest of the dissociative disorders," says Dr. David Spiegel, associate chairman of psychiatry at Stanford University.

Doctors at Atlanta Medical Center have diagnosed "Preston" as suffering from psychogenic fugue, an extremely rare form of amnesia. If anyone knows "Preston," you are encouraged to contact the Fulton County Police Department.

---

"WOW," I said. And I immediately got on the phone with the reporter. "Terrell Weeks, please? This is Attorney Ophelia King speaking." As I waited for the call forwarding, I prayed that this was the break we'd been looking for. I wondered two things, however: first, how had Terrell come by our story?; and second, were there any significant leads so far?

After the salutations, Terrell explained, "You mean, besides the information being all over the six-o'clock news? Well, I did my research, contacted the hospital, and I have to be honest, Ms. King . . . I'm a big fan. I've been watching you ever since the Brady trial. From that one trial I was following you. The Davis girls? The ones who they say plotted to kill their father? Then you won the case against that cigarette company, and picked up the NBA contract, and then the University brought you in as a consultant, and—"

I was laughing. I was amazed. Either this man had my whole career on a chalkboard in front of him, or he was a *fan*. And it felt a little spooky, I can't lie.

"Okay, so it's clear to me that you know a little about my career."

"A little? *A little?* Ms. *Ophelia King,* I am probably your biggest fan. No kiddin'. Oprah first, then *you.* I think God plays a close third to Beyoncé."

Now my laughter grew into a bellow. And it had been a while since I'd heard my own bellow.

"Okay, soldier. Well, since you're on my team, and I really didn't know I *had* a team until this story hit, maybe you can tell me about the inquiries. Were there any?"

"Actually," he said in a most drawn-out, effeminate voice. "There were a few. I'd be surprised if they haven't gotten in touch with you already."

*Damn.* What he was referring to was probably the load of irrelevant boy-crazy women who called me already. Maybe the callers on my voice mail made for a mixture of everything. A stew of lost women looking for a plug-in to this hunk living in my house. Wagging my head, I felt like this was a dead-end call. Except for this spirited energy on the other line. And spirited he was, still talking up a storm. But I couldn't hang up on him. Somehow, he was a resource that I had to make use of. You never knew when—

"Terrell, do you mind if I keep in touch? I mean, having a star reporter on my team can't hurt."

*"Me? Team? The Ophelia King Team?? I think I've absolutely DIED and gone to heaven!"*

I laughed my way off the phone and back to work. I couldn't let this houseguest consume my day. There was a case to win and other work to do, besides.

The phone rang almost as soon as I hung it up.

"Ms. King? It's Terrell again. There *was* an interesting call. I sorta discounted it, on account of my busy schedule and all. But, a woman from McCormick & Schmick's called."

"The restaurant?"

"Yuppers. She said she recognized the face, but nothing more. I did take her name and number."

"Wow. Lemme get that up off a ya, Terrell." And he recited the name and number before I told him, "You are a gem! We *really* need to stay in touch, okay?" We exchanged e-mail addresses and I couldn't wait to dial Bo Humphrey.

"Bo! Guess what!"

## [ TEN ]


## DANTÉ


THERE WERE ALWAYS women in the King household, which was a big tease because I was a single man who was, for lack of a better word, *unappreciated* at the present time. And it wasn't like there was a memo marked *urgent*, or that this want or desire was something at the top of my agenda. Maybe it was a natural "man thing" for me to want to pair up with someone? I mean, big house, luxuries abound, beautiful women all around? *I want some!* Well, as that "man thing" in me began to assess the options, there was a process of elimination. Toni, Ophelia's niece, was apparently messing with some local producer who always came over to help Dancer lay down tracks. So, I suppose the man in me was thinking: *unavailable.* Ophelia herself was claiming the single life, but I couldn't see her as a love interest. She was more of a big sister. Angela was in the office part of the house from nine to four and was the first one to address *me.* And it was pretty obvious that she was single and desperate because many times when I passed her desk or came into the office to use the Internet, Facebook, BlackPlanet, or

Mingle City were Web sites that were open on her screen. Like Ophelia's law, work came second to her finding some dick. She even had me help her with changing her profile picture, as well as she asked me questions about her appearance: *how do you think this would look? You think it would be too obvious if I put my phone number?* And there were other such questions that she asked to help *mold* her online presentation for the best results. Never did I consider how this woman would fit into my arms until she asked me personal questions.

"So how come *you're* single?" she'd ask. And, "Do *you* have a Facebook profile?" And beyond that, when one of her friends was in the office they got to talking about men and even sizing me up and giggling. I acted as if I didn't know they were taking about me. But I guess I was desperate, too, because I actually fantasized about doing Angela. The truth is, I wasn't at *all* attracted to her because, well, she wasn't an attractive lady. In her late thirties, with her beady eyes and bubble forehead, it took a *world* of imagination to think anything sexual about her.

I even forced myself into the state by offering her a foot massage. And I don't know where the idea came from, what made me think I could do a good massage. But it connected me with her body and I could see how my raw, attentive hands on her naked feet were sending spasms through her, even if she pretended not to feel anything. More lotion. The balls of her feet. The insteps. Between the toes.

Of course my conversation was crucial, too: *So when's the last time a man massaged your feet real good? How's that feel? You like that?*

I knew *exactly* what I was doing. No sense in her trying to hide the enjoyment. I wasn't born yesterday. The only thing I had to do now was try to look past the ugly that I saw in this woman. The massage was easy. *That*, however, would take real talent.

The try on Angela went nowhere, because I was side-tracked. While I attempted to be in Angela's face more often, Dancer happened to stroll into the office and needed my help in her studio.

"I can't fix it," Dancer told me, speaking of a light fixture.

This, I know, was *dead wrong*. And I felt like I was taking advantage or something. But something about Dancer was calling me. It began with me fixing a broken light fixture in her studio. Then I got all caught up and sucked in to her singing. One thing led to another, and my hands were all over her. It felt really good to have this woman's hands on me, but it also felt a little awkward: a violation of some kind. It was as if was there was a *law* or a *rule* that said I shouldn't be involved with Dancer. And even though she was six years younger than I, she *was* of age. So, if the attraction is there (which it was), why not? We were two grown-ass adults, as far as I saw it. But of course, I'm *way* certain her mother would see it altogether differently. And as good as Dancer's tongue felt in my mouth, as good as her breasts felt molded in my palms, I couldn't help feeling the authority of Ophelia King in the atmosphere. Ophelia's mansion. Ophelia's daughter. *Ophelia's Law*. Except, as much as Ophelia's influence hovered over me, my body had a mind of its own. It wasn't long until we took things to that next level. From touching, kissing, and petting on the worn leather couch, we somehow sloped down to the floor, until we were animals pushing and pulling and reaching for satisfaction. The strange thing was how Dancer felt so, well . . . *new* to loving. It was how she engaged in the tongue flicking against my foreskin; it was how she held on to me while we were missionaries, and then how she cried and screamed when I was driving into her from behind. In a word, she seemed such a *novice* to the love game. Either that, or this was just the way it was for the younger crowd— younger than I was, anyway. And, in a way, I was turned on by the naïveté and the idea that this—speaking of Ophelia's daughter—was *virgin territory*. As far as I knew, all the noise didn't matter since the studio was soundproof. And we certainly tested *those* extremes.

Out of nowhere, our harmony in the studio was interrupted. The voices were loud—an ongoing conversation.

"And this is the studio where— *Oh. Excuse me!*" The voice caught me off guard, and I almost choked on my spit; or Dancer's, whichever I was consuming while we fed on each other. The sudden noises were compliments of Angela, Ophelia's paralegal, who hustled real estate on the side. *I knew there was a reason I didn't like that woman!* She had barged in while Dancer and I were grinding on the floor, and what's more, she had a couple of prospective buyers just behind her! I felt violated, as if something sticky had spilled all over the carpet; and I was the carpet. *Lord.*

In the weeks that I was a guest there, I respectfully stayed out of the way or found something to do whenever the house was being shown. I had come to meet a couple of the brokers who were trying to sell Ophelia's home, but the real-estate market was experiencing an all-time low,

and I got the idea that the house had been on the market
for a while and would probably be on the market for that
much longer, according to the nationwide economic recession. I mean, everywhere I looked (newspapers, TV, Internet), someone was singing the blues about the economy,
the recession, and the possibility of a depression. Not only
that: I wasn't getting any obvious signals that this home
was about to be sold. Instead, there was every sign of comfort and convenience: the yard being kept by gardeners;
carpet cleaning; pool maintenance; and Ophelia and her
niece continued their shopping sprees. And the showings
where buyers came in to see the house were most infre-
quent. It had been going on a month now that I had been
living in the King home, so maybe it was me; however,
these weren't signs that folks would be leaving soon.

And what did any of that have to do with the price of
oranges?

Not a thing. It was just my mind trying to justify and
make sense out of why and how I *really* fucked up here.
But, now that Angela had popped her big head in without
warning, a *whole* other set of events was likely to unfold.
And here I was thinking that as long as Momma King was
at church, the coast would be clear and Dancer and I could
play. And here I was thinking that living with Ophelia King
would help me find out who the hell I was and maybe get
me back to my pops and granddad. Here I was getting extremely comfortable in this woman's lap of luxury, influence,
and power. Only now, this fantasy film appeared to turn to a
horror flick before my very eyes. I could see how the rest of
this would play out. Angela was surely gonna rush through
the rest of her appointment and would probably be on the

phone with Ophelia in mere minutes. The next series of images that came to mind included Ophelia, her niece, Toni, her ape-faced paralegal, Angela, cousin Ray Ray, and any other manly resource she had access to would be on my ass *hard*, beating me senseless until I'd end up *back* at Atlanta Medical Center with an all-new coma to muddle through. *Jesus*.

At once, I needed to put things into proper perspective. I asked Dancer what her mom would do.

"Nothing. She's not gonna find out," said Dancer adamantly.

"Really. And what *act of God* is gonna stop Ms. Magilla Gorilla from turning us in?"

"Me, that's who." And before Dancer cleared that up for me, she had already zipped up her pink sweatsuit and was now leaving me behind in the studio to pull myself together. Clearly, she had something powerful up her sleeve. And I didn't wanna miss out on the showdown. I was hopping into my last pants leg and nearly fell into one of the studio speakers as I made my way through the door, down the hall, and up the steps to the main floor of the mansion. I took my time and remained out of sight as Angela gave her farewell to the prospective clients. I could also see Dancer waiting there in the living room as I remained out of sight but within earshot.

Angela's heels tapped along the wooden floor as she returned through the entry hall.

"Angela, I need you to forget what you saw downstairs," said Dancer. Hearing this threw me into being an instant cheerleader, realizing that this chick had a potent amount of Mommy's gumption in her blood.

"I will *not*. Young lady, that *vagabond* is an *eyesore* in this home. And I intend to see that he is removed."

"Ahh. It's not gonna be that easy, Angie."

The little perspective I had gave me an okay view of the two in a standoff. Angela had her arms folded, and I assumed Dancer held the same pose except I could only see her back.

"And what do you mean by that, young lady?"

"First of all, you don't need to address me like that. You only do that when you're being condescending. Plus, we spoke about that a few days after you first got here. So cut the crap—"

I could feel Angela choke up, and since she didn't say a word, I assumed the standoff was leaning in Dancer's favor. Although only in my mind, I was pumping my fist in support. *Go Dancer!*

The conversation was ongoing.

"You might not think I know what goes on around here because I'm always in the studio, or writing songs, or zoning out, or something. But I pay attention, Angie. And I been catchin' the foul shit you been doin'. First and foremost, you been dissin' Momma's clients left and right. You're fuckin' rude when they call, when they call back, and it's always everyone else's fault, never yours."

"Young lady, I—"

"Hey, listen. I *told* you about the *young-lady* attitude."

"Well, *aren't* you a young lady?"

"Okay, cute. You call me young lady, and I call you old *bitch*. How's that?"

Dancer's words had to suck all the oxygen out of the atmosphere; if not, then most of it.

"Dancer, that language is *totally* uncalled for." The rich, authoritative Jamaican accent surfaced in Angela's reply.

However, Dancer had her sweet but scathing southern attitude to do battle with.

"Then you *need* to call me by my name. My name is *Dancer*, and if you intend to keep your job; you *need* to keep quiet about what you saw. He's a guest in our home— *my* guest. And you *really* need to stop abusing him like you've been doing."

"Abusing? *Me?*"

"Okay, see that?" Dancer raised her finger, now using it as a wand of some kind. "You wanna get sarcastic with me? *Really?* Please, please. *Pul-eease* do *not* play me, Angela."

"Or *what?*" Oh snap; the gorilla put her hands on her hips.

I'm hearing this, and I'm jackin' my arm and fist back and forth like I'm a team coach watching my star wide receiver closing in on a touchdown. But this latest exchange froze me in midcelebration. Not to mention my hard-on softened.

"*Or* I'll have to explain about the missing bottles of cognac; I'll have to explain about one of 'em and how you got it stashed there to the side of your desk; you know, where nobody can see it? And if *that* don't work, we could talk about Richard."

"*Richard?*"

"Richard," Dancer confirmed. "Ohhh-*ooohh?* All a sudden you got selective amnesia? Must be spreadin' around here. Ahh, *Richard, the pool cleaner?* Did you think I was sleeping when you got it poppin' with him in the gym? On the weight bench? *Really?* Betcha thought I was out with

Moms, din'cha. No, boo. I'm the one who went in there and cleaned your mess off the bench. *Nasty.* But, you know what? Not a problem. I just wanna bet you *any* amount of money that *that's* not part of your job description. And while you decide on that, I wanna see what you come up with when you weigh me and my friend in the studio against you and the pool cleaner bumpin' uglies in our home. Let's see who comes out unmarked. You *really* wanna play with me, Angie?"

*Wow.* I could have heard a pin drop. Dancer went *hard.* I didn't need to hear any more to know this conversation was over. I made way back down the steps, driven by some new energy I couldn't make two cents of. On one hand, I was loving this chick who was brand new in my life, brand new at sex, and on the other, she was *beyond* skilled in the negotiation-and-debate arena. *Damn, she put it on that pain-in-the-ass paralegal!*

I was in Dancer's room (across the hall from the studio) when she returned. I played stupid and waited for her to reveal all. When she did, I acted appreciative and proud. She was the track-and-field winner who came home to show Daddy her trophy. She was the college student who had made the grade and returned home with a big smile and a diploma. She was a singer from ATL (with a power broker for a mother) who just knocked out her opponent, a snob who was trying to throw a wrench in our way. I grabbed Dancer, lifted her short, pretty ass up off the floor, and eased her down from her aerial view so that her lips connected with my own. The kiss was long and involved and there was no *question* that I was ready to be a Dancer fan.

# STACY

This was crazy-good. The credit card company got them balls of steel. But I ain't mad at 'em. And really, I guess that's what they do when they sell people's information to this, that, and a third. Now it was Bank of America offerin' me up a credit card. Only they came to the table with a card for $12,000. But I ain't no dummy. I knew how to spin them folks good. Once I got the offer in the mail, I made 'em wait a week and then I hit 'em back with the ol; *Listen, $12 grand can't do nothing for me.* Of course, I didn't speak that way; I had my lil' proper white voice goin' on. But I told 'em straight up, *If you can't match my current card for $100 grand, what makes you think I'm ready to do business with you? Actually,* I told them, *what you're sending me is really disrespectful.*

Then one thing leads to another, and the manager of approvals gets on the phone. He does some checking on the computer before he says, "Okay, ma'am, we can match the hundred grand if you'll let us assume the debt for your Chase account."

Now, till that point, I didn't know what he was talkin' about. But I acted real quick, put José on hold and called my people, who told me exactly what to say. Next thing I know, I'm agreeing with the supervisor, he's telling me he's gonna approve a new line of credit for $100 gees. Immediately, I'm thinkin' like Lincoln, and I *know* they can't be *serious*. I wasn't fittin' to shut down *nothin'*. And at the end of the day, B of A cut a check and made it out directly to Chase. All that did was clear up the money I spent with

Chase. And now, a chick with *no credibility* had herself $200 gees worth of credit. It was about to be *on*! And the very next thing on my agenda was to go get my man. This foolishness that was keepin' us apart was fuckin' with my head. How he gonna argue with me, then disappear like *that. Poof.* Whatever was buggin' him probably blew over by now, and in a minute he gonna be in love with me as if it was the first time all over again. I know people would think I'm crazy and that I had enough money to go where I wanted and get who I wanted. But I don't care *how* much money or credit I got, can't no amount of money buy a chick a good, dedicated man with a strong work ethic and a wicked back-stroke. Plus, I gave this man my heart, my body, and all the fixins. Ain't nothing more perfect fit than that. Gotta get him back. Period.

I figured I would get back on my real-estate grind while I'm up. Little more 'n a year ago I had close to $40 grand in equity built up, and because of some bullshit I lost it all. So, how I see it, it's only right that I come back bigger and stronger. Not only that, the real-estate market is *sweet* now that the market is all broke. I been checkin' around and found quite a few steals. A house that was once for sale at $115K is sellin' for $40K now. And mansions that enter-tainers might live in could look like a million dollars, but they can be picked up for $400K and $500K. And to qualify for a $400K loan means 10 percent down. Wow. For $40K I can look and live like a million dollars. Sign of the times, for real.

When I mentioned my intentions to Momma, she started trippin'.

"How you gonna buy another house when I already *got*

one? Plus you got these kids growin' out they clothes every two minutes, and gas prices is just crazy. Just like you, wastin' your money."

"Momma, this is *your* house. I want somethin' of my own. Something I can invest in and be proud of. Ain't that what you taught us? Ain't you tell us to have our own so we don't hafta depend on no man?"

The conversation went back and forth until she got personal, talkin' about my ex. You know, I fuckin' *flipped* when she went *there*. It didn't take me long to lose it. I was screamin', tears all streamin' down my face and shit. No question, I was about tired of her shit. So I'm like, *Okay, time for this chick to make her comeback.*

I got on my grind *quick*. I was partying at one of them model events at club Opera, the ones Leo and them be puttin' on. I had some *lovely* form-fittin' pink dress on. Plus, the lace-up, matching leather stiletto boots I had on were turnin' heads like never before.

Naturally, niggas was hollerin' at me and passin' business cards by the dozens. Sam, an old friend from school, was tryin' to talk me into being featured in a YouTube video. He sounded very convincing, try'na make some money 'n' all. But I had to tell him straight up, "I'm focused on real estate and nothing else."

That was in early September.

By October first, Sam, the realtor, was proposing to me across a table in Starbucks in Lithonia.

"Are you serious, Sam? You chose a time like this to propose? Why didn't you just wait till I hit the megamillions and pop the question as they cut the check? *Damn.*"

"I assure you, Stacy. My proposal has nothing to do with

money. I'm doing pretty good in my profession; got you as a client, right?"

I rolled my eyes, thinkin' that if *this* was the best line he could come up with—

"Okay, so you're right. But can you blame a brother? You're an obvious male-magnet. You're set financially. You got the *baddest* ride I seen in a long time. And, yes, you have a head on your shoulders, too. So, I figure there's no *better* time than now."

I was giggling at Sam, while at the same time asking his forgiveness for laughing in his face. Then I said, "If that ain't the lamest sack-a-shit attempt I ever heard, Sam Albert. A luxury truck? Financial security? A woman's figure? That's what you want in a relationship? Nigga, you got a lot to learn about women. You *really* got a lot to learn about *you*, and what you *really* want, 'cuz the shit you just said? Don't you *ever* say that shit to a *real* woman. You want her for her ride, her financial stability, and because she's a male-magnet. Are you *serious*, Sam?" I said this, but then I touched my palm over his hand to let him down easy. Wagging my head now: "You probably do *real* good with the ladies, don'tcha, Sam. Okay, sure, you're probably having a dry moment now, and I know we known each other for a minute, and it's probably *convenient* for you to speak your mind at a time like this, but . . . *not me, Sam*. I'm not the one. Plus, if you want the *truth*? My man is waitin' for me. He's somewhere in New York right now, but soon as this closing is over tomorrow, soon as I get my house right, I'm gon' get my man." I said these words while I showed Sam a picture of Danté and myself on my cell phone.

"That's your man?"

"Sure as the sky is blue. That's my future husband. My future baby-daddy."

Sam cocked his head back some. "He's in . . . *New York?* You sure?"

"I'm sure. What's that look for? You know Danté?"

"Ahh, I got news for you. Stacy, I don't know how to tell you this, but this Danté fella? He's"— Sam stuttered for a second—"he's fuckin' some rich lawyer's daughter down in Cascade. I just walked in on him last week. A broker was showing us a mansion with a studio in the basement. Except"—Sam cleared his throat— "the studio was a little *busy* when we walked in."

The frozen, angry look on my face was more for the rich lawyer's daughter he spoke of than it was for Sam himself. And just then, the business meeting turned real personal. None of the smooth jazz playing in Starbucks, the customers gliding in and out of the entrance, the busy workers and their rituals—none of it mattered.

*What drink can I get started for ya?*

*Will you be having whipped with that?*

*Should I leave room?*

None of it existed for me because I was too busy daydreaming and floating in a place called *nowhere,* and, although he didn't know it, so was Sam. But I couldn't even see Sam; just his lips were moving. His lips were answering every *single* one of my questions. Names. Address. When.

THAT NIGHT, I had to plan my attack. I was thinkin' about fire bombin' a rich lawyer's house. I was thinkin' about layin' in wait for some young, wannabe singer to come drivin' down a long oval driveway so I could ram my truck into that bitch's car. Every- and anything goes at this point, 'cuz at the end of the day, no rich bitch—I don't care if she *is* a lawyer—is gonna get in my way. As far as I was concerned, her singer-daughter was out of her lane. Danté was *my* territory. *My* property. And they might not know it, but I had a surprise for all of them.

# [ ELEVEN ]

## OPHELIA

I'M TRYING TO maintain some sense of a steady schedule, but it's near impossible. Both large and small clients are late with their payments. And that's my fault, really, for being too lenient and allowing payment plans. And it's all added up, weighing on my shoulders. In the end, it all amounts to bills backed up and an unbalanced bank account. If things get way out of hand, bill collectors call, or worse, the sheriff comes with papers to serve. *Embarrassing.*

I was knocked out when the sheriffs came with the court order. But a 5:00 a.m. knock at the door is what woke Ray Ray. And Ray Ray got to arguing with the sheriff, and before long there was a back and forth that grew loud enough to get Dancer and Toni out of bed. I'm told there was a little face-off down there and that it was Preston's sensibilities that put a stop to it all. I'm so glad for that. But I had more pressing matters to conquer. The reason the sheriff came was for the mortgage. Sixty-five hundred dollars a month. And if I'm any later than thirty days, they send the dogs. This is the first time something like this has happened to us, and it was truly embarrassing to be served like this. So, of course I was up in arms and ready to shoot at everyone who owed me money. I put a list together with Angela and came to a grand total of eighty thousand dollars that was owed to me. Again, me with the relaxed payment plans and the sniveling clients. Well, no more mister nice guy.

While Angela got on the phone and gave hell to some of my late-paying clients, I got down and did a little dirty work myself.

"After all, Mary, I don't provide layaway-plan law; I'm a professional who gets results. And that's the way I expect to be paid, like a professional who gets results. I was in court *every day* last week, on time, representing you even when you didn't come on time. There's gas, lunch, other paying clients I have to push aside. It's a lot. So, I understand your woes. I get it that the economy is hurting. But that's not my business. Because whatever the economic climate, Mary, I'm here to represent my clients. . . ."

". . . If it rains, I don't work any less, Charles. Nor do I limit my performance. When it's too hot out, I don't cry the blues. I just dress appropriately, and I get in there and go to work. That kind of performance is *expert* performance; Charles, it's not just talent. Blame economics and cry the blues to everyone else *but me*. I'm the one who's either keepin' the business alive, keeping attackers off the back, or else keeping someone's butt out of jail. Somehow, one of those applies to you, so I can't have you or any other client treat me like I'm not a priority. My bills need to be paid just like yours. . . ."

". . . No, you need to cut that off. And I need to be refunded every dime that you've taken out since July. I did

not authorize any consistent payment schedule, and I don't
need this service on a monthly basis. . . ."

". . . Two fifty a month? For *what*? No, sir. We needed
that service just *one time*. We don't do name searches that
often. Please take us off your list, and please refund what
you took from the account for the past two months. Thank
you."

A new priority was in place in my home. I needed to
tighten screws, buckle down on spending, and call in those
outstanding loans. 'Cuz that's what they were. If you're
owing me money and if your debt is outstanding, I'm no
less a lender, and you are but a borrower. And that's how I
found myself addressing people, no matter if you were a
friend, family member, or a corporation. I found myself
caught between attacking my clients and the moochers
who were preying on my bank account. And at the moment, nothing else was more important than the money.
Because if I could help it, I wasn't about to experience another of those embarrassing sheriff moments ever again.


AS IF time froze, I took a seat and stared at the TV. Barack
actually *won* the election. *He won!* I was so full of emotion
and didn't know how to release it. I cried. I laughed. I gave
hugs to whoever came into arm's reach, got some love. Think
about it: after generations of struggle here in the South, from
lynchings to the White House. *Wow.* If I were to write a
book, that's what it would be called: *From Lynchings to the
White House.* We've endured so much as a people, and there
are so many misdeeds, inhumane acts, and ungodly injustices
that blacks have surrendered, submitted, and succumbed to

that there was just *no way* to seek redemption. Men, women, and children, killed. Human rights deferred. Injustice and abuse of authority, rampant. And all of it has weighed on the conscience of Mother America like a bloody boil. Naturally, growing up as a young girl in the South, I've seen a lot. And what can a woman possibly do to right all the wrongs? I'm just one person making my own minuscule contribution to the universe. It's not like I'm a big politician or a big spiritual leader who can move congregations. But then, seeing this in my lifetime has made my two cents of contribution so worthwhile. My struggle to do good, to walk in righteous footsteps, and to proceed with power and purpose has finally been endorsed by this significant achievement. I can honestly say that Barack is me; that he pushed through muddy waters and climbed the highest mountain imaginable to eventually win the world's highest office on my behalf.

And while I'm telling myself these things, Angela was closing the doors to my office. She did this usually when guests were in the reception area, or when she was leaving me to enjoy privacy as I consulted with clients. This time, however, it was apparent that Angela was looking for her own time alone with me.

"Ophelia, I need to talk to you about something."

"Looks serious. Why don't you have a seat." And as she did, I had to say, "By the way, I want to tell you that you're doing an *excellent* job showing the house. I know these are difficult times and the house will *eventually* sell. So just keep up the good work. We'll drop the price again and see if we can't get it moved for six hundred."

"At that price, I'm gonna need to call a few people

who've already seen the house. I'm most certain to find us a buyer."

"Good. Then it's done. So, what did you need to talk to *me* about?"

"Ophelia, this is a little difficult to bring up, because I've only been working with you for six months, and I *never* get into your family business. . . ."

Up until Angela mentioned *family* I couldn't imagine what might be so important. In one day we had jointly pushed my delinquent clients to make due on at least half of the money that was owed to the King Firm. Thanks to Angela's tough Jamaican attitude and my aggressive courtroom approach, we got it done. So, whatever Angela had to tell me, I was all ears.

Angela took a deep breath and appeared to brace herself. Then she said, "It's about your houseguest."

"Yes?"

She stalled before she said, "First I need to tell you something else. Ophelia, I *promise* this won't happen again. I really screwed up big-time, I know. It was just, well, he forced himself."

I could feel my skin stinging and my heart pounding. *"Preston?"*

"I, no—uhh, I'm so sorry, Ophelia. I never meant to violate your trust in me."

The fire in my eyes was intense. I suddenly felt sick to my stomach. *I invited this man in my house and he forced himself on my paralegal?*

I could already see myself cursing this man and tossing him out of the house on his head and cutting my losses. After all, what, am I gonna get disbarred for my housecleaning?

Just as I began fuming, the phone rang. At the same time, Angela was wagging her head and trying to say something. I put her on hold and took the important call. It was Bo.

"FOUND OUT who your boy is, Ophelia. Want me to come and see you? Or should I let you have it now?"

I was thinking that whatever Bo had to tell me now didn't matter. I almost said what I was thinking, too. But I was more curious than anything else.

"Yeah, Bo. Why don't you let me have it now." I braced myself for what I was already prepared to write off and disregard as irrelevant nonsense.

"Well, for one thing, his name's not Preston, it's Danté. I took the lead you gave me, met the maître d' at McCormick's. She remembers him coming in late for dinner, and she set him up with a reservation at Ruth's Chris. At Ruth's Chris he was the last diner and they even had a credit card receipt to show me. *You're not supposed to know how I got that type of access, Ophelia.*"

"Right. Just like I don't know how we solved so many *other* unexplainable fact-finding missions."

Bo chuckled and went on with his find. "So, his real name is Danté Garrett. He and his family run a business called Mister Fix-It, a company out in Park Chester, a section of the Bronx, up in New York. But, get this: I remembered you said something about him wanting to get back to his father and grandfather."

"Yeah."

"Turns out that's not even possible. Both of them have passed away from the big C."

"Cancer?"

"Prostate cancer. Might be hereditary. But, sure is the sky is blue, his elders are MIA."

"What about his mother?"

"No info on that yet. Still have my hounds out. I did also find his address. Called the super. Turns out he hasn't paid rent in three months. They asked me some questions, but of course I haven't said a word."

I was doing math in my head, counting the two months he'd spent in the hospital and the two months he'd been with me.

"Oh. One more thing. Once I knew his real name, I did some checking with New York State Department of Motor Vehicles. He drives a turquoise Blazer, plate number A72 98FD. When I checked with Atlanta PD; they pulled it up right away. The vehicle had been impounded from being left on the street for so many days with tickets building."

I sat there at my desk, staring at CNN and the postelection commentaries, opinions, and talk of where the Obamas would be spending Thanksgiving. The images got me to thinking about Thanksgiving and how we might be throwing down. I was already tallying the food list in my head, along with how many people would be coming and who would bring what. I figured all this even as Bo was still explaining things.

"Of course, you *know* I had to get to the impound. Whole bunch of personal items that were in the truck. Thought you might like to see them. Dropped off a package at your door early this morning."

"*Wow.* Bo, you are more efficient than a scientific experiment." I put my hand over the phone to tell Angela,

"There's a package at the front door. Would you get it?" And just like that, Angela was up and out of my office. Meanwhile, I was talking to Bo again. "Bo, you *knew* I was gonna want you to tell me everything on the phone, and yet you were offering to visit. *Silly.*"

"Well, you know any opportunity to visit the famous Ophelia King I would not sleep on."

"You're so sweet, Bo. Give my best to the family. And you be sure to bring your wife down here to my Barack Obama party next week."

"Wouldn't miss it for the world. Oh—wait a minute. There's somebody you may want to speak with. His name is Pastor Bishop, from the Bronx. From what I've learned, he's been trying to find our boy and even advocated a missing-persons report up there in New York." Bo gave me the pastor's number before we ended the call and I found myself wondering about this Danté. I've met many characters in my career, but a man like this was a rare find. We've witnessed his hard work around the house and he seemed to be well mannered. So then, what was it about him and Angela?

Angela returned with the box that Bo had left at my front door. I couldn't wait to dig in. Meanwhile, I started to feel myself part of a conspiracy as Angela stood over me more or less like a backseat driver as I picked through the items. That wasn't gonna fly *this time.*

"Have you followed up on the rest of the invites, Angela?" I asked this because if there was gonna be some nosiness going down, I needed to do that alone.

Still, Angela seemed to have something more to say. I

was frustrated with her procrastination and slightly snapped at her.

"What, Angela? Something else you need to tell me?"

Cowering, she replied "No, Ms. King."

"Okay, then let me have some time alone. We'll catch up later."

As she left and closed my doors behind her, I was already into the miscellaneous goings-on in the "Danté box." I scanned the documents such as insurance and registration cards, a mess of various business cards, and even more cards that boldly advertised MISTER FIX-IT. *"You name it, we fix it. Mister Fix-It."* Once I verified the name on all the documents was Danté Garrett, I immediately called the 718 number printed on the business cards.

Just as quickly, the recording came on to tell me that the number had been disconnected and that no further information was available. Nothing unusual there, I figured. I ignored the few other items in the box and pulled open a black leather organizer. Notes. Post-it notes. More business cards. Notations were made all the way up until September, and then most of October, November, and December were blank and unused. Naturally, I began to backtrack through the notes leading up to Danté's hospital visit. The very last note was "Trip to Atlanta with Stacy."

Before those notes were other reminders and such; more or less last-minute activities before Danté's trip to Georgia. My eyes were already smiling, knowing that I had a treasure map of sorts; one that would inevitably lead me to some kind of jackpot. At the same time, I was looking for contacts like Stacy—*a girlfriend? wife?*—and Pastor Bishop.

*Danté Garrett, I know who you are now. I know your clients, your business connections, and your routine.* As I analyzed and negotiated in my mind as to how I would move forward, I looked through the phone-contacts section of the organizer.

*And now I have the numbers for your pastor and Stacy.*

Twiddling my thumbs, taking account of Danté's notes, his help around the house, and then weighing in Angela's argument about his behavior, I changed my mind about tossing him out so abruptly. My big party was coming up, and it would be good to have his helping hand around. And even his company. After all, I had a heart, didn't I?

No question: *after* the party, I'd be putting that boy out my house.

# [ T W E L V E ]

## D A N T É

DANCER HAD ME feeling real comfortable after her discussion with Angela weeks earlier. And I knew damn well that there was more to it; that Angela had probably wanted me and realized that Dancer had just scooped me up and out of her reach. But that was behind me now.

What helped us all to further forget things was how Ophelia had thrown a big Barack party to celebrate the historic election win. To the best of my knowledge, I never saw so many top-level politicians, community leaders, and church officials in one place in my life. And just as unlimited was the food, the drink, and the joyous energy. It was such a prestigious event, too, complete with a jazz flavor, a five-star chef who cooked up southern cuisine, and a singer named Ayanna who inspired everyone with her enchanting voice. I took none of this for granted and did everything I could to assist and to help make this a successful gathering for Ms. King. I understood from my little research that Ms. King often threw fund-raisers and political parties for Atlanta's rich and powerful. Only, something about *this time* was really special. There was such a glow in folks' eyes, some more fogged with tears than others. A sense of renewed hope and energy was thick in the air; rich enough for me to inhale some of it myself. And then I was getting all teary-eyed, too. A lot of people stood before the gathering and said a few words, but when Ophelia spoke, she had the whole place in sobs. She talked about everything from lynching and sharecroppers to her grandparents and parents and feeling disenfranchised all these centuries. She touched upon so many struggles in the South, from affirmative action to Dr. King's "Dream"; from the impact of the Million Man March all the way up till the injustices of the now. She covered everything in so few words, speaking on human tragedies like the Rodney King beating in the West, the dragging of James Byrd Jr. down in Jasper, Texas; then she took it to the East, noting the police killing of Sean Bell. She tied all that into the success of Barack Obama and the idea that black folk, as well as the world at large, were *sick and tired* of the same ol' same ol'. Leaving no stone unturned, Ophelia glued *life* together, and showed how it all made sense, and she did it in more than a closing argument. She did it as would a preacher, a politician, a motivational speaker, and a little home-grown soul. Ophelia King was *brilliant*. And I *knew* from that moment that whatever landed me in her arms—whatever reason that life had to place me in this woman's tender loving care—was *supposed* to happen. I was truly *blessed* to know this woman. And as much as I had felt a large amount of guilt lying with her daughter, Dancer, I felt more empowered now, with a great pride that I was not only *really* feeling this young woman, but that she came from a mother so rich and powerful, with intelligence and wit. Maybe this was a little premature, but I suddenly wanted to make an announcement in front of all those people at the party:

*Hey, everyone! Special announcement! Your boy Preston is part of the family, too!*

*It's Preston King, now! G'wan, Dancer. Tell everyone what the plan is!*

And, of course, Dancer would step out and (bulging stomach and all) announce that we're getting married, not to mention the child we'd be bringing into the world.

Okay, so that much is *definitely* premature. But can anyone blame a brother for wanting in? Can anyone blame a brother for wanting to be a part of the King family? Not for nothin', but as far as my eyes could see, I was just a step or two from paradise *found*!

However, there was one strange moment I experienced in the hours leading up to the event. I was helping Ophelia to position and prepare the dining-room table for the buffet she had cooked. It was the way she was throwing shade my way. I would strike up some conversation—maybe small-talk to her. And her responses would be short and not so sweet. I thought she might be getting those pains in her abdomen again as she did months earlier; how we first met in the hospital. Still, I was encouraged to ask, "Is everything okay?"

She answered with short nod and wag. Her head movement was somewhere between *yes* and *no*. It was somewhere in the middle of *I'm fine* and *things aren't good at all.* And for some reason, I embraced her gesture personally, as if *I* could've done something wrong. But, she didn't dare know anything about Dancer and me. *Or could she?* And another thing: when Ophelia introduced me to her friends who attended her party, she never mentioned my name. It was never, *Hey, Joe, John, or Jack, this is Preston, friend of the family*. It was always, *Hey, meet our friend*, and then I'd have to do my own introduction. It was either that, or she just avoided introductions altogether. I couldn't help wondering what was up with that.

THE DAYS following the party were mysteriously silent, as if the house itself was also resting from being over-worked. Dancer and I had a little disagreement (real stupid) on the night of the party. She came up to my room, for a change, and she still had glitter on her, on her body and in her hair. Even after she came from the bathroom. So, in my mind I'm saying, *Okay, she didn't shower, just wiped off . . . she's in just as much of a rush as I am to do the nasty. . . .*

The thing is, she was gonna lie with me and bring all that glitter in the bed with her.

I hate to be a bitch about it all, but *eww*! I mean, if she was a hooker and I didn't give a fuck, then *okay*. She could come to bed with makeup on, my tongue would touch nothing, and I'd have to wear *three* rubbers. For sure. But I was really *feeling* Dancer. When I kissed her, I was trying to reach her tonsils with my tongue. I was trying to touch everything she had to offer, and then some. I was trying to be *one* with her. Somehow, I didn't see makeup and glitter as part of that. When I put up the slight protest (without any deep explanation) Dancer got offended.

"Oh. So you try'na *change* me?"

"God. You have to take it *all the way there*? You're making something big out of something *very* small, Dancer."

"Well, I think you're making something out of *nothin'*. So there."

And at that instant, I saw our little discussion turn into a *Keyshia Cole: The Way It Is* episode—*ghetto*, with a capital G. One side of me wanted to see Dancer let down from her position on the issue. I wanted her to see I was right. Instead, she kept up her face as if I was trying to challenge her; as if there was even *any* challenge here in the first place. She was being her mom, in the courtroom (a bedroom), exercising her persuasion techniques. *Why?*

And what was *really* bad of me was how, in my mind, I was seeing someone else. It was that *other* woman I was seeing coming at me in my nightmares—the nightmares that were giving me the headaches. A part of me even wanted to give in to Dancer, only to take it out on her in the bed—because that's what our sex had become, me teaching her and her conforming to the things I liked. In the half-dozen times we had mixed it up, I'd felt the imbalance; there'd be a little foreplay until the prerequisite blow job. But always, Dancer brought with her some strong intention to *prove* something to me, as though she were saying, *I can keep up with you just as well as anybody else you've been with*. And as the recipient, I was always getting more pleasure than I was giving—or so I thought. It was possible (and this went unsaid) that Dancer just enjoyed the hell out of giving. Maybe that got her off. Don't know. What I *do* know was the dastardly thought that I had to *punish* this brand-new ass in a way that would earn *me* the last word in our "glitter argument." Yet, in the back of mind, whatever redemption I'd feel from that would be negative. I didn't want to feel that way about her. I wanted to sincerely love Dancer. And so we went back to our respective corners; Dancer remained down in her basement lair, and I stayed in the simple-ass guest room on the second floor.

It was on the second night of our silence that I couldn't sleep. I intended to read, but needed a little coffee lift. I headed out and down the dark hallways, then down the spiral staircase for the kitchen. I didn't expect what would happen next. But I should've known better. The lights were always off in the hallways and foyers of the house, especially late at night. Everyone retreats to their respective rooms, and you really can't hear a sound. Every now and then someone will be watching the big TV in the living room, or the distant locomotive horn will interrupt the silence ever so much, but not enough to rock you out of your sleep. Otherwise, it feels like you're blind in the dark, and the house, with its high ceilings and spacious areas, is some monster vessel that would be unaffected by the actions of any mere mortal. And that's who I was on this late night. Mortal. Human. Maybe it's just me, a newcomer to the mansion, when it feels like everyone else is so comfortable here. Still, I find myself overwhelmed by this huge home.

On many a night I had gone down these steps. And on almost every occasion I had assumed a step was there when it wasn't. It was either a landing I thought was a step, or worse, a step I thought was a landing. Either way, I had tripped on that staircase on too many occasions, and almost had the stumbling down to a science. On this particular night, I was still sleepy, hadn't yet had my coffee, and what

I thought was the landing was actually a step. I buckled. My weight was thrown forward and I tumbled some. But I caught myself just in time so that I didn't *really* fall. What this was (I realized) was a warning of some type. *Slow down* was the message. Where the message was coming from might've been obvious, but I didn't consider all that. I was more concerned with watching my ass. After all, wouldn't it be something poetic for me to tumble down the steps, hit my head, and somehow shake my memory into a reality check of some kind? *Yeah, right. Man*, what Ophelia and her friends are talking about, I don't know. But I'm just fine. My mind doesn't need correction. I don't find myself forgetting anything, and there's no loss of memory as far as I'm concerned. The gods have rolled the dice, and this is my life: where and what and who I am. Why can't they deal with that? The only bad thing is these headaches and some crazy woman interfering with my sanity.

After I got my coffee, I headed up the adjacent steps, the one closer to Ophelia's bedroom. I usually do *not* come this way, just because the walls in the house are not sound-proof. The only soundproofed room is the studio. *Trust and believe*, Dancer and I tested the extremes of that threshold. But the staircase near Ophelia's master bedroom is really an open door into her conversations because she really gets into it. Sometimes, her conversations travel down to the main level with all the energy that she devotes to her phone calls. It could be legal speak, family, or the troubled rela-tionship she'd been having with—

*Okay, so I've overheard a few things.*

Still, I try to afford the respect due. However, on this occasion I was forced to stop. There was a light that fanned from under the door into the dark hallway. But it wasn't that; it was hearing Dancer's voice that froze me in my tracks. I felt like a spy as I inched closer to the door.

# OPHELIA

"Mom, how could you say that? And all this time you've known who he *really* is and you didn't say *nothin'*? *Dag,* Ma!"

"First of all, I just found out the other day. And *second* of all, don't you take that tone with me, young lady. I'm *still* your mother."

"Well, Ma, I might be your daughter, but I'm also a grown woman. And I been locked in this mansion *forever.* And I don't know what you're expectin', maybe you want me to be a nun or somethin', but—I deserve to be loved, too."

"Okay. I know where this conversation is going."

"No. I don't think you do, Ma. I'm twenty years old. *Twenty.*"

I could feel my eyes smarting and my arms naturally folded across my breasts. What she was about to say felt like a seed that had already taken root, only I didn't want to believe it. I had to cut in.

"Dance, the man is from the Bronx. The man has a woman there. Someone named Stacy. Maybe she's his wife. We don't know."

As if none of what I said mattered, Dancer said, "Ma, I'm sleeping with him."

My face had to have the biggest hole in it—my mouth. My arms came unfolded and my hands shot to my hips.

Blood had to be at its boiling point, already filling my pu-
pils; I was *sure* of it. My breathing was erratic. I couldn't
remember ever being this angry at my daughter.

"You *what*!?"

There wasn't even a stall. Dancer just came out and re-
peated herself, as if there'd be no repercussions—or that, if
there were, she was ready and willing to accept them.

I squeezed my eyes closed and asked God almighty for
strength at this moment. My next words came out choppy
and deliberate.

"Dancer, tomorrow I am having that man's truck removed from the police impound. Then I am gonna give
him a few dollars, and I am going to give him his property
I got from Bo, and I am going to ask him to *leave this house*.
It's over. Whatever you had is *over*!"

"Mom. Mom. *Mom!* You don't get it, *do you*! You cannot
just pay someone off and have them removed from my life!
I actually *love* that man. Preston, Danté, whatever. Same
man, as far as I know. He belongs to me, Ma—"

"*Please! Young lady*, I was brought up with *good* home
training. So were you. I DO NOT consent to you having
sex with *any* strange men under MY roof. And besides,
what if he *is* married? Then what?"

"Ma, this isn't about that, and you know it. This is about
control. It's a control thing with you, isn't it? Nothing to do
with good home grooming, Ma. Who are you kidding? Ma,
if you were a devoted member of the no-sex-until-marriage
club, then why does Napoleon stay over? Oh, he's just a
personal chef who, after he cooks, happens to stay in your
room all night. No sex goin' on in *your* world, right, Ma?
Not you; because after all you're not, what? *Married*. You're

fornicating just as much as I'm fornicating. Hell, we're all fornicating."

"Watch your mouth, child."

"Stop it, Ma! Stop it with the *child* bit. Just fess up. Admit that you and Napoleon are—"

"That's different."

"Really? And what's so different about it, Ma? You're an adult. *I'm* an adult. You're in love. *I'm* in love. What's your point, Ma?"

"Don't try and match your situation with mine. I'm your *mother*. There's no comparison here."

"Nah. No comparisons, Ma. Just one lawyer-slash-*blocker* who's tryin' to mess with my groove."

"Your groove? Your *groove*?" I didn't wanna go here, but Dancer was getting a bit too sassy for my taste. It was time for some tough love. "I'll have you know, young lady, that the *man* you say you *love* has laid with my paralegal."

"Is *that* so." Dancer didn't waste any time in attacking my charge.

Wagging my head and waiting for her to give in, I said, "I'm afraid so. Angela told me *everything* a few days ago, before the party."

Now Dancer had her hands on *her* hips. She seemed to be thinking things through, and I could almost feel the heat and pain she was feeling.

"Ma?"

The tone in her voice lowered considerably. The argument, I figured, was over.

"Yes, baby." I was already prepared to drop the armor and take this poor girl in my arms. She'd been used. We all had. I couldn't wait to flush this stranger out of our lives forever.

"Your paralegal is a *big fat liar*. I don't know how we've trusted her all this time. She disrespects your clients. She's *very* rude. And what I *didn't* tell you is that I caught her having *sex* with Richard in the weight room."

"The pool man—*Richard*?" The thought of those two together pulled up a big laugh from deep in my belly.

With a serious look on her face, Dancer said, "I think it's funny, too. I think it's funny that all day long your *employee* spends *hours* lookin' for men on Facebook and MySpace and Mingle City. Not only does she *not* have a life, but she's a big fat *liar*, Ma. My man don't want no *parts* of her. In fact, he *hates* her effin' guts, Ma. So, I *know* she's lyin'. Ma, the truth is Angela walked in on—"

"Your *man*? Your *man*? Dancer, are you *kidding me*? You've known that man for all of two months and you *love* him? *Are you serious*? How does he go from perfect stranger to *your man*? *Please*. I need to know. In fact, scratch that from the record." I had to regroup from this digressive conversation I was having with my daughter. I had to remind myself that this wasn't the courtroom, this was my daughter. This wasn't an assault against the opposition, it was the little girl I watched grow into an attractive woman. I calmed my voice and said, "I don't *wanna* know. I don't wanna hear it, Dance. Listen—this is not about Angela. It's not even about you, baby. It's about *this man*. How *dare* he come into *my* home and—*what?*—have his way with my *daughter*? Is he *serious*? How convenient was this? I'm the Good Samaritan who brings him home from the hospital, and the minute I turn my back he sinks his greasy fangs into—you all *did* use protection, right? *Please* tell me you all used protection, child."

# DANTÉ

I cocked my head back so many times during that conversation; I wanted to push through that door, scream, yell, rejoice. *I love that man,* she'd said. *Wow.* And she'd said this in the midst of our argument phase. I mean, it was one thing to have someone tell you to your face that they love you. It was entirely something else to hear them say it to someone else.

But, other challenges were conflicting here. Ophelia had become unreasonable. Plus, I wanted to smack the *dog shit* out of Angela. *Lyin' bitch.* I got to thinking about the foot massage I'd given her, and not to mention her many questions as to why I was single and the other conversations she'd started with some sort of sexual undertone. And at the time I didn't really think about how this would work against me; me turning her advances down. But now I'd heard it all. First, there was the confrontation with Dancer, and now I gotta hear it from Ophelia's lips that I *what!?* Oh, *I was hot!*

I would've left that night, but the truth is I *did* need the money and the truck she'd mentioned. There's a *truck* I own? Things still weren't adding up in my brain. But one thing I *did* know was that you best have a car in these parts, or else you were SOL. *Shit out of luck.*

———

*DANTÉ? TRUCK? The Bronx? Stacy?* So much was spinning and swirling around my brain so fast that I just wanted to disappear. I didn't have the means to up and leave, but best believe my intentions were *right there*. One thing I did know, even if I didn't know my name, was that I didn't want to be anywhere I wasn't welcome.

Early that next morning, there was a knock at my door—that is, the door to the guest room at the King mansion. *My room*, hardly.

## [ T H I R T E E N ]


## STACY


YES, THIS WAS a little intimidating, even for me. I was
stepping right into the fire, ready for the one-on-one with
my enemies. *But, have I not been through worse?* I watched
my boyfriend get shot up. I lost my home and kids. *Please.*
Although I didn't know Ophelia King or her daughter personally, I still had to look at them as enemies, and with all I
been through, I was *definitely* not afraid of *these heffahs.*
Bottom line: they had my man in their home. According to
the news reports Sam told me about, Danté don't even
know who the fuck he is! Poor Danté. And it was probably
all my fault, too. Soon as I get my boo home, things are
gonna be different. Everything's gonna be perfect. Wait'll
he sees our new home I just got; he won't think twice about
this raggedy mansion.

Of course Sam was with me as we walked from the oval
driveway to the glass-door entrance to the house. But he
was really no more than a pawn; a cobroker who could get
me in though the front door. Far as these heffahs knew, I
was just another potential buyer who had seen a dozen

other homes. But if anything got out of hand, the worst-case scenario here was the switchblade I had in my purse. When all else fails, that would get me the respect I deserved.

SAM WAS the first to speak as a woman pulled open the door. I noticed she used a key to open it first and wondered what *that* was about. *Is you lockin' my baby in here?*

"Hey, Angela. This is my client Ms. Singletary."

No disrespect, but the chick he called Angela resembled a sort of Lady Kong (if there is such a thing) and I was almost afraid to shake her hand. But I did. I knew this wasn't Ophelia since I had done my Web searches and such. I knew exactly what the lawyer looked like, and I was prepared to play dumb once we met face-to-face.

*The things I have to go through for you, Danté.*

Wearing dark sunglasses and my favorite blond wig, being escorted through the house felt a little like undercover work, even though I had done this over and over again during the past two months while speculating for my own home purchase. Not to mention how I had rehearsed this over and over in my head the night before. And now here I was, living my dream as the *take-charge* woman I am, but still nervous as shit.

Sam did his little sales pitch to make it all look and sound good. *My client is very exclusive, so if you don't mind me showing her around* . . . A damn good excuse Sam used, but he knew damn good and well that I was not the usual qualified and interested buyer for this house. I was merely going through the motions. Funny thing about the real-

estate game: everything is always made to look so perfect—
perfect lighting, everything clean, unlived in, as if the new
owner wouldn't have a care in the world. But I remember
well the many conversations Danté and I would have as we
laid together watching the HG channel, discussing how so
many houses were made the same, with much of the same
materials, and for as inexpensive as possible. And sure
enough, as Sam took me to see property after property, I
could see, feel, and almost smell the inexpensive materials.
And everything—the designs, the landscapes, and the
craftsman specials became so predictable. I could easily
refer back to things Danté had told me, and I *knew* that I
wouldn't get taken advantage of.

When I finally found the house I wanted, I stumbled on
an additional sense of security in my purchase. As it turned
out, the man who came out to appraise my new property
was from New York! Not only that, he was a former New
York Knick! In my mind, I put two and two together and it
all made sense. First of all, there was no way this man
would ruin his reputation and just green-light *any* old purchase for me. And second, he was a *homeboy*!

All he had to say was *go* and I was ready to buy. I was
ready to put down a few grand in the event they gave me a
problem with getting an FHA loan. And what's more is the
owner/builder carried the closing costs for me. I was in
heaven with my brand-new three-thousand-square-foot
four-bedroom house, complete with unfinished basement
and plenty of front and back yard. I had my two-car garage,
my mortgage payments would be twelve hundred a month,
and now all I needed was to have my man back to complete
the picture-perfect storybook life I wanted.

I couldn't wait to see him. *Danté*. His name still felt so good on my tongue. Soon, more than his name would be on my tongue.

Lady Kong agreed with Sam's request and found somewhere else to go. On the top floor of the house we went through a couple of rooms, the master bedroom with the queen's bath and Jacuzzi and multijet shower, and a long-ass closet where Ophelia kept so many shoes. In my mind I was saying, *You just wait, baby. In a minute it'll be my turn to live like a queen. And I'll be the one with the thousand pairs of shoes. Just a matter of time.*

I already had an understanding of what the house looked like on account of Sam's details and the printed listing with photos. So, I knew that the studio, the law office, beauty salon, and weight room were the last areas I wanted to see. I was also ready for the possibility of seeing my baby together with the other woman. *God help her if she gives me trouble.*

One of two other rooms was labeled THE EGYPTIAN ROOM. And it was occupied by a young lady who had been on the phone when we knocked. She offered up a quaint smile and brushed past us to allow viewing. I tried to lock eyes with her, but she seemed to be very into her phone call. And if that was the chick I had to fight with, then *whateva*. Now that I had a good look at her, I felt ready. I hurried Sam through this room and we went to another. The Ivory Coast room also had a decor that was distinctly African, *but I'm not here for this*, I told myself, not wanting to enjoy any of this. The only thing I wanted was to be face-to-face with Danté.

Already, Sam was knocking on the next door and announcing our entry.

"Good morning? Showing the home?"

In this room was a daybed back up against a far wall. There was a chair near the bed and a black leather organizer positioned on the chair. I would recognize that day planner from a mile away in an eclipse. And sleeping on the daybed, covered in a comforter from head to toe, was my baby. Our entrance woke him and he was navigating through whatever sleep was still caught in his eyes. I froze as I watched him wiping away his dream.

*Danté.* I wasted no time.

"Sam, lemme have a minute." And Sam knew just what I meant. *Wait in the hallway and guard the door so I can talk with my boo.*

Danté didn't suspect a thing. I had to recall that I was wearing a disguise as I approached him. The sunglasses came off first and I negotiated for his attention, trying to establish eye contact while he busied himself with straightening up.

"I'll get out of your way," he said without looking up.

"*Danté?* It's me, Stacy. *Danté?*"

At least I got his attention. But he seemed to be confused. It was the look you'd have when someone called your name, but you couldn't remember who they were. You couldn't place the face.

"I'm sorry. You must have the wrong person."

*My poor baby.* It was so real and right in my face. This whole memory-loss bit I saw in the online news accounts. And that may be so, but there was no questioning this electricity I felt being so close to him. Still, I did not hesitate to move in closer. What's mine was mine.

"*Baaaby*? You don't remember me? *Stacy*? The love of your life?" Danté seemed to be avoiding eye contact, but the way a shy boy would; one who was being confronted by an aggressive schoolgirl. But nobody did aggressive like *I* did aggressive. Closer still, I touched my palm to the side of my baby's face. "*Aw, sugah.* Is it *really* like they say? You can't remember anything?"

More confused now, Dante's face screwed some. But I had the antidote to this little puzzle in his life. I eased in evermore and molded my body to his. He rejected and backed up, but the wall was right behind him. And now I had him pinned there and my face easily snuggled into the nape of his neck. I immediately began to smell him. *God, how good this felt to smell my man again.*

"Miss? Excuse me, but you got the wrong person."

"Up here? Maybe?" I was pointing to his forehead. Then my arm quickly lowered until my hand was cupping *my* belongings—the package between *his* legs. "But down here? Ain't no mistakin' these, baby."

Danté was startled, as though I might be threatening his prized possessions. But it wasn't that way at all. Not sure of my own aggressive actions, my grip weakened, and with my eyes closed I stroked him. Being up against him like this and breathing him in felt so right; that void I had been living with for months now was being tickled and rekindled. I just wanted to scream as I took my hand from between his legs and put my arms around his neck. I was ready to get the best of a long-awaited kiss.

# DANTÉ

Damn. *It was her.* The minute she took off her glasses—*the eyes.* And how could I not have seen this coming? The irony was there, right alongside Murphy and his pain-in-the-ass possibilities. *Whatever can go wrong, will.* And to think I was *this close* to making my great escape. The thing that spooked me was, *how did she find me?*

Earlier that morning, Ophelia had come knocking at my door. It was a 6:00 a.m. knock that I would've never expected from her. Dancer, yes. Momma O? Not in my wildest dreams. But here she was. And I should've known, really. Especially considering the conversation I'd overheard the night before. Clearly, just about *anything and everything* was possible from here on out.

However, this—I admit—was impossible; from *way* out of left field. *Stacy.*

Ophelia had laid it all out for me, right before she spit the raw truth at me.

*I want you out of my house*, she told me. *You have overstayed your welcome. You've slept with my daughter and my paralegal . . .*

It took a minute to get the superstar attorney to shut it up, but once I got to say my two cents, there were just two things I had to clear up.

"Ophelia, no doubt. This is your home. I've disrespected you. I totally agree. But you need to know two things. First of all, I have real strong feelings for your daughter. She's not just a socket I plugged my extension cord into. Memory or no memory, I gotta feel at least a *connection* before sleeping with a woman. With all these diseases floatin' around, it's life or death, dating out here. But the *other* thing? If I was on an island far, far away, and your paralegal was the last woman standing with a suitcase full of million-dollar bills . . . with a Superwoman cape on . . . and my life depended on sleeping with her? You know what I'd do?" Ophelia stood before me, arms folded, in her courtroom best, most likely on her way to a hearing of some sort. "I'd shoot myself," I said. *"Twice!"*

And of course I gave my best defense, but there was no winning here. Ophelia was judge and jury. I was dead wrong and really should have taken my time with Dancer. Should've known better. She was a lovely woman, talented, beautiful, and in reality (thanks to her mom) *delivered to me on a garnished platter.* Not your average relationship.

"And that's what I'm saying. Okay, so you may *not* be a bad man. You may be the best thing that ever happened for my daughter. But I'm not gonna *assume* that's the case, where you get a *pass* on all those other important *courting* decisions that women have to make. This is just too damn convenient for *any* man." Then, Ophelia said it best: "If there's *really* anything there to go on, you all will find one another in another space and time. But you won't do it under *my* roof." That's about the point when the conversation about Dancer ended. I had no real power or leverage.

After those issues were clear, there was a bunch of other small talk; I guess, her way of saving face under the circumstances. She also handed me a box of some belongings, including a wallet with a car registration, insurance card, and a black leather organizer. The organizer looked familiar, like it could've come from one of my nightmares. Just the same, I scanned through it as Ophelia began to tell me what she knew about me. She had apparently spoken to some people who knew more about me than I did. She also dropped a bomb on me about my father and grandfather: *They're no longer alive, Danté. And you were running the business yourself ever since. Apparently, something happened with this Stacy—I think she's your girlfriend, according to Pastor Bishop—but you came down here with her and somehow you were separated and had the accident downtown.* Ophelia had laid it all out for me, even pointing to some of the notes in my organizer and showing me some of the pictures that were set between clear plastic photo holders. This felt too much like her closing argument and what would be considered exhibit A and exhibit B. I just happen to be the defendant on the losing end of a smoking-gun case. Pictures of me and my father. Pictures of me and my grandfather. A picture of me by a forest-green truck. Magnetic advertisements that read MISTER FIX-IT were applied to both side panels, right under the driver- and passenger-side windows.

Amidst Ophelia's revelations, my mind began tossing ideas and images around. There were instances when I felt pain coming on, but then it stopped. There was that woman again—the one who tried to attack me with a knife in an earlier nightmare—only this time she had a sundress on and he was approaching me with some sultry smile that was more promising than evil. Again, there was my concern for my dad and grand—

*Did she just say that they're no longer alive?* I found myself stuck between Ophelia's words; as if I was literally squeezed within the images, the foggy images, the fog alone. And now, here she was, standing before me with a box of things, passing them to me and asking me to leave her home.

*Here's five hundred dollars to help you out. Don't worry about paying me back. I just want you to get back on your feet. Your truck is outside. Here are the keys.* And just like that, I was expected to be out of her home; out of her daughter's life. I couldn't imagine the repercussions if I went against Ophelia, and I didn't want to, either. By six thirty I was back under the covers, trying to catch up on as much sleep as possible. Long day ahead. And now it was sometime after ten and all of a sudden *this* woman was in my face.

*The chick in the nightmare.*

Her mouth was reaching for mine, but just then I put my palm over her face like a mask. I squeezed as though I had a nice grip on a basketball and I spun her around so that now *she* was against the wall. What I had to say next couldn't be prevented.

"I don't know how you found me, but you need to get the *fuck* up outta my face. Keep your crazy ass out of my life. I'm not gonna tell you *again*." *Again.* I heard myself say *again*, as if I'd told her this before. I was spooking *myself* now. *Whoa.*

She was obviously mortified. I didn't feel any resistance against my hand; no fight in her. So I took my hand from her mouth and I backed away from the confines in which I had her. Her face had turned soft and her eyes saddened. There were some tears caught up, but they didn't fall. It was just a stillness about her. Remorse. Loss. Surrender?

She looked down at the floor.

The door to the room opened behind me, and some guy stood there.

I turned back to her and was shocked by how close she had come. Her hand reached for my cheek and she smoothed it along my skin.

"What happened to us?"

I didn't answer.

Again she asked, "What happened to us, Danté?" The words came out in more of a pathetic sigh and lacked spirit. And now the tears *did* fall. She appeared to run out of gas (thank God) as she stepped around me and headed through the door. Before she was out of sight, there was that last look over her shoulder that said so much and so little all at once.

*Why are you doing this?*

And I had to admit to myself that I felt her pain. Part of me felt sorry while another part thought about the nightmares. For sure, that was her. And seeing her here in what I considered a most secure environment just added fuel to my fire. It was time to go. Where I was going, I didn't know. I just knew I was getting the hell up outta there.


LEAVING THE King mansion was bittersweet. At one point during my stay there I felt embraced, as if I might spend the rest of my life there. Yeah, there was the pool, the great lawn, all the comforts and luxuries that kings and queens enjoy. But it was so much more than that. The mansion was nothing but a building. What made it "home" for me was being fed and pampered, so there was a sense of security and certainty. What made it *special* for me was feeling worthwhile, helping where I could, correcting computer issues, and fixing things around the property, indoors and out. Even if it was to go to the local Publix supermarket to buy hornet spray and then aim and shoot it at a nest that plagued Ophelia's sense of calm. Sure, this sounds so simple, but it was through these acts that I felt a sense of contribution and inclusion on various levels in the King home. It could be something simple like cleaning, mopping, or spackling tiles in the shower. It could be more involved, like when I spent all day cleaning the garage. *Whatever.* This felt like *family.* It felt like something I really missed. But then, add to that the love and attention I was getting from Dancer, and you could say I had the best of all worlds.

And now I was suddenly stripped of all that in one wave of a wand. It was as if a decree came down from the queen: *off with his head*! It was drastic and I wondered why Ophelia didn't just cut my *dick* off!

# [ FOURTEEN ]

## STACY

MY PROBLEM WAS more serious now because I had not changed my mind about wanting Danté back and yet I couldn't reach him. It was damn frustrating, to tell the truth. I still didn't have Danté's cell number—his old number had been disconnected. It was hard to tell if he even had a cell phone still. I had Sam do some more spying for me, since he was privileged still to go in and show the house whenever, to whoever. Shit, worst-case scenario, he could get a friend to go in, show them the house, just so he could follow through with *my* wishes. And it wasn't like I wasn't invested in Sam. The new home I bought made him at least $4 grand in commissions. So, really, I wasn't try'na hear the word *no* to any of my requests.

*Sam, I just need you to keep an eye out for me.* That's all I had to tell him. And sure as Sam came through in the past, he came through for me again. Only this time he wasn't giving me information that I wanted to hear.

"I don't understand. We were just there the other day," I

told Sam on a call. "What do you mean, he's not there any-more?"

"I'm tellin' you, Stacy. He's not there. The room he was in before is *empty* now. Saw it for myself."

"Okay, so maybe he moved in with—" Just the thought of it made me wince.

"Ahh, before you go jumping to conclusions, here's what I figure. His truck is gone. The green Blazer you told me about? The one we saw in the driveway? It's not there any-more. I stayed out there almost all day yesterday; lined up potential buyers for the entire afternoon. No sight of this guy. I even ran a few things by the paralegal who works for her—you know, the one who let us in? And trust me, by the look of relief on her face, that boy is *gone*."

"Okay. So where did he go, Sam?"

"Stacy, I am *not* the FBI. But I will say this: if this rela-tionship between your guy and the daughter is worth any-thing—"

Sam's suggestion made sense, even though a part of me rejected the idea. Taking a step back and looking at this all with another set of eyes, I'd have to say I was in denial. But, I *know* Danté knows who I am. I saw it in his eyes the other day when he pushed me up against the wall. And sure, he scared the shit outta me when he grabbed me like that; and I honestly don't know what I did to get him so angry. But my only other guess is that he's tryin' to shed his past. For whatever reason, he's playin' dumb so he can start this new life; a new life without me? Well, if that's the case, and if my Danté is really trying to play me so he can work this new piece-of-ass singer he's fuckin'? He's got another thing comin'. I'm just *not* about to give up that easy.

# DANTÉ

My days and nights tend to go by fast. And thank God for the good weather here in the South, because it makes it a whole lot easier for me to live in my truck. Oh, the truck is no longer a truck, but a van. I traded the Blazer in a few days after I left the mansion, and I was able to get my hands on a sturdy cargo van. It was big enough so that I could fit one of those fold-down futon beds just right; a little lucky move I got from Craigslist for eighty bucks. So, I sleep comfortably at night, in long johns if need be. That was another investment I had to make, some hand-me-downs from a local thrift shop. It was but a week's worth of clothes that I wash twice a week—you do the math. Most times I'll wear clothes for two days and even fall asleep in what I'm wearing. And if it gets too cold I'll run the truck and warm it up for a while, or for the whole night, depending on how cold. I learned that no matter how erratic gas prices get, the cost of heating the truck for a night beats paying a monthly rent or mortgage any day. And the economy calls for this nowadays, the low-cost living and the low-cost state of mind. In my case, I just see it as breathing room for a guy to stack some paper.

Speaking of paper, the documents in the wallet that Ophelia gave me were useless, except for the registration and title for the Blazer. Thank God I had *that*, otherwise I'd have nowhere to sleep. That five hundred dollars she gave me, if used for a hotel or motel room, would've run out before my second cup of coffee. Now, as for the license and credit cards, the license was as good as gold—everyone

needs ID. And there was no disputing that this guy pictured on the license looked just like me. I mean, hold it up
to my face and we're identical except for my new scraggly
hair style and the six-o'clock shadow on my face. But otherwise, what could I do with these rough playboy looks, get
cash? None of the credit cards in the wallet was working.
Even the bank debit card was worthless because I didn't
know the PIN code. When I went to Bank of America (the
issuing bank, printed on the plastic and a book of checks),
they told me the account was blocked for some reason. I
thought nothing of it since I wasn't familiar with any bank
account. So, I figured, *nothing ventured, nothing gained*.
What am I gonna do, argue? I wouldn't feel right. Because I
honestly *don't remember*.

There was also a black leather organizer that Ophelia
told me she had looked through in order to find some contacts. On the day I left, she pointed out a few highlighted
names for me; people she'd contacted herself. One was a
bishop of some kind, and it was marked URGENT in red.

"I strongly urge you to call Pastor Bishop," she said on
that morning she kicked me to the curb. "He says he knows
you well, and—" yada, yada, yada. There was also some
woman named Ms. Thomas that was highlighted. Apparently, Ophelia had talked with her as well and there was
talk about her being one of my *number-one clients* and that
if I needed someplace to stay, her doors were open. Well,
that sounded good, and it would be great; that is, if it
weren't a door that was opened halfway across the country.
And I did plan on calling these folks, but another thing I
needed was a cell phone. The phones out here are cheap

these days, but you need credit to get the service; and according to the Sprint and T-Mobile stores I went to, my credit was jacked up. Something about a *charge off* on my record. I shrugged at the idea and kept it movin'. They had *no idea* how perfectly fine I was with that. But I at least had to get one of those prepaid phones to call Dancer. No matter how twisted her moms had acted in this whole mess, I still have strong feelings for her. I still wanna see her.

Meanwhile, I thank God I don't have kids I need to look after. That would get in the way *big time*. What would they do, sleep and eat in the truck with me? What would they do, shower in LA Fitness and eat Cup-a-Soups all day until they were blue in the face? Not to mention their momma. *Yeah right.* So then, my only responsibility right now is to take care of myself. Odd jobs here and there to take care of the minor maintenance like laundry and food and a membership at the gym would be just fine. I figured I'd go with the whole Mister Fix-It title since (according to what I've learned) that was supposed to belong to me anyway. And I guess I'd be the handyman that most people can call on when there's a need. A little ad on a community bulletin board here and there and word of mouth would work. Maybe in a year or so I'll have enough money saved up and I can dive into one of these foreclosures that have been popping up every week. All the handymen would get paid off those bad boys, 'cause the truth is we *like* to work. It's the comfortable, lazy folks who got ahead of themselves with their spending that led to the foreclosures. It's the people who didn't have backup and contingency plans that are caught up in this nonsense. Of course, not *everyone* can be included in those statistics. But I got my own opinions, and I guess *what will be will be.* I'd just like to grab a bunch of these folks and get them in some kind of boot camp. Give 'em a crash course in discipline and survival skills.

But I guess if I'm talkin' that way I gotta walk the walk. And it's probably just karma that I found myself doing that very thing in those post-Ophelia days. The reality is that I had to crawl before I could walk. I have to admit that the first few weeks were rough, getting myself situated after living so comfortably. My first purchase, besides the gas to keep my van alive, was a "stinger." It's basically a hot pot that you buy from Walmart; you plug it in and *shazam*! The water is superhot in minutes. I could use that for oatmeal in the morning, Cup-a-Soups at any other time. My other rituals would be bagels that I could heat up at Starbucks— thanks to Starbucks for those toasters and miniovens they put in a lot of outlets, because that kept my stomach full on *so* many occasions. There's also those little tuna lunches I'd get from Walmart for a buck and change—just the whole low-maintenance thing. I was able to get a membership at LA Fitness, which helped me to knock out two birds with one stone. I'd get my workout on and my shower. If my body needed a little pampering, LA Fitness even had the Jacuzzi, pool, and sauna. I'm not a fat boy, nor do I have a weight problem, so the sauna isn't for me. But it's nice to know there's the option. All told, I'm happy about my slim physique and my health.

Meanwhile, I spend hours at Starbucks reading local papers and looking for opportunities. Okay, and *yes*, I run into a pretty woman now and again to keep life interesting, but you'd never catch me jumpin' up to speak to every one of them who passes. At other times, I use the computers at Smoothie King, where you only need buy a drink to access the Internet. So, I go there to place ads and search for jobs and opportunities online.

Dancer still comes around. It felt different to make love to her in the days of my homelessness because we'd use hotel or motel rooms. I won't do her in the back of the van because I have too much respect for her; or maybe it's because I know the type of living arrangements she's accustomed to? Either way, I have strong feelings for her and want us to build something more substantial than just a quick fuck in the back of a truck.

Something else I had to be prepared for: once I *do* plant myself somewhere, it's gonna open up a whole new can of worms. The information about where I am (even in what city) will be more or less public. I'll have to trade my driver's license off and I wouldn't be able to get the new Georgia license unless I had a utility bill. No utility bill if I don't have a lease. So, in essence, I'm *forced* to live somewhere even if I don't want to. That *sucks* because I was appreciating this being somewhat invisible and unable to be reached. There was freedom and liberation that came along with homelessness; I guess that's one of the "pros" to go along with the "cons" of feeling disenfranchised and feeling like I don't belong. So, for the time being, I absorbed myself in the attitude, the state of mind, and the consciousness of a hobo; only I wasn't necessarily on foot. It was a way of life that was different and foreign, but it was one that I wasn't about to give up that easy. To make things so much more comfortable, the weather in Atlanta could be classified as *vacation weather.* Regardless if it was sunny or rainy, the climate would average around seventy to eighty degrees. So, the weather I could live with, especially if it was mine to enjoy for little or no cost.

AS FAR as doing business goes, it wasn't as hard as I thought it would be to build a client list down here in Georgia, but it wasn't *not* easy, either. Nevertheless, I got creative and met a few general managers in this or that hotel. In doing so, I could camp out in the hotel lounges, where there are microwaves, coffee, and even free breakfast if I hung around long enough. I thought about the Tyler Perry story, the Eartha Kitt story, and the Jim Carrey story, and how they all were homeless for different reasons and periods of time. But I was no singer or actor, and I wasn't necessarily good with the Rubik's Cube like Will Smith showed when he acted out the Chris Gardner story. I didn't see myself as a promising talent like those cats; not as a handyman, anyway. I mean, how many people would pay to see a movie about a handyman? Not many, I'm sure.

Now when I look back at those rough times, I'm sort of glad I went through them. Being homeless toughened my Teflon, and it kept me focused on things I needed to do for *me*. But I also have the utmost respect for those who've been living homeless for years and years. They must be stacking paper like crazy; either that or they just live free, without too many responsibilities. I just knew I couldn't be out there forever like that. I had way too much going for me in the way of energy and knowledge. No sense in that going to waste when it could be useful to other people. And if I can get *myself* working, especially after what I've been through, then others should be able to do it, too. But then, giving advice like that, I guess I'd have to be Danté the teacher, not Danté the handyman.

JUST FORTY days into my new routine, my itch for trouble must've needed scratching, because Trouble showed up unexpectedly, in threes.

It was one of those every-other-week get-togethers that Dancer and I had orchestrated. It wasn't too frequent, because her mother still had the iron fist on her ass. Hey, if Moms is in control of the roof that's over your head, and your singing career is not quite where it needs to be for you to be out on your own with bills paid; and if Moms is footing the bill so that you at least have a solid shot at making it happen, why argue? *Why go against the grain? Let Mom think she's getting what she wants, I suppose. And work your magic until your dream comes true.* That was my advice to Dancer. Yet, we still had our carnal desires and the want to maintain that very familiar, very sex-driven compulsion to be with each other, folded together and locked inside our own ways of satisfaction. So I decided it would be La Quinta Inn this time, except Dancer wanted to add some *spice*, she called it.

"Why can't we do it in the van?" Dancer asked, shooting me this deceptive smirk I'd seen in bed, mostly when she was about to get—she said—*naughty*. And the crazy thing was, my van was so tidy on this particular day. I had cleaned it out, deodorized, washed my clothes, and—*hey*, that's how I'd be living otherwise, right? Truthfully, everything was so orderly because I knew Dancer was coming to see me, and I suppose a part of me wanted to show her I was *okay*. Part of me wanted her to see that just because I was homeless didn't mean I had to *look* and *act* homeless, too. People didn't have to know my business, or that I was down on my luck. I wasn't trying to impress anybody. Well, maybe except for Dancer.

"You know how I feel about that, Dancer. Just because I'm on the futon doesn't mean *you* have to—" And there she went, with her spontaneous ass all up in my face, climbing from the front of the van into the back, showing me (rather than telling me) that she was all game. *Damn!* I loved the way she did this impulsive shit. Never planned. Never predictable. She'd just jump right into stuff without warning. And most times, the Dancer addict that I was, if she led the way, I was the tagalong, her number-one fan.

"Alright, hold on, Dancer. Lemme at *least* park the van out of sight or somethin'."

The girl didn't even answer. She was already back there doing a strip tease, pulling her blouse over her shoulders and making it clear that life was about to get interesting for us.

Now there was an urgency. *She* may not have realized it, but I did. At least the windshield offered a clear, head-on view of the inside of my living environment. So, whenever I wanted privacy, I'd park somewhere off-road, even a Walmart or Lowe's parking lot, and I'd pull down a dark green Hefty bag like a curtain. Even at night, my battery-powered light could be hidden from anyone passing by. But this was broad daylight, and if this was gonna be the usual bang-out between Dancer and me, then I'd need to more or less bury our existence so that the rocking and loud noises wouldn't be heard.

Just off I-20, in Lithonia, there's a big industrial area with a lot of auto-repair shops and other one-story factory-type buildings. I've parked within this environment on a few occasions already, as I have in areas across town, or in the middle of busy shopping areas, or even in a church parking lot. This was just my way of staying hidden in a world where *everything* costs money, including parking. Thank God parking is very liberal here, except not when you're knockin' boots.

I COULDN'T *wait* to work this out there in the back of van. I know I was trying to be a gentleman and all, and I know Dancer is not that type of chick. But, quiet as I kept it, this girl was one spoiled so-'n'-so. At home, she had every luxury a young girl could imagine. Her life had been paid for and cushioned through adolescence and puberty and then as a young adult. So, my giving it to her rough and rugged (but affectionately so) in the back of my van was *just* what her bourgie doctor ordered. Maybe it wouldn't make up for the crying she must've done through the years to get what she wanted, but it had to be a *start*!

Hefty bag secured, I climbed in the back and dived on top of her pretty, silly ass. I bit her neck unremorsefully, tickling her all over her half-naked body. I provoked giggles and convulsions and screams, and it didn't matter how loud she was. It didn't matter how much the van rocked. We were in a section of vacant commercial properties that hadn't seen commerce for months, maybe years. Not only that, I parked way back from the road and closer to the railroad tracks. Some sort of trash compactor blocked any possible street view of the van. So nobody was gonna hear or see us. And that was a *good* thing, because I was about to *murder* that pussy.

It didn't take me long to find Dancer's belly button. That was *the spot* on her body I knew was so sensitive that she'd squirm. But today, at seven o'clock in the evening, on the side of the railroad, I made a meal out of her navel. There was still enough room to kneel on the floor of the van, even with the bag of folded clothes I just cleaned at the laundry. Most everything else, like food and sneakers, were neatly packed in the crawl space under the futon. Leaning over my prey, I kept Dancer stretched out and I overpowered her with my left hand so that my strong grip kept her wrists constrained. At the same time, my right elbow and forearm pressed against her thighs. No question I had her trapped inside my intention to torment and tease and pleasure her. Her haunting cries only encouraged me to nibble more, and I eventually found myself between her legs, lapping and kissing and still teasing. Dancer knew that it was special for me to give her pleasure like this. And I could tell that she wanted it since she was freshly shaved; part of a past conversation we had about grooming and what it would take for me to *over*indulge. So that's what I did: I *over*indulged.

It was okay to release my grip now, since I was so sure that this was more of what she wanted, as opposed to the slight bondage and torment I had been executing. I have to say I got great joy out of seeing Dancer pulling her hair, biting her wrist, and basically going through the give-and-take of this excruciating pleasure. She managed to reach up enough to scratch at the side wall of the van, ripping a front-page newspaper article I'd taped there. I grunted, knowing that it was a collector's item she ripped—Barack on the cover of the *Atlanta Journal-Constitution*. Instead of getting angry and screwing up this perfectly sizzling moment, I got even. I pulled away and kissed her thighs with light pecks. I took my time, too, grazing my tongue close to her hot spot, then backing away again. And again. I could see that this was killing her, and I guess she didn't wanna be too bold and beg me to go back to the tongue kissing I was performing on her clit. And that was just the point: to have her spoiled ass do things she wasn't accustomed to. To bring her nose from "up there" to down here with us regular folk.

Now I stopped altogether. In the van, there's no music system yet, so I use the iPod that was with my personal property, and there's a dope set of headphones I got from that thrifty store, same place I got my clothes. On the iPod was a superdope remix of the Tony! Toni! Toné! hit "Anniversary." So, while that jam rocked, I caressed Dancer's leg while she lay there with that exhausted look on her face. It was part frustration, part satisfaction, and part *I want more*.

Dancer had done her little strip tease to set it off, so it was my turn now. Wiggling like I knew what I was doing; like I was the new Chippendales trainee, I made my little ugly faces as I showed Dancer the six-pack I'd been working on at LA Fitness. She smiled and soon had her nose against my abs like she was trying to smell *all* of me. But in Dancer fashion, she began eating at my abs, licking row by row until she was pulling my underwear down. I made it that much easier for her; I grabbed a bunch of her hair and manipulated her body around so that she was now kneeling on the floor with me sitting on the futon. I wasn't rough about it, but just rough enough for her to enjoy my bit of puppeteering. Next thing I know, Dancer had a mouthful of Geppetto. And although she didn't know it, I was the one being controlled by *her*. All I could do was sit back and enjoy this, hands either managing her head or stretched back. I got into my own husky moans and groans and couldn't have cared less about how loud I was.

"Turn over for me, baby."

The look on my face was *twisted*! Dancer had toyed with me on other occasions, flicking her tongue against my ass, and teasing me there while giving head. But never had she gone about it with any such determination as she implied at the moment. In fact, she went so much further. While I'm on my hands and knees up on the futon, naked from the waist down, Dancer reaches up under me, pulls my swollen penis back, and begins sucking me from behind. She shifts her attention back and forth, licking, sucking, and eating at my three most-sensitive areas. No lie, this woman had me cryin' like a wolf. I wanted to turn around, toss the girl on her back and pound her into submission, but true story—*I* was the one submitting! And between the work she did with her mouth, and the way her hand was grabbin' at me like I was a cow being milked, I lost all control. I guess it was reflex, but a spasm shot through me and at the same time I clutched Dancer's head so that she caught all of me in her mouth. I became so weak that the satisfaction left me a little dizzy. I reached for a bottle of water there on the floor. But before I could be rude and drink some for myself, Dancer grabbed the bottle and gulped down a third of the water. I was frozen by the seamlessness of it all: how she swallowed me, then washed it down right after. *Damn*. I couldn't say the words, but her actions had me so in *love*! And not that nasty defines what love is for me, just that Dancer so embraced spontaneity. She had such a raw rebellion about her, and I loved every raunchy second of it.

Still speechless, our quiet, undefined moment was rudely interrupted by three loud bangs on the side of the van. No question, I could've shit myself. And I'd later learn that the way my head jerked in response to the banging was the cause of three days of neck pains.

I pulled the Hefty bag aside to see a blitz of flashing red and blue cruiser lights. I was also blinded by bright halogen spotlights pointed directly at the windshield, not to mention the smaller flashlight rays that were swinging to and fro.

Squinting, I was sure that something was wrong here. But I was also sure that these were police officers; a *lot* of them.

"Put your hands where we can see them!" shouted an authority.

I carefully slid the plastic farther out of the way so as not to confuse these guys with what they could or could not see. I didn't have a single weapon in the van, unless you were counting Dancer, the most lethal of them all.

"How many are in the van?" a voice shouted. I still could not see the faces, merely ghosts amidst all the bright rays of light focused on me. I could see at least two cruisers, one of them unevenly parked on the embankment that leads to the train tracks. Another facing the driver's-side door, officers perched with guns drawn. *Fuck!* The critical importance of this was all so suddenly real.

"Just the two of us," I shouted back so they could all hear me beyond the confines of the truck. Then, to Dancer I said in a soft but hasty tone, "Girl, put some clothes on!" From the side glance I shot at her I could see her expression and how she was questioning my hostile attitude.

I could only think to myself what a *spoiled brat* she was. But that was *so* irrelevant right now.

"Okay. We're gonna need you to step out of the vehicle, slowly, one at a time."

That was a little confusing since we were a *mess* and that I had a choice to go through the side or the front. For the sake of stalling—time for Dancer to get herself together—I climbed through to the front driver's side and eased out so that I was standing with my hands reaching over my head. Yes, it was a little chilly out, and I didn't think to grab a coat or sweatshirt, but even *that* wasn't relevant right now. In my mind, while officers were frisking me, pressing me up against the truck and waiting for "the star of the show" to step out, I'm still wondering, *How did they find us?*

I could already hear the apprehension and upset in Dancer's voice as she made her way out of the van.

"I'm *comin'*. And could you get that *light* out my eye, *please*!?"

As I'm hearing this and while I'm being manhandled by these strangers in uniform, I'm also wagging my head, wishing I could disappear. The rest is a blur: *You're being charged with indecent exposure. The holding cell? Why are you putting handcuffs on me?! Or central booking? Do you know who my mother is? Young lady, you need to calm down before we restrain you. You're already restraining me!* Again, Dancer is crying out, *Do you know who my mother is*!? And while all this is going on, the activities in the immediate vicinity swirling around me like a small storm, I'm realizing some next-level energy in my life. Not a positive energy, but a force that was sweeping me into it.

I sat with my hands cuffed, in the back of a police cruiser, while one officer asked me a bunch of questions. Who was the girl to me? Why were we out here and not in a hotel room somewhere? Who was I? I wanted to say to him: *That's a damn good question, Officer.* Still, while I'm going through that, I watched officers as they investigated the back of my van, picking through my personal items, laughing and chatting among themselves. In my mind I'm thinking of everything in there, knowing there could be nothing incriminating, nothing that could take all this to another level. I noticed one officer who seemed to be in charge of everything got on a radio and I imagined him calling in the ingredients of this nasty soup being cooked before my eyes. In another police cruiser, Dancer sat in the back. I could see the distress on account of the fogged-up window where she was being held, as well as the vehicle rocked some as if an angry captive was confined within. *Who could that be?*

Maybe it was the sixth sense working, but something told me to turn around and look in another direction. Down the way, alongside the abandoned commercial building, a sharp, shiny white car sat idling with the headlights on. Whoever sat in it was on a phone call. Just as I assessed that, a sparkling black full-size vehicle rolled past where the white one was. There was a dust-raising sudden stop in the immediate vicinity of the police cruisers.

What happened next was something out of a movie. Ophelia King, all suited up in a red skirt suit, got out of her parked Mercedes and stepped up to one of the officers. Part of me was so happy right now; if there was anyone who was capable of straightening this out, it was a power attorney. The other part of me was saying, *God—no! Not her mother*!?

Ophelia was directed to see the officer in charge, and the two of them spoke there in the open, staged right there in the middle of the headlights and police strobe lights. Maybe the cops didn't realize this, but this was open court and this was Ophelia's justice.

Ophelia with her arms folded, listening to the officer in charge.

Ophelia's attention shifting to the left, where Dancer was detained.

Ophelia looking in my direction, the culprit. *Jesus*.

Ophelia with her brilliant smile and charismatic gestures.

Ophelia's manicured nails, piercingly beautiful eyes, and jet-black hair pulled back in a bun.

The commanding officer escorted Ophelia to where her daughter was seated. The window was lowered so they could speak. The conversation lasted all of one minute before Ophelia nodded at the officer. Next thing I saw was Ophelia's eyes swinging in my direction. The air was sucked out of my body as I braced myself for the consequences.

I'm not sure she could see my eyes, but I could surely see hers. It was Ophelia's wrath that (to me) was worse than any handcuffs, any judge, or any jury. Call me a coward, and a coward I will be, because I was suddenly more afraid of this woman than I was a lightning strike.

I squeezed my eyes and through closed lids I begged: *give me the guillotine.*

When I opened my eyes, and as if my prayers were answered, I watched as the officers released Dancer. Dancer and her mom walked to the Mercedes, and just as Ophelia was opening the driver's-side door, she stopped and looked in my direction. There was no anger or hate there. There was no emotion at all. In those eyes, it was all too clear: *justice is served.*

# [ FIFTEEN ]

FRIDAY NIGHT. RICE Street. Processing. Fingerprints. Police radios. Keys. Appraising eyes looked at me with every passing moment as both uniformed and plainclothes officers passed me. I was so far out of my element, seated on a sturdy wooden chair and cuffed to the chair's arm. Police lockers were standing to my far right and they were opened periodically as I awaited my fate. This was a world apart from the environment at the King mansion, and even the isolation of the van that I now called home. *Is that still home?*

"So, how serious are these charges?" I asked.

The officer winced, as if this was but a nuisance charge.

He shrugged as he explained, "It's nothing, if you ask me. I mean, if you look around here, this is a busy place with *real* crimes to solve." Shaking his head: "Yours is not a real crime, Mr. Garrett. If you'd just be patient with the process, I'll see if I can getcha out of here."

The relief I felt from his words gave me the second wind I needed.

To help things along, I said, "Listen, whatever the fine is, just let me know, I can get it, and you'll never hear from me again."

"I gotcha, Mr. Garrett. Just let me work things out."

"One more thing, sir. My van—"

The officer put his hand up. "Mr. Garrett, everything in your van is safe. It's been secured. I have your keys. I'm tellin' ya, it's all gonna be alright if you just let me do this."

I gestured that he wouldn't have any trouble out of me, and while 9:00 p.m. turned to 10:00, I recorded this place with my eyes and ears; not necessarily the law breakers that were escorted in, but the men and women who peopled the Fulton County police force. They were the characters in an unscripted play. Comedy. Drama. All of it entertaining me as I dozed off and thought hard about how I got here.

My daydream was cut short when a woman, bottle-shaped and black, in her forties, came into the squad room. She seemed to have the attention and respect of everyone present.

"Is this him?"

"Yes, Major."

The woman stood tall-like over me, her uniform dressed with insignias, credentials, and the requisite badge. It was obvious that she was the HNIC when she signaled the processing officer to give her a rundown. This was done right there, within feet of me.

When she heard it all, simple as it was to explain, she said, "That's it?"

"Afraid so, Major."

"Willis, let me have a word with you." The major spoke into a mic that was attached there on her shoulder. I soon learned that the Willis she spoke to was the commanding officer; the one who officiated at the proceedings where we were found and where only I was arrested. Yes, I thought about why just I was arrested when it was the two of us, Dancer and I, who were in the van bumpin' uglies. But I just as soon shook that from my mind every time it surfaced because I really didn't want her caught up in this. If I had to take the fall, pay the fine, or whatever, then *let it be.*

Major Chambers was apparently more in charge than I had gathered. I was escorted to a bench just outside her office and the vent overhead lent me some insight as to the truth about my circumstances.

"Willis, please tell me you not bringin' charges against this man and fillin' up my jail with nonsense when we got more important criminals out there to find?"

"Major, I followed protocol and called it in. Spoke to Lieutenant Chavez and we were about to issue summonses. But—"

"But *what*, Willis? I *know* Lieutenant Chavez told you to set 'im loose. I *know* he had to. No priors on this guy. The girl was of age, I understand?"

"Yep."

"So, where's the beef here? Git this joker out the judicial system. It's Friday; no need for no on-call judge. No need to tie up my jail any more than it is. You *know* we already overcrowded. Ain't no way this man gonna stand 'fore a judge within seventy-two hours. Even a mini-DA and attorneys is gon' tie up my complaint room. *Come on,* Willis?"

I was so *deep* into this conversation that I wanted to shout. I wanted to shout OPHELIA KING, DAMMIT!

Because I *knew* she was the key component here. I *knew* this Willis guy wasn't comin' clean with the major, and that it was likely Chavez (the officer who *wasn't* present) who had some kind of allegiance with Ms. King. But I held my tongue. This seemed to be working out in my favor, and I didn't wanna screw it up. There was also the conflict here: sure, this was no big deal to the police, and maybe it was Ophelia who called the police, maybe following Dancer and me until we had the van shaking? But then again, with me this was still feeling like a violation, especially after what I had been through just a month earlier at the mansion. The other thing was, I didn't want to see this get any more complicated than it had. Okay, yes: Ophelia King was probably using the police to attack me for jumping her daughter's bones. But how could I blame her? If it was me, I'd probably use a nuclear warhead if I could to interrupt some stranger trying to make moves on my daughter. *Probably.*

Thing is, I *know* I'm a good man. Sure, I have my sexual pet peeves, but who doesn't? And really, what part of sex *is* considered *normal*? Is it the act itself? Is it the state of mind you need to have to get aroused in the first place? And what is and isn't considered permissible by religious standards, or even by pornographic standards? I mean, isn't this all just semantics and don't we all just wanna be loved to the limit? *What's so bad about that, Ms. Ophelia King? Didn't you engage in the same so-called ungodly activity to bring Dancer to life? So why not cut a brother a break?*

I was talking to a wall to think that what I had to say could be heard by Dancer's mom. It was that much harder when you considered the emotions of a mom and what type of man she might consider worthy of her daughter's coochie.

# OPHELIA

I've gotta say I felt so evil to use my resources like I did, to get that man locked up. And I'm supposed to be the woman to keep men *out* of jail? But we're talkin' about my daughter here. And I can't explain it any other way—I don't care how mad Dancer is at me. But finding love has got to be more challenging than Mom bringing home a stray pup from the hospital. She can stay locked in her studio for a month if she wants. Mom is right in this case.

"Lieutenant Chavez, please." I couldn't sleep until I knew Danté was out of custody. Plus, I had Dancer back and I had settled down from the high; all the commotion near the railroad tracks. *The railroad tracks! Jesus, I've raised that girl so much better than that. Sex in the back of a van near a railroad track!?* I coulda screamed when I heard this. When I got the call from Chavez. It sure pays to have friends in high places.

"Hey, Lieutenant. I was just thinking that I might've gone too far to have that boy locked up, and I was wonder-ing— *Really?* I see. Well, does he need bail or anything?"

When I hung up the phone it dawned on me that nature had taken its course. Apparently the girl named Stacy got involved. It was the one noted in Danté's organizer; the girl that Pastor Bishop talked about when I called. And so it was true: he did have a woman he loved, and who loved him. I only hoped Danté could get back to being himself, with the family that loves him. He did seem like a good man, and if that's the case he should find some resolution in his life. Every good person deserves resolution and closure.

## STACY

This has worked out so much better than I expected. I mean, I expected to break up their little rendezvous. But I didn't think the police would actually let him off the hook without so much as a citation? Because, even though Danté and I have been going through our issues, he's the last person I want to see hurt. In the end, the truth is, his hurt is my hurt. And now that I've reached a certain level of success, I didn't want any more hurt. No more pain.

"Why you lookin' at me like that?" I asked Danté. He was sitting in the passenger's seat of my brand-new Lexus, the very place I've pictured him over and over again. "Why do you think I wanna *hurt* you, Danté? All I ever wanted to do was *love* you. We had so much going. We were soul mates. We *are* soul mates."

It didn't matter how Danté was staring at me. All that mattered was that I had my man back. Sure, he was a little (what did they call it?) insubordinate. But that was, I guess, a consequence of the big picture. But *wow*. I can't begin to explain how incredible it feels to have him back. And I couldn't wait to give him that warm welcome home that he deserved.

"Don't worry, Danté. I have all your valuable stuff in my trunk. I didn't wanna see anything happen to it out there near the deserted area."

"What valuable stuff?"

"In your van. And whatever happened to the Blazer? Oh, it doesn't matter. I can buy us *ten* Blazers if we need it." I couldn't understand why he had this *crazy* look on his face. I mean, was that what they meant by *crazy* love? "And I had your truck brought to my house, so *that's* safe, too."

"What the *hell*?"

"Baby, it's *okay*. Really. You need to know that *whatever it is, I got you*. Listen, I couldn't wait to tell you this. I know you gonna be mad at me, but let me tell you the whole story before you trip. Remember I was cleanin' up at your apartment back in the Bronx? I used to organize your papers, your mail, and so forth? Well, baby, it will take a lot of explainin' and a lot more understandin' on your part, but you and I are the proud new owners of a five-bedroom home right here in Fulton County. I can't wait to tell you how I did it. . . ."

# DANTÉ

I felt trapped. It wasn't just that she had all my personal property *and* my van in her possession. It didn't have *anything* to do with her showing up at the police precinct to bail me out or rescue me; it was so much more than that. To end my run-in with the Fulton County Police Department, there was no bail. I found out that Chavez, whoever he was, screwed up seriously by going along with Ophelia King's influence. To let Dancer go without so much as a record and to put me through the ringer, so to speak, was (as I thought) dead wrong. Favoritism, I figured it to be, although

I'm sure there was some other legal or official terminology for it. Either way, to squash things and keep everyone happy and healthy, I guess Major Chambers put her foot down and cleared me of all charges. She was real, extra, super-duper nice to me, too, even passing me her business card and mentioning that I should call her if I had any issues. *Wow. And did I ever have an issue now.*

I walked out of the police station sometime later expecting that I'd have to take a cab or something to get to my van, and look who pulled up in the shiny white Lexus. It was her again, only she didn't feel threatening, at least not to a man who was down on his luck.

"Hey, superstar." If she was trying to be dazzling, it worked. She had some form-fitting jeans on, a tube top that allowed for a good look at her chiseled midsection, and a jeans jacket to match her slacks. "Goin' my way?"

Don't ask why it was so easy for her to talk me into the ride, but I didn't see a reason why I shouldn't. I didn't see her as a threat. Not at all. And now we were together in the warm, leather seats of her car, driving Lord knows where, to a house she said she bought for *us*?

"Where we headed?"

"I was thinking it's Friday night. I was thinkin' we might need to get a little weight off our minds. Mind if I treat you to a drink?"


IT WAS a good thing this spot had food, 'cause I was starved. I didn't take the time to add it all up, but I had cum *real hard* earlier that night; there was the whole exhaustive altercation with the police, and now I was in the hands of a woman who I had been having head-throbbing nightmares about. A brother could use a good chicken dinner right about now.

Club ABC was so busy with well-dressed black folk that I couldn't help being proud for the owners who put it together. The music was on some just-right soul tip, the flat plasma screens all over the place either had the sports, the videos, the news, or advertisements goin' on all at once, and the furnishing wasn't cheesy. It was a comfortable at-home plush atmosphere with sectional couch arrangements and cushioned stools parked at a generous amount of high tables.

Within minutes, Stacy and I were seated at an intimate setting for two, set apart from the crowd of a hundred or so. Soon thereafter, I was munching on a salad and waiting for the barbecued-shrimp platter we'd ordered.

"I see you still on the eating-good routine."

"Sure. I love to eat good. And this is close to the only unfried foods they have on the menu. Salad and shrimp work fine for me. How come you not eatin'?" I said.

"I just enjoy watchin' you. A couple of these will do me right. I'm celebratin', baby."

I couldn't figure it out, but sitting across from Stacy felt okay. Talking to her felt so familiar. Together with the food and drinks, this all was no different than one much-needed massage on my mind and body.

And that's just what it became awhile later.

We were in this brand-new home that Stacy said was recently built. She had shown me around, pointing out that she was still in the planning stages for furniture, as well as the paint she wanted. The home smelled so new and everything was so untouched and fresh, and it was all so intoxicating but also conflicting in my head. I knew I deserved this and that I'd one day have it all, but for it to be handed to me on a (so to speak) platter like this was something out of a storybook.

"And this is the master bedroom. Isn't it lovely," announced Stacy. And she spun around with her arms outstretched like a fourth Dream Girl.

*Your closet. Your side of the sink.* The his-and-hers towels. In this room is where *you* can set up your little desk to keep all your papers, invoices, and stuff related to clients. You'll have your own office right here at home, baby! And she did this throughout the house: this will be *mine;* that will be *yours.* And so what if the smallest closets and smallest bedroom were set aside for me. It got to a point where I thought, *Up until now I kept everything in a cargo van, so what the hell.*

If the purpose of showing me the house and all the talk about how she was gonna *upgrade me* and whatnot was meant to get a broke man excited and all absorbed into this new *Stacy experience,* then it was surely working. The drinks we'd had earlier didn't hurt, either. Of course, I was *tellin'* myself that I was clear-headed. But truthfully, she could've told me the sky was green and I would've believed it, especially with the great food and white wine. Because, at this point, what reason did I have *not* to believe her? And as for Stacy, she was very animated about it all, so buzzed and so talkative and tossing all sorts of promising futures my way. She was full of suppositions and dreams already fulfilled. This will be the baby's room. This will be the guest room. This room will be for my shoes and clothes. I can't lie: I was standing there spellbound, feeling a little like Cinderfella, if there was such a character.

Somewhere after midnight Stacy popped open another bottle, some 150-proof cognac this time. I urged her to make mine a *real* small shot. I heard it wasn't good to mix liquors, but I was sure a little bit wouldn't hurt. After a somewhat uncommitted toast, my host, rescuer, and sponsor put on some Isley Brothers, and even on an MP3 player with miniature speakers, this music was soothing. And that's the mood I was in, soothed and relaxed like some clay; putty in Stacy's hands.

The drinks were enjoyed in a warm Jacuzzi, where we talked more about the future, as well as Stacy going to great extents to remind me about our past. *Remember when we first met in the elevator? Remember when I gave you hell that night at the bowling alley? Remember when we went to see Keyshia Cole and Donnell Jones and I met that actor? Remember when we got all crazy at Uno?* Stacy's recalls were bouncing around in my head, and I honestly tried to put the pieces together, but I kept on drawing a blank. At a certain point, she gave up, frustrated with me, but in a friendly, understanding way. And she went back to all the jibber-jabber and how the basement would be the family room and how there would be another "private" area down there where she could hide from the world.

"And I can't wait to get you the *new* Cadillac Escalade, and a *new* wardrobe, and—" On and on and on she went with what she was gonna buy, while in my mind I'm wondering, *Why do I need a new Cadillac Escalade?* And, *What's wrong with the clothes I already have?* And, *Kids? Don't we hafta be in love first?* All those questions in my head were battling with the mother of all questions: *Where she's getting all this money?*

We took turns executing hot-oil massages and I came to love the softness of her skin and the fullness of her breasts. Something told me her breasts had been augmented, but I was too buzzed and too excited to care. It was all good, as far as I was concerned. The intimacy graduated to kissing until both of us embraced in the oily water, inevitably becoming one body. I found myself attached to Stacy even though images of Dancer still popped up in my mind. From the Jacuzzi, to the large jet-stream shower, Stacy and I eventually headed for the bedroom. I was still toweling myself dry when she switched on the iPod and set it to play one of those old-school songs by Lenny Williams.

"Remember we used to let this play back in Park Chester? And we used to make love all night with the windows open?"

I tried to keep from making a face; to keep from showing the confusion that was there anytime she brought up *the past.*

*"I looooooove youuuuuuu. I neeeeeeeeed youuuuuuuuuu
Oh-oh-oh-oh-oh-ooooooooooooooooooh"*

After swallowing down the last of my drink, I went to lie on an air mattress that sat about two feet from the floor. And as if she needed to give me an excuse, Stacy said, "It's just temporary until my furniture arrives. Remember, I just moved here two days ago."

*Babble on, sister.* I wish I could've just come out and said *shut the fuck up* because every other minute there was an excuse, a promise, or *something* sensational coming from her mouth. I just wondered if there was a *normal* thought in her brain; like the stuff that average, broke folks like me might want to hear about. At what point was I supposed to say, *None of that highfalutin shit you talkin' matters to me!* But of course I kept my mouth shut because that would've ruined the moment—a moment that had encouraged me to grow hard and erect and ready to find a home, *figuratively.*

A DUD. That's what happened when we finally got into it. Yes, my dick was hard and I was excited and ready to make it happen with this girl. But I didn't really need to get off, since that had been my reality just hours earlier, with a woman I *really* had feelings for. Forgive me, Father, but for the moment I was just going along with this to get a head start and to maybe end the struggle ahead of me. Blame it on the cognac if you will, but I was feeling real scruple-less right now. I was ready to start livin'! Except, lil' Danté had other plans. The erection I took to the mattress started to die fifteen minutes into the blow job she administered. It wasn't her fault, I can attest to that because she was doin' *marvelous* work down there, like she was a professional at it. Like she was once a—

And that's when my erection got soft, even with my eyes squeezed shut, trying my *damnedest* to maintain. It was a no-go. The images of this woman somehow manufacturing these feelings in my mind, the thoughts that this was all contrived and phony caught me off guard, like some swift left hook to my conscience. Those images mixed with thoughts of Dancer and how she must be crying her eyes out. The police came into the picture with the flashing red and blue strobe lights and I felt myself rocking, like Dancer and I were in the van; only it wasn't Dancer and I, it was me rocking inside Stacy's mouth, trying like hell to keep this up when it was already feeling so *over*. I did start to grow stiff again. But then my eyes eased open and I could see Stacy's sudden smile there in the glow of the moon's light. At that instant I got a strange look into her mind (through her eyes), and I got this weird idea that she thought she was *succeeding* here! But I also sensed some sort of deception in those eyes of hers, even as she went back to work on me. Somewhere under my closed eyelids I saw the white Lexus parked out there where the police had trapped us off. And then I thought about the ride from the police precinct . . . in that *same* white Lexus? *Oh shit. Of course! It wasn't Ophelia who called the police. It was Stacy. And she sat and watched it all from her car!* And that did it for me. I fell back off my elbows and crash-landed into the small pile of pillows.

"Baby, what's wrong?" she asked.

I lied and said, "Maybe it's just been a long day. I have been through a lot." And maybe there *was* a little truth in that. But I also knew my body and mind. And my mind was telling my body that this was *just not happening*.

Stacy shrugged and shifted her body so that she was lying against me.

"It's okay, boo. I understand. Besides, there's more to love than making love, right? Remember you used to say that to me? Well," Stacy touched her finger to the tip of my nose before she said, "I'm in agreement. Let's go to bed."

And that's just how it was left. I dozed off into the dead

silence that rural America ensures. No dogs barking. No police sirens. No shouting neighbors. But that's just what I was seeing and hearing in my sleep. The phone was ringing and someone was asking for their sink to be fixed because *we can't wash our dishes.* A police siren was shooting past and at the same time someone was blasting Big Pun. My dad's head reaches under the sink where I'm working and says, *Hey, soon as we finish this I wanna head over to Home Depot over near Whitestone. They're closing and everything is half price.* From the conversation under the sink I somehow found myself in the back of an ambulance, where I'm crying man-tears, trying to be tough while my grandfather is lying on a gurney, the EMS workers going through various procedures to keep him alive. Somewhere along the rocky ride through the Bronx streets I realize it's not my grandfather but my father on the gurney. The image faded to black and there was a flat line.

I was shaken by all that transpired in my sleep and found myself sitting up with my hands over my face. I was sweating and shivering all at once. I was also alone in the bed.

*"Stacy?"* Everything was dark in the master bedroom except for the red and green indicator lights on the DVD player and digital clock radio. "Stacy." I was a little louder, a little more concerned. She wasn't in the bathroom or the walk-in closet that extends past the bathroom. I checked the other three bedrooms on the second floor and they were empty. What made me check the closets in those rooms, I can't say; I guess it was just instinct. And that's the way I did it through the rest of the house. The rooms. The closets inside the rooms. I even checked outside the house,

the backyard, and the garage. The Lexus was still parked beside my van. *Nothing.*

Back inside the house, I cut on the kitchen light and stood with hands on my hips.

I noticed coins on the floor leading to the pantry, and I stepped over and pulled open the door. Sure as there were cans of soup, bags of chips, and paper plates, Stacy was curled up in a fetal position on the closet floor, 100 percent naked. She had been crying, and her glassy eyes looked up at me with fear and then anger.

My first thought was that she needed help. So I bent down to give her my assistance.

And as if she were a tiger and I was reaching for her food, the woman scowled at me.

*"Get away from me!"* The growl in her voice was enough to give me goose bumps. And I immediately backed away. Before I could think twice, she came again with, *"You don't love me!"*

*Wow. Is this some kind of delayed reaction from earlier events?* I couldn't imagine how she had come to this conclusion on her own, unless I had been talking in my sleep. And I can't even rule *that* out of the equation. But if I was never spooked before, I sure was now. She wouldn't come out of the closet. When I reached for her, she seemed ready to scratch and kick.

I couldn't sleep. I wasn't sure who this woman was, even if things were clearing up for me. Even if I was beginning to put the pieces to my puzzle together. I just knew I'd had enough and that it was time to go. The house, the promises of peace and comfort and security were all part of an illusion to sugarcoat something that wasn't there. *Love wasn't there.*

What was complicated was that this woman had my belongings in the trunk of her car, so she said. She also had the keys to my van. And what's more, one of the tires on the van had apparently caught a flat since I'd driven it the day before. I did have my wallet and a couple hundred in cash. But I wanted everything back. I *deserved* everything back without so much as an explanation as to why—why I needed to leave this woman once and for all.

# CONCLUSION

Why didn't I just ask her to let me have my stuff so I could leave? Why didn't I just give it to her straight—no chaser the next morning? Well, the truth is, things were more complicated than that. I didn't *have* to ask Stacy for my stuff. She brought it to me, along with a few other surprises.

I was in the kitchen, pouring milk into a bowl of Rice Krispies when Stacy appeared, still in her bathrobe. It was about 10:00 a.m. When I woke up a half hour earlier, she still wasn't in the bedroom. But I gave up wondering and worrying. Right about now, it was time to plan my escape. Just the thing I was thinking when Stacy showed up.

"You're leaving me, aren't you."

I said nothing. Just turned to her and gave her the once-over with no expression in my eyes.

"You all are always leaving. You never stay. Well, I'm not

gonna stop you. *Here.* I gotchu your shit. And here's your keys, too." I hadn't noticed, but she had a box of my things at her feet. She thrust it forward with her toes. Then the keys were tossed on the counter where I was fixing my quick breakfast. "At some point we're gonna need to talk about dissolving our partnership."

My face squeezed into its own level confusion before I asked, "What does *that* mean?"

"Well, you were out of touch for a while, but I didn't see any reason why I shouldn't proceed with our plans to get our house, to settle in Atlanta; you know, all the stuff we talked about. Remember that night at Uno's?"

I used my hand like a duster, wiping all the imaginary dust from the air between us. *Screw all that; what we talked about, what we used to do. I remember none of that, and wasn't trying to.* At the same time, I asked, "Do you mind speaking English about what you mean?"

After a deep breath, Stacy said, "Well, baby, I sort of had you cosign for me on a few things." I cocked my head back. But she was still explaining. "And that's how I've been able to build our nest egg. I had to build my credit, and *use* the credit so that *more* banks would issue credit, to the point that I now have a few hundred thousand dollars in credit. Remember that first credit card I received? Well, it wasn't *exactly* a surprise. Thanks to you, that card was guaranteed. So, yes. We're partners."

"So, you used me. You—you stole from me?"

"Not really, baby. We were virtually husband and wife, almost. And you would've agreed anyway, right? I mean, I would do it for the love of *my* life."

"Stacy, I don't remember cosigning any—"

"See, and that's the real *beauty* in this situation, Danté. You *don't remember.* So then—" She stalled for a minute, then she said, "Actually, you *did* cosign. I remember even if you don't. It was back in the Bronx when—"

"You're a *liar,*" I said, spilling some of the Rice Krispies as I confronted her.

"Are you gonna choke me out like you did at that woman's house?" Stacy was bold, bracing herself for a fight while she spoke.

I thought about back then and how I had snapped. I stopped myself. I had more discipline than to get rough with a woman, even if she *did* deserve it. But that didn't stop me from raising my voice.

"You know what, Stacy? You're poison. *Poison pussy* is what you are. And your ghetto past is gonna catch up with you."

"*You're* from the ghetto," she responded, as if that was evidence to condone her actions.

I was still close enough to put my finger in her face. "I'm not talkin' about where you live on this planet, Stacy. I'm talkin' about where you live *up here.* In your *brain.* The way you think is *twisted,* and it's not righteous. You can say whatever you want, it cannot be justified—no way, no how."

Stacy stood there with the whole *well what are you gonna do about it?*

"You know what, Stacy? I may not have *all* my memory, but I *do* have my common sense. I have common sense enough to know I'm done with you. And nothing you did can hold me or keep me. I'm gone. *Gone,* you hear me!?"

"And you're leavin' all *this* behind."

By the way she said *all this,* I could swear she was also

implying her body was part of that package. I huffed when I realized she was helpless and didn't get the point here.

"*Whatever.* Whatever you did doesn't matter. I don't care. I'm doin' just fine with what I got and I don't need a shiny car or a five-bedroom house to prove it. You just go on with your life, and let me live mine," I said, calm and collected now.

"Danté, you really are lost. So different from the man I once knew. But you know what else? I *ain't* stupid, Danté. I'm thinkin' you're choosing to block certain things and certain people from your memory."

"Why would I do that? That's the stupidest thing I ever heard."

"I remember you once said to me that you were tired of the grind up in the Bronx. You were feeling alone without your father and grandfather in business with you. Now you get down here, you have an accident, you get introduced to the good life—"

"What good life? You? *This* is the good life?"

Stacy wagged her head and twisted her lips. "Naw. Not me. You were livin' in a mansion for a minute. Plus, you had some of this good southern love that we got here. You likin' it down here, and it's a new way of life for you."

I approached Stacy again, close enough to feel her nervous breathing. "I'm not likin' it, Stacy. I'm *fuckin' lovin' it.*"

"Well, thank you for that. Now, if you don't mind, I'm just gonna finish my inexpensive breakfast and—matter fact, your Rice Krispies are stale." *And I'm not just talking about the food.* I poured the bowl into the sink and ran water behind it. The sooner I got away from this woman, the better.

"So that's it. You don't want any of this, any of the fruits of my labors—"

"*Your labors*? You're tellin' me you used me as a cosigner to get credit, and that's *labor*?"

While I'm saying this, I'm thinking of all I'd seen and heard. I'm listening *now* to stuff she'd said *then*. I'm thinking about the credit cards in my wallet and how I'd tried to use them but found they were blocked. I'm thinking about how I tried to get a cell phone at Radio Shack and how they told me my credit wasn't sufficient. *For a simple cell phone, my credit wasn't sufficient?* I was getting sicker by the moment. This woman had ruined my credit? And I figured I had to have credit at one time, or else where did the credit cards come from?

The headaches were starting. And while I was holding my head with two hands, I was seeing a big IKEA truck and a bunch of people jumping out of vehicles with loads of shopping bags. I could've exploded. Instead, I grabbed my box of things she brought to me and headed for the door. I pulled the door open and exposed the dark and troubled house to a bright Saturday morning. But even if it had been raining, this was a liberating moment. Flat tire and all, I drove slowly out of this crazy woman's driveway, determined that I'd never see her again. This meant *freedom*.

# NEW YEAR'S EVE

It's been almost two months since the drama in Fulton County. But I've learned fast how things can change without notice in this lifetime. I keep in touch with Dancer, but only via e-mail. We've agreed to let our relationship breathe so that we could both work on getting our lives together. I've also apologized to her mom, to try to mend things. But after the apology I had another issue to discuss with her. And come January 2, I was gonna be a client of hers so she could go after Stacy for the financial fraud she committed against me. Ophelia assured me that Stacy would choose to go for a financial settlement rather than face criminal charges.

Stacy also has some other issues. Now that she has property closer to where she once lived, her old enemies have come out of the woodwork and have vandalized her Lexus and her house. I felt bad for her, considering how much I knew about her past and that none of that mess was her fault—the ex-boyfriend being shot up; the sisters of the ex blaming her for a setup. But, now that I know what I know about her, I often wonder if that was something she might've done. I mean, if she'd commit fraud and try to sabotage my life, if she had so many twisted states that she could ease in and out of without a moment's notice, then what else was she capable of? The resolve for me in that case was to rest on the idea that *you reap what you sow*. So then it would be up to a higher power to determine her fate. But that wasn't stopping me from my meeting on January 2.

As far as my sorry life goes, Mister Fix-It was still my company name. Except, I changed my direction. I'm living out of my van still, and keep myself a good forty minutes southeast of Cascade, up in Conyers. Yes, I still fix the plumbing and electrical problems. Yes, the market is great for skilled people like me, and I always get calls from real-estate investors. But that's all secondary income now. I now use the company name for my new profession.

THE WAY the promoter oversold this event on New Year's Eve was a damn shame. Two hotel rooms at the Hampton and two strippers were definitely *not* enough to satisfy the demand. There must've been 150 women between the two rooms. I needed air! Thank God he had it set up so that me and the other stripper, "Joe the Plumber," were to switch rooms every half hour from 10:00 p.m. to 1:00 a.m., with a fifteen-minute break in between. That meant Joe and I had to put on a total of five performances between the two rooms.

But this wasn't just any old New Year's Eve party. This was a bachelorette party for a chick named Cindy. And if Cindy wasn't the finest woman I've met in ages, then I had to be deaf, dumb, and blind.

Joe the Plumber is my partner, who I call to do two-man shows, and we split the $750 to $1,000 that I charge the promoter. A lot of times I deal directly with the girlfriend, the sister, or whoever is organizing things for the bride-to-be. And dealing direct is sometimes better; sometimes not. The promoter that can do his job and fill up the party is worth his weight in gold. And he'll make a few hundred dollars from the gig. On the other hand, without the promoter there's no tellin' if the party is gonna be packed, and in that case Joe and I wouldn't make a lot of tips. And tips can turn a $1,000 night into a $1,500 night, easy. For New Year's Eve, our fee was doubled, and I was hoping to leave with at least $1,500 of my own so that I could walk into Ophelia's office with some hard cash for our meeting. Only thing is, I had to keep Joe focused.

While we were changing outfits, Joe said, "Hey, Danté, this one's a killer."

"Yeah, it will be, if they keep tippin' like they are."

"Naw, man. I'm talkin' about the bride. She's hot to death."

"No doubt."

"Hey, you ever bang a bachelorette right before the wedding?"

I chuckled and said, "I should be askin' *you* that. You know I ain't been doin' this as long as you. *You* ever get lucky?"

"Nope. But I think I'm gonna get lucky tonight. The bridesmaid—the one who helped to organize things with the promoter? She asked if I would bang 'er."

"The bridesmaid?"

"No, not the bridesmaid. The bridesmaid wants me to bang the bride."

"Wow. 'Cuz she told me the same thing."

"*Giiiit* the fuck outta here."

"Yup. But you know we can't do that, right? The woman's getting married in a week. We can't fuck up the marriage, you *know that*. That would fuck my business up *big time*."

"Yeah, you right. Somethin' to fantasize about, anyway."

"I appreciate that, Joe. Let's keep the Mister Fix-It brand strong, now. Discipline, m'man. *Discipline*."

"Gotcha, boss."


ON NEW Year's Day, Cindy Blackmon, the bride-to-be who I had danced for the night before, was snuggled up close to my LA Fit body. It was close to 9:30 a.m. when she got up to use the bathroom. When she returned, it was to talk, not sleep.

"What now." Cindy's words were more a confession of guilt than an inquiry. Her arms were folded as if she were cold or naked, waiting for me to wake up and join the conversation.

"What now," I sighed in my own *admission* of guilt. Once I was sitting upright, I said, "Cindy, whatever you were missing in your life, you got last night. Nothing more, nothing less. It was great, don't get me wrong. But your husband is probably set—a doctor, right? I can't do battle with him and his resources. I'm just a handyman with an okay body, tryin' to scratch two nickels together to make a dime. You have to be realistic. He can offer you a lifetime. I can only offer you a weekend."

Cindy seemed convinced and confused, both. She pulled her clothes on erratically and did her best to avoid eye contact. But all I did was look at her. She had the most amazing body. And her sex sent me back into amnesia, if only for one night. When I saw her to the hotel-room door, she abruptly turned around and grabbed my face and pressed her lips to mine in some last-minute attempt to, I guess, memorialize our involvement. I have to say it was a cute and spontaneous move. And I wanted to pull her back in and lay her back on the bed. But I just eased the door closed and fell asleep hard.

After a day of sleep I went to meet with Ophelia at her second office: the one she uses for certain clients who she doesn't want to come to her home. That would include me, since the whole incident with Dancer.

There was no receptionist to invite me in, just Ophelia, who came out to greet me real quick and asked me to have a seat till she finished with her client. And as I waited for Ophelia, I noticed the BE RIGHT BACK sign on the reception counter. The office space wasn't cramped and it wasn't too overwhelming in size, yet it was impressive in luxury and simple in decor. I wondered secretly if Ophelia herself wasn't an HG fiend like I'd once been.

While still reminiscing about my eventful New Year's Eve, I scanned over a few magazines. My name was eventually called and I barely looked up as I lifted myself from the couch. I almost collided with the appointment that was just leaving Ophelia's office in a rush. Recognizing the face pulled me back down in my seat like some gravitational force. My eyelids froze open and my mind spun. I *knew* this guy. The sight of him threw me more than just physically, it threw me mentally. As the man continued on his path out of the office, I felt as though his wrath was left behind. I squeezed my eyes closed and tried to cope with the reality, but I was feeling like I'd dived off a cliff, falling into an atmosphere of images, names, and people, some still life while others were moving. The work on Mr. and Mrs. Gilmore's water heater, the shower door for Mrs. Fraoli, the light bulb for Marsha Thomas. And while these things were all mashed together, all of them pushing through my head, and while I was looking back toward the elevator at Ophelia's last appointment, I wasn't paying attention and tripped over a mat: THE KING AGENCY. I guess this was supposed to be a welcome mat of sorts, but instead it was a switch: *lights out.* I found myself stumbling face-first into the pane-glass door that separated the reception area from the back office—the inner sanctum of the Ophelia King enterprise. There was a point when I crash-landed and my head jerked; however, none of the small amount of broken glass cut me. I had fortunately fallen to the side between the doorjamb and the end of the reception area. But while all this was happening in real time, my mind was somewhere else. I was in the Bronx, a spectator at the Puerto Rican Day parade, and then there was Stacy and me posing in front of some graffiti. It wasn't just *any* graffiti, but a mural of the late rapper Big Pun. Stacy and I were striking a pose, then another. Now it was Ms. Thomas with me, except I was cool and she was extra, trying to be hip-hop with her old-school ass. Dad and I posed in front of the mural, too, and then Grandpa. A preacher stepped into the camera frame, asking anyone if they needed a taxi ride. Then, somehow, my family was replaced by the Singletary family, both the North and the South. Those thoughts were swept away by the King clan. And the very last thing I remember was Theodore Jefferson Barnes. He stood there alone in front of the Big Pun mural with his pants sagging, his chains hangin' low, and his fresh new kicks loosely laced. His arms were folded so you could see his muscles and tats, and he had this mean, twisted grimace that showed some of his gold teeth, all of this daring anyone to try him.

I soon realized the significance of this one man, and how he played an indirect role in bringing so much havoc into my life. First off, according to Stacy, he shot her ex-boyfriend. So, Stacy may not have traveled to New York to stay with her aunt if not for Theodore Jefferson Barnes. She would've still had her house, her kids, her man—all that. Then there was the bum rush they tried to put on me in downtown Atlanta. Again, Theodore Jefferson Barnes. And I know it was him on account of his spooky hairstyle and the patch over his eye. The fucking guy is a modern-day pirate in a thug uniform! Add to that, if I hadn't had the accident, I would've never been to the hospital, I would've never run into Ophelia King, or Dancer. I would never have made Momma King angry, nor would I have had the run-in with the police in Fulton County, and I *definitely* would not be homeless, living out of an LA Fitness locker, a cargo van, and stripping for a living. I would not have been in bed with Cindy, the bride-to-be, and I *surely* would still have my credit, because Stacy would have never gotten close enough to my personal papers and access to my finances. Theodore Jefferson Barnes, you fucked up my life, and you probably don't even know it.

The receptionist was the first person I saw when my eyes opened. Ophelia King was standing behind her, wagging her head. Just then, I thought I'd died and gone to co-incidence heaven.

"Man, we gonna hafta get you a Seeing Eye dog. You walked right into the daggum door." The way Ophelia said this was not harsh but friendly; something I could smile at. She could never get me upset because she was just too beautiful a person, no matter what had transpired between us. The thing that confused me was the coincidence here—it was her receptionist. She was stroking my brow and then helping me off the floor. Ophelia came over to assist and we all moved toward her office; all except Cindy.

"Cindy, please get him some cold water. And hold all my calls."

"Yes, Ms. King."

It was Cindy Blackmon, the perfect body and bride-to-be that I had lain with on New Year's Day. She worked for Ophelia King.